DESERT
MOJITO

DESERT MOJITO

a novel by
NAZLI GHASSEMI

MUSEBERRY PRESS

This book is a work of fiction. Names, characters, places, and incidents either are products of the author's imagination or are used fictitiously. Any resemblance to actual events or locales or persons, living or dead, is entirely coincidental.

Copyright © 2012 by Nazli Ghassemi

First trade paperback published in the United States of America by Museberry Press.

All rights reserved. No part of this book may be reproduced, scanned or distributed in any printed or electronic form without permission. Please do not participate or encourage piracy of copyrighted materials in violation of the author's rights. Purchase only authorized editions.

For inquiries, please contact:
Museberry Press
1286 University Avenue #589
San Diego, CA 92103
www.museberrypress.com

ISBN 978-0-9853009-0-6

Edited by The Threepenny Editor
Book layout design by Phillip Gessert
Cover design by Niyaz Azadikhah

Printed in the United States of America

10 9 8 7 6 5 4 3 2 1

This book is dedicated to entertaining the displaced, misplaced, and in-placed people in all popular and unpopular places near and far.

Perhaps travel cannot prevent bigotry, but by demonstrating that all peoples cry, laugh, eat, worry, and die, it can introduce the idea that if we try to understand each other, we may even become friends.

MAYA ANGELOU

ACKNOWLEDGEMENTS

I wish to thank and acknowledge the following people and organizations (in no particular order) without which this book would not have been possible.

All the hard-working, lovely baristas at my various "office locations," especially the following: Starbucks, the one next to Duo on The Walk, Jumeirah Beach Residence, Dubai; Caribou Café in the Greens, Dubai; E Street Café in Encinitas, California; and my friends at the Costa Café Eppco gas station next to the Greens in Dubai.

The Kickstarter Desert Mojito campaigners—the amazing international circle of naughty and happening people, friends and family every writer dreams of having by her side—for believing in me. For their encouragement and support and promotion of this book, special thanks to: Parviz Ghassemi, Sussan Mossafa, D. V., Pedar (Dr. R. A. Ghassemi), Touran Ghavami, Maziyar Shakourzadeh and Layla Saiy, Jila Nameni, Abu-Ali, Mireille Boyadjian, Bita, Mahsa Vahidi and Arman Paymai, Roya Parviz and Soheil Nasiri, Maryam Mortezaiefard and Mina Mortezai, Reikimoto, Rez G., Ali Ghadiriyan, Azad Ghassemi and Jennifer Yang, Borzou Ghassemi and Shahrzad Sadeghi, Shahram Lalehzarian, Sarah Ronaghy, Club–XTR Tasis, Maysam Mostafavi, Delyar Amirsadeghi.

Afsaneh Modiramani and Shervin M.T., my favorite calm and gentle friends, who encouraged me to take my love of writing and telling of humorous stories, seriously.

My parents, for supporting my unusual choices in life and loving me unconditionally.

Emirates Airlines, for flying me safely to my favorite destinations: Tehran and New York and everywhere in between.

Anna Soler-Ponta, my agent, for her enthusiasm, hard work, encouragement, and belief in me all along.

Sarah Cypher, my amazing and super-intelligent editor, for her calm and all her brilliant guidance in paving the way to preparing this book for publication; for patiently deciphering my words; and for getting my sense of humor.

Jane Galvin—the Blithe Spirit—for her reflections and advice on the manuscript throughout, as well as for being the inspiration behind one of the characters in the book. (Wink!)

Mireille Boyadjian, the sweetest friend one could ever be so lucky to have, for sharing her "amusing" stories about Dubai and Beirut.

Scott Ollivier—the soul surfer—for his musings and for skillfully dancing us through the social media waves.

Phillip Gessert, for his devotion and absolute brilliance in working his magic on the book layout design.

My grandfather, whose eyes still sparkle with the magic of wonder at age ninety-nine, for encouraging me to write, dance, laugh, and travel.

The Brotherhood—Ramin and Rokni Haerizadeh—for their constant support and love; for cultivating my imagination through their "family" movies and more.

BF—Mahsa Vahidi—my beautiful, smart, and super-efficient creative director for her brilliant ideas and for her selfless dedication to creating an amazing book campaign.

ACKNOWLEDGEMENTS

Tony Valenzuela, for all his invaluable advice and guidance; and for introducing me to his professional, awesome group of contacts.

Robert Ferrante, for sharing his story and painting a vivid, beautiful portrait of celebration of love, which became the inspiration behind one of my personal favorite chapters in the book.

Niyaz Azadikhah, for her unique vision and her sexy-poetic cover design.

Hesam Rahmanian, for his unconditional kindness and generous contribution towards the book cover.

Josh Hunter—the Dream Illustrator—for sharing his design expertise, wealth of wisdom, and artistic vision in building the book.

My one and only Funny Valentine since childhood, for his constant support throughout my life and connecting me to the right people and airlines.

I would also like to acknowledge and extend a special thank you to the great commercial publishers: Bloomsbury, Random House, Grand Central Publishing, Penguin, and Doubleday. They were "so charmed" by the book, "couldn't put it down and read to the end!" and thought that it "strikes rich chords of comedy," and that I took them "into the strange and foreign world," and that I ably ground my story "in familiar and relatable" life, and that they "loved the setting" and found "the characters…fresh and funny." Thank you for your positive rejections that kept me going.

QUESTION:
What is the meaning of life?

ANSWER:
"Try and be nice to people, avoid eating fat, read a good book every now and then, get some walking in, and try to live together in peace and harmony with people of all creeds and nations."

SIRI, IPHONE 4S

JUST AN ILLUSION

Universe: "Next."
 I walk up.
 Universe: "Hey, it's you again. What's up? Going for another ride, eh?" Universe has a friendly surfer dude accent for some reason.
 Me: "Hello. Yes. It's me again. I just need to go back one last time to hopefully reconcile some pending last minute stuff with one of my exes, get my poetry published…and, you know, the usual…to become a more conscious human being…blah, blah, blah."
 Universe: "Blah, blah, blah?! How many lives will it take you to do that? And to deal with your exes and just move on? Please. We don't just *give away* lives here. They are precious."
 Me: "I know. I know. It's just that last time I ran out of time. I had managed to almost forgive him and erase all corresponding karma, but then I expired."
 Universe: "That's insane. You *were* ninety-four years old."
 Me: "Actually ninety-three and seven months."
 Universe: "Whatever. Time is of no concern. It is all eternal. Your essence is eternal. And if you had paid more attention and not wasted your energy on the trivial, you wouldn't need to keep going back and forth, back and forth."
 Me: "I'm sorry. I just keep getting distracted. It's not as easy as it looks you know. I promise to pay attention this time and become eternal. Which brings me to the next very important reason why I want to be born again."
 Universe: "Let's hear it."
 Me: "Gossip has it that humanity will be going through some major revelation in the next fifty years, and I want to be

a part of that. You know, kind of like reaping the fruits of my hard work throughout all my past lives."

Universe: "That's swell. But don't believe everything you hear around here."

The Universe hesitates for an instant, lets out a sigh, and says: "All right. All right, I will give you another chance. I can see that your beloved ex is also in line. Just keep your life's mission in perspective this time around. Don't lose sight. Remember, you are going back to awaken your consciousness. The rest is just an illusion."

Me: "Wasn't there a song with that title, 'It's Just an Illusion?'"

Universe: "Totally. It was by that European group, Imagination. I love Eurotrash music. Good stuff."

Me: "Me, too. You are so cool."

Universe: "I try. All right. Get over it. Come on. Get a move on. Don't waste my time."

Me: "I thought you said time is of no concern and it…"

Universe: "How do you feel about being born a mute this time around?"

Me: "No. Please. No. I'm sorry. I'll stop talking now."

Universe: "Do you have any gender, status, place preferences?"

Me: "I believe you already know the answers to those questions."

Universe: "I sure do. Go stand in that birth line and wait for your turn. Have a safe journey."

Me: "Thanks. Bye for now."

✺

BOP!
Born on planet Earth.

A STAR IS BORN

Maya Bibinaz Rostampisheh-Williams. The progression of my name from simple to the impossible is an indication of nothing special, other than a typical case of marriage between the East (my Iranian father) and the West (my American mother).

Intercultural marriages tend to stretch parents' imaginations—and their children's names—across borders and hemispheres. I would say my name rates three on a scale of one to ten; one being appalling and ten a not-too-ear-petrifying mishmash of Eastern and Western.

But looking on the bright side, a peculiar name does develop character, giving one the chance to practice fighting to fit in from the very first breath.

❂

Of course the name on my résumé reads: Maya R. Williams. Could you imagine a promising career path if I advertised my full name, which alone takes up half a line? I think not. I can just imagine a potential employer saying, "Yeah. Right. I bet she is as much a handful as her name."

I'm lucky to have such a malleable name, one that allows me to camouflage myself for the job at hand. Job being, living a decent life in this indecent world.

That is, up until I landed in Dubai, where all résumés must also include a six-by-four picture—to save time, energy, and discomfort in the process of both racial and facial discrimination. I can no longer appear as American as I once did on paper. So, here I am, posing as myself, working as a freelance commercial photographer and writing poetry on the side.

DESERT MOJITO

What to do? (With an Indian accent.)
That is just the way it is here.

❂

My patched-up name, nationality, various places of residence, and consequently my personality have managed to confuse other people a little, and sometimes a lot, over the years. These days, there are many of our type around; citizens of the world with multinational parents, mixed and confused features, multiple passports, and colorful backgrounds; twenty-first-century hybrids. You know you have come across one when the simple question, "Where are you from?" requires a two-minute explanation, almost making you sorry you ever asked.

❂

My father Sohrab met my mother Rebecca while studying in Detroit, Michigan in the late sixties. According to him, he fell for her long blond hair, and she for his dark, bushy mustache. It seems that hair played a major role in their union.

Eight months into their relationship they got married and I was born shortly after. They were on their way back from a road trip passing through Oshkosh, Wisconsin when, BOP! Here I came rushing out, three weeks before my due date, making my grand, unexpected, fabulous entrance into this world.

We moved to Tehran, Iran when I turned four.

❂

No major memories from my childhood stand out except for a revolution in my presence, followed by a war in my absence

A STAR IS BORN

from Iran. I also remember that as a little girl, I secretly believed I had all the right elements for stardom and was destined for the limelight whether I was ready for it or not.

I attended a public elementary school in midtown Tehran next to our house. I was certain my name and features were distinct enough to secure my entry into fame. After a careful consideration of various creative versions of my name: Maya Bibi, Mayabinaz, Baby Naz, Bibi Maya, I finally decided to introduce myself as Maya Naz. I would be one in a million amongst the other girls with typical Persian names: Maryam, Naghmeh, Nazanin, Mojgon, Roya.

The name turned out to be a total catastrophe. An embarrassing disaster, which backfired immediately, having the exact opposite effect intended. The problem was that it sounded too much like "mayonnaise" to some obnoxious people. They made a mockery of my star name, making it sound even worse in their drawn-out, lethargic, Farsi accents, "Meh-you-nez," they would shout out in class, and burst into laugher. At the end, to save face, I had no choice but to settle for just Maya.

This little setback did not discourage my dream of stardom. The name was just the beginning. I had a sea of hidden talents and obvious qualifications that contributed to my inevitable fame, whether I liked it or not: I spoke fluent American English, danced very well, sang not as well (on a good day I sounded just like Bronski Beat), but I knew that the voice had great potential once trained. I was tall for my age with black, almond-shaped Persian eyes, and thick, straight, light brown hair with streaks of gold, and a funky looking bony nose. Last but not least, all my classmates not only knew I was born in the United States, but they thought I was from Hollywood, California. I figured a little white lie was appropriate, considering all my other fabulous traits. As far as I was concerned, no matter what I said or did, my road was paved all the way to stardom.

❂

I made my first and last television debut when I was ten years old, winning the district dance competition with four other girls in my group. I thought my discovery was imminent: I would be spotted by some Hollywood agent who just happened to be visiting Tehran looking for candidates for the new, up-and-coming show which nowadays would be called, *The Talented Non-terrorists from the Middle East*. Then it will only be a matter of months before I would be a pop or rock star, and nominated for a Grammy. I'd come strolling down the red carpet at Staples Center in Los Angeles with my best friends, who after many visa rejections will have finally managed to make it to the U.S., thanks to my fame, fortune, and powerful connections.

❂

But much to my surprise, I was not discovered that day or anytime soon after.

NO MAN'S LAND

Whoosh! Whoosh! Whooooooosh! Wham!
 I hear strange voices. They are coming from above.
 Above my head that is.
 Or is it inside? Inside my head.
 I hear people…people talking…I can't make sense of anything they are saying.

Voice 1: "Weyn zoja?"

Voice 2: "What did that guy say in Arabic?"

Voice 3: "He's asking where her husband is."

Voice 4: "Elle est mort?!"

Voice 5: "No, she's not dead. She seems to be breathing."

Voice 6: "Bbreeedding? Bbreeedding?"

Voice 7: "Dios mio! Bleeding?"

Voice 6: "No. Madame. Bbreedding. Air. Air. In nose. Nose."

Voice 7: "Chi shodeh?"

Voice 8: "Ma'am? Ma'am? Ma'am?"

Voice 9: "Don't bloody move her."

Voice 2: "What're they saying?"

Voice 3: "The Indian guy's trying to find out if she's breathing and the British guy's saying something about blood."

Voice 10:	"Ana napilas?"
Voice 2:	"What about her nipples?"
Voice 10:	"Vaat nipples?! NAPILAS! I vas vonderrring iv she's drrrunkk?"
Voice 1:	"Mahal el horma fel beyt."
Voice 3:	"Now the Arab guy's saying a woman's place is in the house."
Voice 2:	"Is he referring to the drunk Russian woman or this one?"
Voice 11:	"Please clear the way. Sir. Sir. Step back please."

✪

Men and women speaking in tongues. Oh my God! Have I died again and gone to heaven? Of course, being the Goddess of Optimism, the thought of being in hell does not even cross my mind.

Well, that was a short, lovely life. I missed my midlife crisis by a few years. What now? Where am I? My legs feel weighed down by what feels like twenty tons of bricks, and my head is light as a feather. Maybe I'm in purgatory. Somehow my head has made it to heaven and my legs are still stuck on Earth. Crap! Way to go in messing with all the religious doctrines known to man, Maya. I knew I should not have had all that bacon yesterday. Let's not mention the many glasses of wine. Oh! And I almost forgot the little premarital sexual activities. Oh. Forget it. Too late now. I am officially beyond redemption.

I realize my eyes are closed. I wonder if I can take a peek around. As I begin to slowly crack open my lids, the voices around me begin to fade out. And then, I cannot hear a single sound. It's total silence.

Maybe I was just dreaming.

Or maybe not. Little by little, miscellaneous faces come into focus. I am reminded of group pictures we used to take in college; we would place the camera on the floor, set it on self-timer, and then huddle in a tight circle with our heads pressing against each other, staring down into the zoom. "Everyone, say CHEEESE." Click! Except that under the present circumstances I am playing the camera's role, staring into faces as multi-national as a Benetton ad.

Entertaining the idea of a Benetton ceiling mural in purgatory, much to my amazement, the Indian model in the ad leans down and gives me a huge smile, his white teeth shining blindingly bright in my face. It takes me a few seconds to realize that the light beam is coming from a tiny flashlight pointed into my eyes. Kneeling beside me are two young European-looking guys. One is shining the flashlight into my pupils, and the other has his finger on my wrist, taking my pulse. The Indian man seems to be operating independently of these two guys, as well as from the other motionless heads with their frozen stares crowding above me.

He bends down closer and says, "Are you okay, Madame?"

I stare back at him in a daze. I want to ask him where I am, but no words come out. Then I notice that everyone is wearing matching blue jumpsuits, black gloves, and huge black boots.

All of a sudden I realize it is cold and I am freezing.

Okay. I am now certain that I am definitely in purgatory. I must have just somehow died and been thrown here until my sins are tallied and a final verdict is submitted. In the meantime, I am amazed and pleased to be among such an international crowd of fellow sinners, here in limbo. I love it. Maybe I can make some good friends.

❂

I did my best while alive. But I thought surely a longer life was planned for me this time around. When my turn is up, I must have a heart-to-heart with the universe. This wasn't the arrangement we negotiated.

As I am figuring out my longevity request speech, a new but familiar face pushes into the crowded heads above me. It's a woman. Is it my sister? It cannot be. Because I do not have one. The woman is wearing a pink knitted cap with Escada written across the front in huge black glittery letters. What is up with all this branding in purgatory? She takes off her pink, mirrored goggles and looks into my eyes. She has clear hazel eyes, a perfectly round face, high cheekbones, a chiseled nose, and a tiny beauty mark on the side of her mouth. Ah-ha. I recognize that mark. She is my friend, Michelle. She is wearing the same ugly blue jumpsuit as everyone else. We must have died together. Poor thing. She was only twenty-eight. She pushes through my audience, sits next to me, lifts my head in her lap and says, "Maya? Can you see me? Can you hear me? Maya. Maya. Please say something."

I blink and say, "Hi."

She smiles back at me and says "The medics are making sure you're all right. Don't move."

"The medics?"

"You skied head-on into a steel pole and passed out."

❂

Whoosh! Whoosh! Whoosh! Bam! Oh no! Everything is coming back to me in bits and pieces.

After spending a very nice day at the beach, Michelle and I had decided to go shopping. When at the mall, we passed by the Ski Dubai area and Michelle spotted her latest fling interest, Paul from England, getting on the lift and heading up the slope. She convinced me that taking a few runs on the slope was exactly how we needed to finish off a perfect day.

So there I was, skiing down the manmade ski slope, enjoying the perfect manmade cold weather and the manmade snow, when from the corner of my eyes I saw him. The perfect God-made man, six feet tall, dusty-blond wavy hair, a high forehead, a strong jaw, and a classic Greco-Roman God nose, skiing skillfully around the moguls. I looked back quickly to point him out to Michelle, who was cuddled up next to the Brit on the lift, flirting her Lebanese ass off. Waving my poles frantically in the air, I finally got her attention and pointed to my right and mouthed, "Wow." She nodded, and gave me the a-ok signal, and I gave her the thumbs up and…

That is the last thing I remember. I must have slammed into the pole at the height of bliss and passed out.

I touch my head, which now feels heavier than the giant ski boots on my feet. There is a huge bump in the middle of my forehead. I have probably done some major damage to my Third Eye. Bummer.

I turn to Michelle in total desperation and whisper, "Did you see the tall guy I was pointing to?"

Michelle nods.

"Is he…one of these people…around me?"

Michelle shakes her head no. I lie back down, close my eyes.

✸

DESERT MOJITO

The medics disperse the crowd and my one-woman show is finally over. But, to further prolong my embarrassing moment of fame, they insist on carrying me down the slope on a stretcher. I enjoyed the ride down, bouncing up and down on the manmade ski slope, looking up at the cement-domed sky and its bright ceiling lamps. Once we get to the bottom, the medics unstrap me and instruct me to slowly stand up. I assure them that I am fine and I just need to get out of the cold. One of the medics and Michelle walk me out of the ski area and help me take my boots off.

"You may need to take some painkillers for your head and have it checked out by a doctor tomorrow," the medic says. "You're a very lucky lady not to have broken anything. Hope to see you back safe on the slopes soon." He winks at me, smiling.

"We'll be back. Hope to see you, too," Michelle says flirtatiously, batting her lashes.

I roll my eyes at her and thank the medic.

"All right, girls. Keep out of trouble." He waves goodbye and walks back to the slope.

❂

Once again luck has intervened. That is my life story. In general, luck is on my side, hand-in-hand with lessons in humility.

LOONEY DUNES

I am proud to be a Dubaian, to be part of this great wonder of the Middle East in the making, this city of sand, glass, glitter, and fake grass—an oasis, a mirage.

The world intersects here in Dubai. And, it is not so much about East meets West in the Middle East, as it is about everyone meets everybody else with a smile on the outside and prejudices tucked away on the inside. Just follow the loudly unspoken rule: Pretend you respect one another regardless of each other's race, religion, and political views, and head to the mall.

Malls. Malls. And, more…malls. Day in and day out, malls are the first and the last destination in this fascinating, fabricated city.

Tourist, terrorist, resident, expat, and Emirati alike. United, we *mall*.

The future Longman's dictionary, second definition of the verb, *to mall*, will read:

mall /mol/ *v.* to perform a series of activities such as shopping, eating, going to the movies, checking out and being checked out by other people, skiing (exclusive to the United Arab Emirates in the Middle East), watching mall entertainment, and, last but not least, aimlessly walking around in a mall; *Last night while we were malling at Wafi center, a group of international professional thieves robbed a jewelry store, driving through the mall entrance with their getaway car.* **maller** *n. Some of the mallers were able to capture the incident on video, and have posted it on YouTube.*

DESERT MOJITO

It's Friday morning around eleven. I have been up for an hour checking e-mails. No one misses me except for Amlak (a local financing company), and Emaar (a major property developer). They have invited me to their "special" upcoming property launch.

No thanks, not today.

I hear a text message beep in. I check my phone. It's from Janet, my six-foot-tall, thirty-two-year-old friend from Arkansas, U. S. of A. Her passion for traveling has taken her to the four corners of the world. She stays in any one place only for a few months—until she landed in Dubai, the intersection of the four corners, where she found the Middle Eastern flair mystifying enough to stay and explore for a while. She has taken to the city's glamorous façade like a moth to a flame, and has replaced her globetrotting shoes and backpack with an assortment of glittery sandals and tiny purses. Facials, manicures, pedicures, weekly massages and beauty salon appointments, shopping, malling, eating out, and dating are some of her other adopted weekly activities. She is also the first to sign up for all the miscellaneous classes offered around the city: Feng Shui, sailing, cooking, fencing, and God only knows what else. She would have been a perfect example of the Dubai-coined term, "Jumeirah Jane," except that she is not a stay-at-mall British wife/mother living in an upscale area in Jumeirah with a Filipino housekeeper and an empty fridge.

I met Janet at a job interview. I had applied for a communication skills position and she was one of my interviewers. I did not get the job. (I obviously did not have the skills to communicate my own skills.) I later found out that although her colleague had found me 100-percent-qualified for the position, she had convinced Janet to go with the other candidate, a 50-percent-qualified guy who was 100-percent-American-bred, as opposed to the suspicious, American-born, but technically a 50-percent-bred one, me.

Janet and I ended up becoming good friends after running into each other several times at the gym. She is a breath of fresh air in this humid desert, where the American light-hearted optimism and uncomplicated attitude are as scarce as camels in New York.

I open Janet's text message, MORNING HABIBTI, U AWAKE? WANT TO MALL? CATCH A MOVIE?

I did not mind a bit of *malling*.

I text back, AWAKE. LET'S MALL. MOE OR IBN? These are our acronyms for the malls in our vicinity, Mall of Emirate and Ibn Battuta.

HOW ABOUT MOE, 7ISH? she texts.

SOUNDS GOOD. C YA :)

✤

Driving to MOE down Sheikh Zayed Road, the main freeway running through the city, I almost get killed by a driver in a Hummer with darkly tinted windows. He or she overtakes me from the left side, barely missing me as I change lanes to exit. I immediately look over, in case I need to later identify my murderer's face. But all I see is a flash of bright yellow tank zooming by, displaying a triangular yellow hazard sign reading, "Child on Board," on its back window.

It is such a universal natural reaction to look over to see a reckless driver's face. This may be to gauge the intensity of our own reaction, depending on the impression on his face: Sorry? Righteous? Bitch? Asshole? And sometimes the only reason we look over is for him to enjoy the charming expression on our face, regardless. These snapshots of sneers and spell-casting stares are the only permissible mute reactions drivers can resort to in Dubai. Any offensive verbal and non-verbal forms of communication, be it by hand, finger, arm, tongue, mouth, or what have you, when driving, are punishable by law if reported by the recipient.

"*Baka*," I curse at the driver under my breath, which means idiot in Japanese, and make it to the mall in one piece.

I text Janet, AM HERE. NEED TO BUY CAMERA BATTERY @ CARREFOUR. WHERE ARE YOU?

WATCHING THE SOUTH AMERICAN MUSICIANS IN FRONT OF BORDERS. COME OVER.

Mall entertainment is another major attraction of *malling* in Dubai. You get to shop, eat, go to the movies, and in between, be entertained by South American musicians, Azerbaijani dancers, and Serbian gymnasts. These events, which escalate during the Dubai Shopping Festival in January, are taken very seriously—so much so that all the local newspapers allocate a section to "Mall Entertainment" and provide a timetable for the interested *mallers*.

On my way to Carrefour, I pass a group of flashy Lebanese women in designer clothes and expensive haircuts having lunch at Paul's Café. Despite years of war and struggle back home, the tough-skinned Lebanese make you appreciate a nation holding on to its high spirits and high fashion, come what may from high above, rain or shine or bombs.

I make my way to the supermarket along with an army of other nationalities and Indians—many, many Indians. Families of this peace-loving nation are strolling slowly down the aisles as if in a park on a beautiful sunny afternoon. They are in groups of five or more, talking, socializing, and having a jolly good time grocery shopping. Their kids are running around and rolling on the floor of the clothes section while their mothers, some in their colorful outfits of pants and long tunics, chitchat and catch up on the gossip. The men are checking out gadgets in the electronics section. At times I have to remind myself that I am in Dubai, in the United Arab Emirates, and not in some South Asian city. I have no idea how the local Emiratis feel about being a minority in their own land.

I am standing in the express checkout line when I hear a guy's voice from behind speak in Farsi: "Come here. This line is shorter." I glance back to see a boy and a girl in their late teens whose nose jobs, spiked-sprayed hairdos, Spock-shaped eyebrows, and designer jeans and shirts scream out, "Tourists from Iran!" The Iranian youth are living proof that there is an inversely proportional relationship between social pressure (forcing down) and hair growth (pushing up).

✦

As I get off the escalator next to the bookstore I spot Janet, towering over others, watching the contortionist. Her blond hair, proud posture, red lipstick, ready smile, and non-discreet presence have proved to be head-turning qualities. In other words, you would not want to take her along when robbing a bank or engaging in any undercover activities. Her pale face makes her stand out even more among the tanned, happy *mallers*. The sunburned people are either tourists or now-pinkened Dubai residents from cold, rainy European countries, Russia, Kazakhstan, Australia, and South Africa, who have been gladly converted to Dubai's cult of sun-worshippers.

I make my way to Janet.

"Hey, *marhaba*," I say.

DESERT MOJITO

"There you are. *Marhabtayn*. How are you?"

"Good, other than almost getting killed by a Hummer man, or...maybe woman."

"Tinted windows again?" She rolls her eyes.

"Black as tar. They've got to start implementing the law against these stupid black windows. Sometimes I imagine a guy in the back seat pointing a shotgun at me and here I am innocently making faces at him. Then BAM! I'm shot...right in the middle of my forehead, with my tongue hanging out."

Janet raises her eyebrows, chuckles, and says, "Not a pretty sight. The black tints are illegal in the States."

"And it had a 'Child on Board' sticker on the window. Is the driver referring to himself? Or is he enjoying driving like a maniac while the child is 'not on board?' What's up with that sticker, anyway?"

"That's so inappropriate. 'Let me do what I want because I have a child on board,'" Janet says, as she takes out her lip gloss to sparkle up her red lipstick. "Driving is crazy here. Sometimes when I'm in the fast lane it looks like I'm towing the car behind me on a short cord."

I laugh. "Tandem driving. My car insurance guy told me that there's this unspoken understanding that the fast lane is for 'them,' meaning the local Emiratis, and to stay away from that lane."

"That's so annoying."

We are both distracted by two young Emirati men waltzing along in their crisp white ankle-length robes—*kanduras*—greeting another group of three guys. As we get closer my nose is shocked awake by a strong scent of a floral perfume.

"They always smell amazingly good," I say.

Janet nods as we continue to watch the men shake hands and do the local nose-rub greeting, bringing their faces close enough to let the tip of their noses gently rub against each other. Emirati gone Eskimo. Two of the men are wearing the white headscarf—*gutra*—and the other three have on the red and white one—*shimagh*. They have casually wrapped their scarves in various fashions around their heads, and one of them is wearing the black cord—*igal*—over his scarf. He grabs the tip of his *gutra* and slowly flips it over one shoulder only to wait for it to fall back down again, before he ceremoniously throws it over across the other shoulder. The expertise of Arabs managing this fabric is comparable to women using their hair as seduction means: twist, twirl, flip, throw, and flick. My favorite is the scarf-chignon, bunching the *gutra* like a bird's nest over their heads.

"Their feet are always super-clean, too," Janet says, drawing my attention to their shiny scrubbed heels and pedicured nails in their designer sandals—*na'als*.

All of them are wearing huge dark sunglasses. "They really enjoy tinted stuff, don't they?" I say.

Janet chuckles. "I can relate."

"Oh. I forgot. You do wear your prescription sunglasses to the movies."

She continues to laugh. "I always forget to bring the right pair." She shuffles through her purse and looks up, "Yup. Forgot them again."

"Whatever works. Ok. Let's *mall*. What time's our movie?"

"The next-best one isn't for another forty-five minutes. It's a comedy."

"I can do comedy."

"Do you want to get coffee at Costa while we wait?"

"Sure," I say.

I am about to ask her who stars in the movie when the sound of "Allah o Akbar, Allah o Akbar," of *azaan* echoes loudly through the overhead speakers around the mall, letting everyone know it's time for the afternoon prayer. This reminder of God comes amid all these ungodly haute couture stores, which have now shut off their music out of respect for the call to prayer. It is as surreal as the ski resort we passed on our way to Costa.

We pass a cart selling assorted t-shirts, stuffed camels, and other Dubai souvenirs for tourists. Janet says, "Do you remember how before all this global financial crisis, at the height of Dubai's construction-rush…"

"You mean when we had to pay a year's rent in advance, and rents were ridiculously high?"

"Yes. Then. Do you remember how the developers had those fancy scale-models of the high rises and residential community projects set up in the middle of all the malls?"

"Sure do."

"You could not walk into a mall and not run into at least ten of those miniature mockups scattered all around."

"I miss those," I say. "The tiny perfect communities, with perfectly lined trees, perfect kids frozen midair on swings, the perfect fountain, steps away from the perfectly green golf course…The miniature version of an Arab dream."

"The perfect family—without the dog, of course," Janet says, chuckling.

"Yeah. I took a palm tree and a tiny red car as keepsakes from a set once."

"Maya! How did you manage that?"

"There was no one around. I just stuck my hand in and tore them off the set."

"That's stealing."

"I know. That was stupid of me and I was lucky not to get caught, 'cause as soon as I put the tree and the car in my purse, a cute Lebanese guy approached me and said, 'Can I interest you in a prime spot property today? We have a special promotion at the Jumeirah Lagoon Water Island Falls of Emirates Sea Shores by the Marina.'"

Janet laughs out loud. "I love the obsession with water-related names here."

"It's quite understandable, helping to create the illusion of *not* being in the middle of a desert," I say, rolling my eyes.

"It's either that or excavating the sand and filling up the hole with water to create artificial ponds."

"And, then they pour the excavated sand in the gulf to create artificial islands. And *voila*. Problem solved. Now we have our land and water where we like them to be; water where sand was, and sand where water was. As man intended. Good luck, nature and wildlife."

"And goodbye, prosaic desert," Janet says with a smile.

"Hello, prosthetic skyline."

"Aside from the poor Indian laborers, nobody works more efficiently and harder than Dubai developers and real estate agents."

"You mean *worked*," I say. "They're all out of money and jobs since the crash."

"True. It has slowed down."

"Do you remember how many cranes we used to see when looking up at the skyline?"

"Oh. Gosh. Yeah," Janet says. "But I still have to take detours around construction sites. Like this morning. Just overnight they had decided to close off the main street that leads out of Greens and I had to take the back roads through Al Barsha to get on the Sheikh Zayed."

"*Habibti*, if you aren't living near, next to, or in the middle of a construction site, then you are not in Dubai."

"True," Janet says.

✸

We get to the coffee shop and get in line behind a young Emirati girl in her early twenties. She is wearing a sparkling, black robe—*abaya*—with sparkling colored studs, and a matching scarf—*sheyla*—framing her round face. The *sheyla* is artfully twisted around, draped over a huge bun-shaped protrusion in the back of her head. She is carrying a designer Dolce & Gabbana leather purse in one hand, and whispering on her diamond-studded pink cell phone in the other. She continues talking on the phone as she pays the cashier and starts walking towards a table, taking deliberately long graceful strides with her shoulders back, head held up high, all the while avoiding all eye contact.

Once she is out of earshot I say, "Look how proudly she walks, and it appears that she doesn't have a care in the world."

"She probably doesn't. A Lebanese friend told me that an Emirati woman's elegant stride and demeanor is compared to the beauty and grace of a camel in the region," Janet says, intrigued. "Apparently this is a compliment of the highest degree among the Arab nations, who consider the camel to be the most beautiful and precious of all animals."

"Huh? Now, that makes sense," I say, "since the word *jameel*, meaning beautiful, takes its root from the word *jamel*, or camel."

"There you go," Janet says.

The Filipino behind the cash register politely waits for us to finish our bridge-across-cultures discussion before he smiles and says, "Hi, ma'am. What would you like to order?"

"We'll have a pot of green tea please," Janet says.

"Ma'am. What?"

"A pot of tea, green."

"For here or to go, ma'am?"

Janet sneaks a look at me before she says, "For here."

LOONEY DUNES

✣

We get our tea and settle down in a corner. Janet has a suspicious smile on her face, which in the female world only means one thing.

"Let's hear it," I say. "Who's the new satellite?"

She laughs and says, "Love that term. How did we come up with that term again?"

"We didn't—you did, darling. You suggested how we, the women, can be thought of as the center of the universe and they, the interested men, as satellites orbiting around us."

"Ha, that's right." Janet grins, leans close and says, "Yesterday I decided to do a Body Combat class at the gym. When I get to the locker-room I realize I've forgotten my tennis shoes at home but decide to do the class anyway. I come prancing in, five minutes late to class, wearing my leopard print flats."

At this point, I am unable to display the corresponding shocked-verging-on-amused expression on my face; my first Botox experience of two weeks ago has settled in and an attempt to frown and raise my eyebrows proves futile. So I just resort to an exaggerated tone in my voice and say, "You didn't!"

"I did." She shrugs her shoulders. "Eh. Who cares, I even went and stood in front of the class."

"Oh! Janet! You're too cool, especially when you do all this uncool stuff."

"I know. I know. Anyway…I make it through the class, avoiding the jumps and the kicks…"

I am thinking, *What's left? Did she just stand there and wiggle her booty from side to side?*

"It wasn't too bad," she says, sounding confident and satisfied. "So as the class ends and I'm walking out, I hear this guy whisper from behind. 'Nice shoes,' he says."

"Lovely. Who was it?"

"No one I knew. His name's Nabil. He's from the UK," she says and waits for me to ask the obvious.

"Where're his parents from?"

"Not sure. Probably India. But he was born and brought up in the UK and has a lovely British accent." She tilts her head slightly back and says, "Yes, daalin.' The devilishly handsome chap works for IBM."

"Eww! That was petrifying. You sounded like a Brit from Arkansas."

"I know, that was awful, wasn't it? I tried." She laughs out loud. "Anyway," she continues to say with her nasal Arkansan drawl, "we get talking, and—to cut a long story short—we're going out on a date this Friday."

"Satellite landing. You got a date."

"Well. Not exactly. He didn't come out and say, 'I want to take you out to dinner.' We were talking about this new beach bar that had just opened on Jumeirah Palm, and he suggested meeting there for drinks on Friday. And then we exchanged numbers."

"Sly. That's not putting himself on the line."

Janet smiles, sits back in the leather armchair and takes a sip of her tea. "I know. Sly, but also witty and funny. He made me laugh a lot in the short time that we talked."

"I wonder if he'll tell you any Indian jokes and do the accent," I chuckle. "Love those."

"Not sexy at all," she says, disapprovingly. "Hey, did you know I've met more guys at the gym than I have going out to bars and clubs? Going to the gym after work's like going to happy hour."

"Hmm. Maybe. Instead of looking for someone at their usual corner at the bar you look for them on their usual treadmill or machine, panting and sweating. Have you ever noticed how funny guys look when lifting weights? Holding their breaths, flaring their nostrils, squinting their eyes as they get red and redder in the face. Enduring, pulling, pressing those giant stupid weights."

She chuckles and says, "They do look funny, don't they?"

"It's fun checking them out," I say. "I have a gym story, too—from a Body Balance class."

"The one with the blond girl farting during the child's pose?"

"Farting child pose," I say, laughing. "I forgot about that. I never saw her again. She might've left town that night. I would've if I were her."

"Poor girl. So what's this Body Balance encounter you've been keeping from me?"

I sigh and say, "Well. This is a while back. I needed to stretch and relax after spending a very long hot day, running around Dubai Creek sweating, taking pictures of water taxis and transportation."

"Was that the freelance assignment one you were telling me about, for the Dubai Department of Tourism?"

"No this is another one for the Dubai Transit. So, listen, here I am in the Mind and Body studio at the gym, with my mat spread out in the back, waiting for the class to start when a tall cute guy walks in and sets his mat right behind mine. He looks familiar, except that I didn't know him."

Janet smirks. "All handsome men look familiar to me, too."

"I know. Except that all of a sudden I remembered where I'd seen him before." I pause, sigh and say, "It was the guy who had caused my skiing accident. Remember?"

"You're kidding. I remember you telling me about your little brush with death. I was in Qatar for a seminar that day."

"That's right. So, forget balancing. I was totally distracted the entire time. Conscious of my ass sticking out in his face during the downward facing dog."

"I'm sure he enjoyed the sight."

"You're most kind. Anyhow, just in case my ass had not impressed him enough, at one point I managed to almost take his eyes out doing a back leg-lift."

"I'm sure he found you quite entertaining."

"Right. So, here I am, done with all my unbalanced, ungraceful poses, lying next to Prince Charming, asking the universe if all this embarrassment is really necessary, when I hear the instructor say, 'Now this is the moment you've all been waiting for. Relaxation time. Just lie down and take the most comfortable position on your mat, close your eyes and…' I didn't hear the rest. My eyes were already closed, imagining the various most comfortable positions I had in mind with my desired object, a mere mat-distance away."

Janet and I are giggling like little girls as I look past Janet, my face freezes mid-grin.

"What? What happened?" Janet asks.

I am tongue-tied.

"This is freaky. Don't turn around. It's him," I say, dazed. "The Prince, walking right towards us."

"No! That's impossible. Quick. Tell me how that story ends before he gets here."

"Shhh. It doesn't end. That was the last time I saw him. He's looking this way. Don't turn around. How do I look?"

"Good, good," Janet says, watching me brush my hair back as I sit up straight.

"I'm going to laugh now, just play along." I wait a couple of seconds then burst into laughter, throwing my head back like I have seen done in television advertisements. I continue making awful fake laughing sounds. "That's so funny. Hahaha."

Janet is staring at me astonished, completely oblivious to my childish scheme of making us appear like two commercially hip, hot, happening girls. Finally, against her better judgment, being the true girlfriend that she is, she starts laughing along. By the time Prince is at our table, we look like a couple of chicks without a care in the world. Just like the ones you see in the Lipton tea commercials, tickled out of their wits, just because the tea is oh so intoxicating.

I pace myself to look up just in time to meet his eyes as he is about to walk past us. Our eyes lock. I tone down my Joker laughter into a Mona Lisa smile and wait for him to say something.

He stops. "Hi," he says, smiling.

I tilt my head to one side, keeping the ridiculous, mysterious smile on my face. "Hi?" I say, sounding uncertain, pretending I do not recognize him.

"From the gym?" he says, innocently refreshing my memory.

Oh. Good job, Maya. You have managed to impress him after all. He has remembered you.

"Oh. That's right! How are you?"

He looks at Janet, who is sizing him up with an awkward huge smile on her face. I introduce her, "This is Janet and…I am Maya."

"Mark. Pleased to meet you." He shakes our hands. "I haven't been to the gym since the time I saw you."

I am thinking, *he must have asked for a refund, complaining about life-endangering members in classes.* Maybe I should have skipped town with the farting blond girl.

I keep my thoughts to myself, smile and ask, "And why not?"

"Just being lazy. I'm not too much of a gym person, anyway."

"Great," I blurt out.

He looks at me suspiciously. "And that Balance class…" He grins, sighs, and says, "Not really for men, is it? I was too embarrassed to walk out after the first five minutes. Too late."

"You should try the kickboxing instead," I say, teasingly.

"Not much into kicking, either." He points in the direction of the giant glassed-in ski slope across the hall and says, "Have you tried Ski Dubai?"

If only he knew the downward-dog girl was also the flying blind bat on the ski slope. Janet sees the blank look on my face and comes to my rescue, "We haven't. They say it's not that bad."

"It's all right for a mall slope. I've been there once before. Today I've got some out-of-town visitors, colleagues, who wanted to check it out, too."

"Is it fun?" I ask.

"It's odd. Skiing inside a mall. But you should give it a shot," he says. "Well…I should get going. Nice meeting you girls." He looks at me and says, "Maybe I'll see you at the gym."

"Yeah. Take care. Bye," I wave goodbye like a six-year-old.

It takes me a few seconds to land back on earth, catch my breath, and look at Janet. I throw myself back on the couch, covering my face with both hands, "Oh, my God!" I say, at a loss for how I feel each time in his presence.

"You didn't tell me he was American."

"I didn't know he was American."

"He seems like a gentleman. How old do you think he is?"

"Mid to late thirties, maybe?"

"You better start going to the gym more often."

"Yeah," I say, still dazed.

"I wonder if he is from the East Coast," Janet says.

"He's from the moon."

"Well, well, Maya. I've never seen you this smitten by anyone. Come on. Our movie will start in five minutes."

"I need a mojito," I say.

"That does sound good. We'll get one after the movie. Come on. Let's go, *habibti.*"

I grin and pull myself together as I get up to follow Janet, thinking, *Mark*.

A CELEBRITY–REVOLUTIONARY IN EXILE

Deep inside, I really like to blame the delay in my international fame on the Iranian revolution, which took place in the late seventies. Becoming the first American–Iranian revolutionary was not exactly what I had in mind. I was quite taken aback by the detour fate had taken on the road to my stardom. But, if a detour was written, then so be it: A detour was my *kismet*, my destiny. For all I knew it could have been a shortcut to my global recognition. Madonna gone Evita. Bring it on.

Unfortunately, my new role as a dancer–singer turned rioter was also very short-lived. My parents knew I had a special knack for both manipulating and being easily manipulated by the mob. The mob being my school classmates. They figured that if I had managed to choreograph their dance moves, it would not be long before I coordinated them into staging their revolutionary demonstration moves: "Five, six, seven, eight… Raise those clenched fists…and…clap. Clap. Clap. One, two, three…now stomp. Clap. Clap. Stomp…Everyone shout out loud: DEATH TO THE DICTATOR! Now RUN for your lives!"

One month after my mom caught me practicing a rally routine in the backyard, I was shipped off to the safest, quietest country on earth. A place where the word revolution was, is, and always will be a myth. A place where, "Maya, la Star," turned, "Maya, la Heroine," will go unappreciated. A place where its neutral state and natural beauty are living proof that life is unfair. A place where the huge white plus sign in the middle of its bright red flag attests to its eternal state of optimism.

Switzerland, land of chocolate and silence. Shhh.

My time will come, I thought. Even if I am shipped off across the planet to a country with a minus sign marking its flag; even if I am bounced and dragged around the globe many times, the day will come when I will fulfill my destiny, and the world will know me, whether for my artistic endeavors and misdemeanors, or revolutionary heroic freedom fighter acts.

The world will know Maya.

I shall sail all oceans, climb all mountains, chase all pavements.

I have what it takes.

Justice must prevail.

I am an American. And I have the attitude and the birth certificate and the passport to prove it.

❂

Ah, the passport. Let us consider the passport: the determining, and in many cases the *terminating*, tiny booklet administering one's right of passage to the azures, the greens, and the browns of this mysterious marble planet as it floats through space. It is another piece of paper documenting our luck on the scale of existence in the material world.

In a perfect world, one passport is as good as another. A person could travel the world and the seven seas 'cause sweet dreams are made of these. But since some of them want to use you and some of them want to abuse you…Many are to waste precious time in visa lines.

The best-case scenario for a citizen of this world would be to have, not one, but a set of Yin and Yang passports to compliment each other. The two would complete each other, just like the Chinese Yin and Yang philosophy of interconnected but independent opposing forces giving rise to one another. The Yin passport, associated with the hidden and the subtle, would permit entrance to developing countries and the East; the countries making the news, where spontaneous upsurges, blasts, violent eruptions, and deaths are due to human (inhumane) acts rather than natural causes. And the Yang passport, associated with the clear and the obvious, would cover entrance to the developed countries and the West.

So here I am supposedly holding the ultimate, the über set of Yin and Yang passports. The Yang passport, the "Blue One," my American passport, eases my right of passage to all countries suspicious of my Yin passport, the "Maroon One," my Iranian passport. And, vice versa.

❂

I feel right at home here in Dubai, the hub of other multi-passport refugees and shady people.

@ THE GYM

I have been sick at home living on Michelle's homemade soups for the past three days. I caught a cold at the movies, thanks to the desert heat outside and freezing air-conditioning inside. All in line with Dubai, the great wonder of pseudo-nature.

Being stuck in bed at home without anyone to take care of me and fret over me in this strange desert city, I'm feeling exceptionally sensitive, melancholic, and sorry for myself. I need to have a good cry. I try to provoke the tears out by listening to depressing music: Maria Callas's *Madame Butterfly* aria, "La Bohème" by Charles Aznavour, "Mosabeb" by Darius, Antony and the Johnsons's "Imagine," and Assi El Hellani's "Bab am Ebki." The songs stir my emotions and bring me just to the verge of crying a river, when at the very last minute tears change their mind and retreat. It is time to turn to a visual invoker. I turn the TV on and switch to CNN news. It never fails. News therapy.

So here I am, crying my heart out for a few minutes over some crazy guy who shot himself in the head after opening fire on a group of people at a bus stop somewhere in Europe. The police have increased security at all public transportation stations. What? Like he is going to come back to life and kill more people?

How can increasing security save us from ourselves?

I continue to cry, flicking through news channels for ten minutes, until I have no more tears to shed. I feel a lot better. But now my sorrow has given way to a set of appalling sentiments—watching the devastating news from around the world, I feel guilty about being one of the privileged, and am ashamed of my miserable self-pity. I turn the TV off. Sit and stare at the black screen.

I have not been able to stop daydreaming about Mark ever since our last run-in at the mall. I cannot afford to be sick at home when he may be out at the gym, being entertained by someone else's downward dog. I must get myself out of the house.

I text Michelle. HEY. WHAT'S UP? GYM TODAY? SICK OF BEING SICK. NEED TO GET OUT OF THE HOUSE.

> STILL AT WORK. GOING TO THE GYM. DOING BODY ATTACK @ 6:30. COME. YOU WILL FEEL BETTER. HAVE NEWS OF MY AHMED :).

It is no secret that women of all ages tend to use pseudonyms when referring to guys of interest. We do this to protect the guy's identity in case he, his friends, or more importantly, other female rivals are around. Since eight out of ten guys may be named Ahmed in this area, Michelle and I decided that it would be inconspicuous to call all our potential interest guys "Ahmed." We just use different pronouns or adjectives to identify which Ahmed. We have my Ahmed, your Ahmed, my old Ahmed, your new Ahmed, your bold Ahmed, my American Ahmed and so on. Janet and I use a more descriptive system of pseudonyms for our satellites such as The Jacket, Last Minute Doctor, Rolling Stone, Liar Liar, Twenty-Four, and so on.

I text Michelle back, confirming I will meet her at the gym.

✪

The gym is on the top floor of an office building, with a rooftop pool overlooking the Persian Gulf.

@ THE GYM

I am waiting for the lift, sniffling away, searching for a handkerchief in my pockets, when the elevator door opens and two Emiratis in starched white *kanduras* walk out with their gym bags. At the sight of men in Arabian robes, time and again, I lose touch with reality and feel transported to another existence, time, and location: a scene out of *Lawrence of Arabia*. I smile at the young men. They smile back. I get in the elevator and push the button to the gym.

✪

The gym is usually crowded, swarming with fit, gym-chic twenty – to forty-somethings, huffing and puffing with as little sweat and as much splendor as possible on the equipment. I make my way down to the ladies locker room, looking for Michelle. I pass the sign, *Don't cause offence. Please use your towel. Preserve your modesty*, and manage to chastely change into my gym clothes. IPod in hand, I head upstairs to the main floor and spot Michelle talking to one of the Filipino personal trainers. She sees me, winks, and keeps on talking. She nods okay as I point to the treadmill area.

I get on the treadmill, put my headset on, and start walking. By the second song I am already feeling much better, bouncing to Madonna's "Give It to Me" when Michelle hops on the treadmill next to mine.

I sneeze right as I open my mouth to say hello.

"*Sah*. Still sick? But, you look much better than three days ago."

"Ahh. I hate this cold. I'll never go to the movies again in Dubai. How are you?"

Michelle smiles coyly, her eyes sparkling. "I have news of my Ahmed."

"Finally."

"He sent me a friend invitation on Facebook two nights ago."

"That's great. Did you accept?"

"Not yet."

"Why not?"

She hesitates and says, "I just finished reading, *Why Men Love Bitches*."

"And bitches don't accept Facebook friends?"

"Men are hunters by nature and they like tough tasks. Apparently they like it when you make them work for it."

"So how long are you supposed to make him wait before accepting his hunting invitation?"

"I don't know. Should I do it now? Forty-eight hours is enough waiting. Come on. Let's go to the members lounge and log on. I can show you his Facebook picture, too."

As we make our way to the member's lounge, the iconic Burj Al Arab comes into sight. "I can't get over how privileged we are here in Dubai," I say, still feeling guilty about the lucky cards I have been dealt. "Can you believe our gym is right next to two of the most talked about places in the world: The seven-star, sailboat-shaped hotel on one side and Jumeirah Palm on the other?"

"Yeah. Sure," Michelle says, dismissively as she pours herself a coffee and walks over to one of the Mac computers. "Too bad we can't see Burj Khalifa from here." She chuckles.

"Not really. I don't like that building much. I know it's the tallest structure in the world or whatever. I like Burj al Arab's sailboat much, much more. It's cool."

"Okay," Michelle says.

I'm sure she has not been listening. She is busy logging on to her Facebook account. Here we are at the gym checking out guys both actually and virtually.

@ THE GYM

Michelle's Ahmed's real name is Stephan, a blond German in his twenties. He has just moved to Dubai to work for BMW, and probably drives one, too. They met in the elevator at her building. During their fifteen-floor ride up the elevator together, he asked her about nice bars in the neighborhood. Michelle had teased him a little, saying that she is a Muslim and does not know about the bars, but that there are two mosques in the vicinity. She said the look on the guy's face was priceless. And how he had turned magenta as he apologized. Michelle had then let him off the hook by showing him her necklace with the cross pendant, flashing some cleavage in the process. They had a good laugh at her joke and exchanged cards. She said the reason she liked him was because he appeared friendly and confident enough to strike up a conversation in the elevator. And he was cute, in a German way. Whatever that means.

Michelle confirms his Facebook friend invitation, winks at me, and crosses her fingers before rushing off to her Body Attack class.

❂

I make my way back to the machines, looking around for Mark all the while. But there is nobody even remotely resembling him in sight. What to do? I get back on the treadmill with Madonna the Immaculate to once again daydream about Mark the Incredible.

I am just getting ready to start my fifteen-minute power run when a hand reaches from behind and pushes the treadmill's pause button. I turn around to see none other than Asif, my British–Pakistani friend.

Asif used to live in my apartment complex when I first moved to Dubai. We met at the pool every Friday to sunbathe, gossip, and check out guys. He moved out of our building when he started working for Emirates Airlines, which provided him with accommodations. Another reason we have seen less of each other the past year is because he has been in a happy relationship with an American guy, Peter, who trains pilots in the Gulf area.

Asif encourages safe promiscuous behavior for available singles, and is a strong believer in spreading love and opening up your chakras, especially the first chakra. Many times I have tried to explain how the rules are different in the heterosexual world; that when pursuing a person of interest, both men and women enjoy the chase, even if the intentions are purely first-chakra-based. At which point he would roll his eyes and say, "Honey, don't come running to me when your first chakra shuts tight, forever." And at times when I have actually gotten some action and would boast about my sexual adventures, he would make a comment like, "You're such a little slut." Then I would call him a bitch, and that pretty much sums up our deep, intellectual conversation.

I jump off the treadmill. We hug and make a lot of noise, inviting unnecessary attention to our union.

"You look great," I say, touching his Tin Tin–styled hair.

He flicks his hair with the tip of his finger. "I know. You like?"

"Yes. I like. I miss you so much. Where have you been?"

"Missed you, too. Honey, do I have news for you," he says, looking at me with a sparkle in his eyes. He checks to the left and to the right, and then over both shoulders, before lifting his left hand to show off a beautiful gold and silver trinity wedding ring on his ring finger.

"NO!" I scream, drawing more eyes to our already high profile scene.

"Shhh! Maya. Contain yourself. Yes. And—it's Cartier," he says, looking smug.

"I can't…I'm shocked. When? Who?"

"Well, Peter of course. We got married last month in Boston."

I tilt my head to one side and give him the proud look of a mother to a child. "I'm so happy for you. Congratulations, my love." I hug him again and pinch his ass, playfully.

"We got back two weeks ago. I was going to call you, but I've had to work overtime. Have hardly been in town."

"Bad, bad Emirates Airlines, making our newlywed work hard," I say, frowning.

"I'm actually very happy with my job. But Peter and I haven't had any time to—you know, tell people and digest it all." He pauses then whispers, "We're throwing a small party to celebrate in a couple of months."

"Where? In Boston?"

"No. Here." He winks.

"That'll be the first," I say.

"No worries. It'll be fine. And you're the first guest on my list."

"I'm honored, even though I'm sure you say that to everyone."

"You aaaare."

"Okay, okay, but, seriously, tell me, how's that going to work out here? Won't you guys get in trouble?"

"Of course we won't. There are no laws against men living together. What they don't know won't hurt them, or us for that matter. Right?"

"Right. Don't ask don't tell," I say. "It's against the law for unmarried couples to live together here, but since homosexuality is not even a recognized legal option you get away with living with your partner. But then, I guess since you're a married couple, living together would be technically legal.

Or…I'm not sure how that would work here? Anyway, how lucky is that, living on the edge of law."

"I'm very lucky to be gay, love. Sorry to see you suffer in your sad restricted heterosexual world."

"Oh! Shush." I sneeze and hop back on the treadmill.

Asif promises to give me a call soon with an update on the commitment ceremony. He blows me a kiss and walks off, gaily.

❂

What a strange world. I'm thinking about Asif tying the knot as I look up at the televisions lining the front wall, broadcasting the different realities of the world we live in; Lady Gaga pawing her way through a bad romance, while a suicide bomber somewhere has successfully managed to kill herself and four others on the Al Jazeera screen, while breaking news of floods, hurricanes, and earthquakes flashes on the bottom. And on the positive end of the news spectrum, Dr. Phil's special on the miracles of cosmetic surgery assures us that we can manage to look young and beautiful as we live through it all.

I put my earphones on and press shuffle. Bob Sinclar's remix of "World Hold On" comes up next. This song will never get old. Yes, world, hold on indeed. Hold on tight.

SWEET DATES

At first glance Dubai may appear to be the dating paradise of the world. It offers an assortment of vivacious people from all around the world, right at your fingertips. It is the second Mecca of the Middle East; this one is intended for the love and appreciation of God's creation, instead.

Ladies' eyes sparkle when they learn that the male to female ratio here is two to one. But it does not take long to find out that the choices are: (1) Indian laborers, (2) married or "committed" men away from their families and girlfriends, (3) lots and lots of single, capricious men in shiny fast cars; knights in shining armor who have done away with all mores of chivalry in favor of a different kind of "nightly" code. All of whom are here for purely mercenary reasons or are literally a hired mercenary on a hush-hush mission.

What adds a twist to the dating scene in Dubai, rendering it more chaotic and confusing than other places, is the city's transitory nature. Adding transit to the noncommittal nature of a typical male is like adding oil to an already slippery fish.

A man in Dubai is like a child in a candy store. He takes a bite of this and a bite of that and moves along to just bite and bite as many as he can get his teeth into. He is happy because the candies are plentiful, diverse, and close to hand.

If you are a woman done with your candy-striped days and bite marks, and looking for a serious relationship, you may be in for a rude awakening.

Janet, a professional dater, jokes about writing her memoirs about Dubai and calling it *My One Thousand and One First Dates*.

DESERT MOJITO

✲

Janet and I are heading to the annual rude awakening day: the Dubai World Cup. Ladies, gentlemen, and horses will be out prancing in all their glamour at the magnificent, super-duper, imperial, state-of-the-art Meydan Racecourse.

I have spent an arduous day beautifying myself at the hair, nail, facial, and wax salons. The lovely Lebanese hair stylist had disapprovingly twisted, twirled, and turned my hair into a high beehive, complaining the whole time about my lack of style and how I should wear my hair down and fashion it with a ladylike hat, just like all other women attending the World Cup. I did not dare tell him about the five golden bumblebee hairpins which were going to take up residence on the beehive once I got home.

✲

At home, while I am putting on my favorite black and yellow psychedelic sixties dress, purchased years ago at a vintage store in Melrose, Los Angeles, a text beeps in from Janet.

WILL BE THERE IN FIVE.

She has been looking forward to this event for the past week, dragging us all over town to look for the perfect hat to match her fake Lanvin red dress. She had the dress made for her at one of the expert Indian tailor shops in Satwa, the South Asian neighborhood, and finally, she found a hat worthy of it at a stand in Marina mall—medium-brim, veiled, black one with miniature red and white roses and glossy feathers.

"Maya. You look amazing. Love your bumblebees," Janet says as I step in the cab.

"Thank you. So do you darling. Love your rosebush."

"I'm sure we'll be photographed by Gulf News and others," she says with a huge smile on her face.

"For sure. With my bees and your roses, even Dubai House and Garden will be honored to have us on the cover," I say, looking at the Indian taxi driver who is trying hard not to eavesdrop.

Janet reaches into her purse to check a text message that has just beeped in. "It's from Kate." She chuckles and reads the message out loud. "'The first case of a number-snatcher misjudge. John just called. Wants to meet at Bubble Lounge at the races.'"

"What's a number-snatcher?" I ask.

"That's what Kate calls a guy who takes your number without intending to ever call."

"Oh yeah. I've met a few of those."

"They're all over. I've become an expert at spotting them," Janet says, with a sense of achievement.

"Do share, girlfriend."

"Okay. Here's how to spot them. They're usually in the company of other male comrades. Their attention's all over the place. They ask your name and forget it immediately. They're too relaxed and nonchalant when asking for your number. And they use the words 'swamped,' 'work,' and 'travel' one too many times." She rests her case with a content smile on her face.

"But why do you think they feel obliged to get our numbers if they're not interested? Is it a power trip thing for them? Is it just the challenge of getting the number?"

"Who knows. Maybe they have a list of numbers reserved for rainy days. Or maybe to them getting the number is as good as getting the girl. I've no idea," Janet says.

"Or better yet, maybe one day a guy discovered what an ego-booster it is to get a woman's number he's not interested in. His buddies all liked the concept. The word got around, and now it is part of the global male unconsciousness," I say, getting excited about my theory.

Janet laughs. "Good one, Maya."

"Thank you. And, we have to put an end to it before it becomes part of the universal consciousness."

"We must. Or we can do what Kate does."

"What's that?"

"She tells them that she won't give them her number if they're not planning on calling her." Janet rolls her eyes disapprovingly.

"Oh! Like that's going to scare them off. What's she going to do? Chase them and beat them up if they don't call?"

"I know. If I were a guy, number-snatcher or other, I'd just run away if a woman told me what Kate tells these guys. She's already putting pressure on the guy for not calling and he doesn't even have her number yet."

"Poor men."

We both chuckle.

"They say it's going to be hard finding a cab back after the race," Janet says.

"Then why didn't we take my car?"

"Zero tolerance, remember?" she says, referring to the no-alcohol policy for drivers.

"I hear they don't bother with stopping single women."

"Maybe. But it's not worth it, *habibti*. There was that woman, remember? She got in an accident after one glass of wine, and they threw her out of the country."

"All right. Let's have fun tonight then," I say.

Our taxi driver tailgates every car in sight, chasing them off the lane, zooming down Sheik Zayed Road.

SWEET DATES

✸

The entire city is here at the sci-fi Meydan racetrack. That includes the local Emirati men who rarely mingle at social events with expats, walking around in their national robes. And some have done without their scarves, wearing only the *taqiyah*—the cap, usually worn underneath the scarf to keep it in place.

We are welcomed and escorted inside by a parade of jugglers, clowns, and stilt walkers, festively dancing and prancing among the crowd. Everywhere around us are inviting spaces—fancy lounges, lawns, and shaded seating areas with huge television screens showing the race, which is taking place somewhere on the premises.

I am walking around, looking for the racetracks and the horses, while Janet is taking her first of many powder-and-lipstick breaks in the ladies' room.

"How's it going, love?" It's a man's voice. I look over to find a chubby guy of the British kind, leaning against a fence, smiling at me. He nods and winks at me, beer in hand, his dress-shirt hanging over his pants. He looks drunk already and the night has barely begun.

"Hi," I say, just to be polite.

"Are you having fun, love?"

What's up with *love*? So annoying. "Yes. Thank you."

"Are you by yourself, bumblebee?"

"No." I can tell he is working himself up to getting more irritating by the second and will have to throw him off his dead-end flirtatious track. "Where can we watch the races from?"

"Do you have tickets for the race, bumbles?"

"No."

"Are you related to the sheikh?"

I stick my neck out, look him straight in the eye and firmly say, "Yes."

"Are you his fourth wife?" He laughs out loud, enjoying his own joke.

I am thinking that now would be a good time to kick him, when all of a sudden Janet grabs my arm and says, "Come on, Maya. Let's go. Follow me. Hurry."

"What are we doing?" I say, finding it challenging to walk gracefully with high heels on grass.

"We're getting into the VIP lounge with this Lebanese woman I met in the bathroom. She's waiting for us."

I see a woman in a white chiffon, off-shoulder, low-neckline dress wave Janet over from the VIP lounge balcony.

"Why would she invite you?" I ask Janet, suspiciously. "Did you say lesbian or Lebanese?"

"She liked my hat and asked me to join her and her friends for a drink. She's very straight and Lebanese. You'll see."

✺

The VIP lounge is filled with ladies in hats, men in suits, Arabs in white *kanduras*, and Indians in turbans, all either lounging on white leather seats or standing around socializing. Free drinks and appetizers are served on silver platters. VIP indeed.

For an instant, I imagine myself in the middle of a real-life James Bond movie (Sean Connery's Bond, of course). I have been assigned to help James find the Russian–American double agent who is posing as one of the jockeys. He is going to steal Sheikh Mohammed's prized horse, Night Pass, and blame it on Israel. Talk about a plot with major consequences to follow.

I snap out of my mental moving scene and follow Janet to the Lebanese corner at the bar.

Janet's ladies' room friend sees her and rushes over to greet her, dragging her to their table. I follow them. "Janet, this is Fadi, my cousin," she says, ignoring me completely. Fadi is a short, scrawny man in his early forties with glass green eyes and a golden salon tan. He takes a puff of his thick Cuban cigar, takes Janet's hand in his, brings it to his face, stares into her eyes in silence, before puckering his thin lips to lightly place a kiss on her hand. "*Enchanté*," he says.

Oh! Please. Spare me. I'm thinking it is time to come up with a quick escape plan. This is not going to work for me.

Janet loves the attention, smiles a big smile, and says, "*Enchantée.*"

I am standing there wondering if the Lebanese chick has any of her original parts—ones that have not been nipped, tucked, pumped, or plumped. There are five people in the *enchanté* group, three women and two men, all looking equally alien in their perfection.

"Maya, this is Jamila," Janet says.

"Nice to meet you," I say, in an unfriendly tone. I make sure Janet notices my "whatever" attitude through my stare.

Jamila does not like me, either, and musters a fake smile. She notices my bumblebees. "Interesting," she says. She then looks back at Janet with a sweet smile on her synthetic face. "You are so tall, Janet."

Janet, who has noticed the presence of an obvious absence of interest in the Maya–Jamila spontaneous-combustion encounter, tries to lighten the mood and says, "Maya's half Middle Eastern, too."

Jamila looks like she has just gulped down a shot of sour milk.

Poor Janet does not know that her comment has devalued me in the eyes of this Jamila, who probably considers herself

Western Asian bordering on European, or anything else other than a Middle Easterner.

The blank stare on Jamila's face is blinding. I feel sorry for Janet, who likes us to all get along. "I'm half Iranian," I say, "Where're you from, Jamila?"

"I'm Phoenician."

"I thought you said you were Lebanese," Janet says, innocently, looking at Jamila in confusion.

"*Habibti*, we are all Phoenicians in Lebanon."

Janet does not look convinced. "But…"

Jamila interrupts her and says, "Tell me about you, Janet. Where are you from in the States?"

Janet smiles, her perfectly lined white teeth brightening up her face. "Arkansas," she says.

"*Habibti*! Alaska?!"

"No! No! Aaarkansas," Janet repeats with a drawl.

"*Habibti*! Where is that? Is that…"

"Sorry to interrupt," I say, non-apologetically, "Janet, I need to find out when my favorite horse is racing." I wink at her. "I'll be at the bar if you need me."

"Oh! Okay *habibti*." She gives me a concerned are-you-okay? look, to which I nod. As I turn to walk away, Fadi orders a round of champagne for the Phoenicians and the American.

❂

I turn around to walk to the bar when I spot an Emirati man in his early thirties, sitting by himself at a huge table with a mountain of sweet dates and Arabic treats piled on a huge silver tray in the VVIP corner of the lounge. His jet black wavy hair, arched eyebrows, and piercing dark eyes stand out like lines of calligraphy against the bleached white of the leather couch, which he blends in with perfectly in his robe and scarf.

Immersed in watching the race on the TV above the bar, he seems oblivious to his surroundings, as if he is lounging in his own living room.

Men in the Gulf area must get married at an early age, latest by twenty-two or three. When asked why, one of my Emirati friends half-jokingly said, "We need a head start if we are to have more than one wife and many children." It appears that to people with his mentality, marriage is more about serving a useful religious and sociological function rather than love and unity.

The women are not as willing to put up with the concept of polygamy and the new generation of men seem to lean more towards monogamy. But the road ahead is still unpaved and long.

The handsome Emirati in the corner probably has at least two wives shopping for him in the mall. Which means he is off my list. Going out with a person involved in a relationship is like resigning myself to being with someone who is already cheating on me.

I settle for entertaining myself with the young, and most probably, single Spanish bartenders making a spectacle, juggling bottles to the music, mixing cocktails. Pedro, Antonio, and José are professional event bartenders and for the next two hours they make sure I try their favorite exotic cocktails with erotic names.

The last time I checked, Janet was slow dancing to George Michael's "Careless Whispers" with the Lebanese Don Juan. He was swinging and twirling her around, unable to pass his arm over her higher-than-usual head with the flower garden hat on top. Each time he tried, he kept hitting her in the forehead.

I'm still feeling odd being at a racetrack, cheering on bartenders juggling cocktails instead of watching jockeys racing horses. When I share my concern with Antonio, in his adorable Spanish accent he says, "Hurry, go there," he points to a large area behind us. "Public grandstand there, go see who wins six million dollars."

"Wow. Six million dollars," I say, shocked.

I look for Janet at the Lebanese corner. No one's there. They have all vanished. I try calling her cell phone but there is no reception. I realize that the final race has already started and it is too late to make it to the grandstand. I am ashamed not to have seen a single horse, but otherwise I feel giddy and good.

I say *adios* to my bartenders and stumble down the stairs to the main field to find everyone in a chaotic state of revelry. The scene reminds me of my childhood and how we all must have looked at the end of a birthday party. Just like tonight, getting to the party, everyone was well behaved and orderly; boys with their hair neatly combed back and shirts tucked tightly into their pants, and the girls in colorful dresses with their hair in bows, ribbons, and flower pins. Cut to three hours later, departure time…No shoes, no tucked-in shirts, some rips and tears, no clean dresses without cake or soda stains, a wild bunch of flushed and sweaty kids, hair in disarray, are ready to be picked up by their parents.

Same. Same. Women are walking around barefoot, high heels and hats in hand. I take my shoes off and join the birthday crowd. I make my way to the fenced off open area in the middle of the grass field where everyone has gathered.

"Hey, there's the sheikh's wife," I hear a guy shout out as I pass a table of what looks like a group of inebriated refugees. I recognize the pestering man who had called me bumbles. Eh…I feel too tipsy and happy to be angry. I wave to him and walk on.

"Maya." I hear Janet's voice. "*Habibti*, Maya. Over here." I turn around and see the Lebanese congregation with Janet in the middle, sitting on Don Lebanon's lap. Her hat is on his head. Lovely.

Janet jumps up to give me a big hug and whispers, "I'm drunk," in my ear.

"Where were you?" I whisper. "Listen, I don't like this Lebanese guy at all."

"We're just having fun. He's a producer for the Middle East Fashion TV, but…Please, please make sure I go home with you."

I nod, wondering who is going to make sure both of us get home.

I then turn to Fadi and say, "The hat looks good on you."

"Everything looks good on me," he says, sneering at me.

"I'm sure it does," I look at Janet, wondering how she can stand him. What decent guy talks like that? He sounds like a bitch.

Janet intervenes and drags me to the table next to us. "Kate, this is Maya," she says.

"Hey there. Are you having fun? Isn't this fun. I'm having so much fun," Kate says, staring in the general direction of my face. Before I have a chance to reply, she turns to the guy with his back to her to confirm whether he is having fun. I'm wondering if that is John, the number-snatcher, when he turns around and my jaw drops.

It is Mark.

I sober up three degrees, enough to quickly scan the people he is with. There are several European-looking men and three women, all in their late twenties or early thirties. The woman sitting directly across from Mark has a friendly face with round honest eyes, shoulder-length hair tucked behind her ears and bangs across her forehead. She reminds me of Angela Merkel for some reason. Next to Merkel is a pretty blond, wearing a wedding ring and getting busy kissing a guy.

My eyes come to rest on the last female in the group, sitting next to Mark. She immediately sets off all my feminine instinct alarms, signaling code red. She is a petite brunette with shiny long hair, dazzling skin, dark brown eyes and a ladylike way about her. The type who stirs up the male protective instincts, making them feel like more of a man. She is sitting way too close to Mark for my comfort. She is pure danger. Penelope Cruz kind of danger in all her cute, sexy, feminine ways.

I make a quick assessment of my two potential competitors, and decide I can take on Merkel, but Penelope is going to be a challenge if she has her eyes on him. She is out of my league unless I resort to ruthless, conniving, ladylike psychological warfare.

As I am busy strategizing, Mark sees me, smiles, and nods hello.

I nod hi back. Why is he being so discreet, I wonder.

I need to get a hold of myself and stop overanalyzing.

He notices me blankly, staring at him, gets up, and walks over to me. My heart skips a beat. I wonder if Damien Hirst can draw the butterflies now flying inside me.

"Hi, Maya," he says, smiling.

"Hi, you. Are you following me around town?" I say, trying not to sound nervous.

"Your personal stalker," he says, shyly looking down for an instant.

"Are you having a good time?"

"This is crazy. The entire city's here," he says as he looks around.

"Did you watch any of the races?" I ask.

"I'm afraid not. Quite embarrassing."

I sigh and say, "I'm so relieved. Now I don't feel that bad." From the corner of my eyes I see Penelope turn around to check on Mark. Her gaze slides past him, to me.

"I was warned about that earlier," he says, chuckling, oblivious of Penelope's wandering eyes. "Apparently most people here don't see a single horse at the World Cup."

"Sad but true," I say.

All of a sudden he bends down to pick something up from the grass. When he comes back up, I see he is holding one of my bumblebees between his fingers.

"Oh! That's mine."

"Hmm, a bumblebee," he says, curiously. He looks at my hair. "Should I put him back on the hive?"

"Eh. Why don't you keep it."

Our eyes lock for an instant, he gives me a sweet smile, and puts the bee in his pocket.

"Are you here with your girlfriend?" Crap! Where did that come from? I wish to evaporate into a tiny particle never to be seen again. I can't believe those words just escaped my mouth.

He chuckles. "We're with friends."

We who? What does that mean?

"Are you here with your boyfriend?" he asks, grinning.

My heart is ready to leap out of my chest. What should I tell him? Should I lie and see how he reacts? I am too drunk to be smart and come up with a clever answer, so I just say, "No."

❂

He was about to say something else when Janet walks over to me and says, "I'm not feeling well. I may get sick any second. Do you mind if we leave now?" She then notices Mark and says, "I know you. You are the…"

DESERT MOJITO

Drunks are like children. They speak the truth. What if she says, "You are the one Maya has a crush on," and then I nod in confirmation. I cannot trust myself or Janet under the circumstances. I cut her off mid-sentence and say, "Come on, Janet. Let's go. Nice talking to you, Mark. See you around."

"Do you need help?" I hear him say as I'm walking away with Janet on my arm.

"We should be fine. Thanks."

A gentleman, too. Could he be any more perfect?

Kate turns to us and says, "You're not leaving are you? I want you to meet John." She winks at Janet and whispers, "The number-snatcher." She points ahead to a guy holding a beer cup, stumbling towards us.

I am not sure if I am drunk or if he really is the same guy who was calling me bumbles and the sheikh's wife. As he gets closer I realize that, unfortunately, it is he.

"I don't feel good. I'll meet him another time," Janet says, holding on to my arm, walking in zigzags.

I snatch her hat off the Lebanese guy's head as we stumble to the exit gates.

✸

By the time I get home it is past three in the morning. All I can think about is Mark, and how one of my bees made it into his pocket. I wish my bumblebee had Cupid's power. And that it would come to life, just for an instant, to sting his heart and make him fall in love with me, forever.

I RAN, YOU RAN, WE ALL RAN, FROM I-RAN

Shortly after my exile to Switzerland, the revolution succeeded without me (believe it or not). But my return home was further postponed due to the breakout of the Iran–Iraq War. Not only did I miss the revolution, but I was missing the war, too.

I was too young to know how to make sense of my emotions. While stranded safe and sound in an Alpine haven trying different flavors of Swiss chocolate, the Iraqi missiles were targeting Tehran, forcing my family and friends to take refuge in the mountains. Mountains were the only common denominator in the two scenarios. Talk about not knowing how to feel: Good? Bad? Fortunate? Guilty? Grateful? Helpless? All the good feelings were for selfish reasons, which made me feel guilty and bad, no matter how many Swiss chocolates I gorged down.

✺

Darius (not the great King of Persia but the great Iranian singer in exile) put it best in one of his songs, comparing Iran at war to a bird with its feathers drenched in blood. My cousin, who had also fled the war, used to listen to that song and drink whisky on weekends in Irvine, California whenever he felt homesick and miserable.

A dejected expat.

Many years later, when he moved back to Iran, he still listened to that same song and drank whisky on weekends. This time around he was miserable and homesick in a place he could no longer call home.

DESERT MOJITO

A disillusioned patriot.

✣

There seems to be a direct correlation between one's distance from a war at home and guilt at heart; the farther away from the front lines, the greater the guilt. The expatriate diaspora of all war-stricken countries are sneered at by their compatriots when back home, while the compatriots at home are made to feel equally guilty by war veterans who were on the front line.

Compatriot: Were you here during the war?

Expatriate: No.
(already feeling guilty)

Compatriot: Where were you?

Expatriate: Away.
(ashamed to name any place other than Iraq or Afghanistan or some other troubled country)

At this point, usually the look on the compatriot's face displays a mixture of envy and resentment.

Compatriot: You were lucky.

Expatriate: Yes.
(Translation: Guilty as charged. I am sorry. I wish I could have taken the whole country with me.)

✣

I RAN, YOU RAN, WE ALL RAN, FROM I-RAN

"No roots, no tree, no family, no me," Faithless sings faithfully while I'm mopping the kitchen floor, in my four-hundred-and-seventy-square-foot studio.

❂

Home does become a fluid concept for those who have voluntarily or involuntarily moved from place to place more often than nature intended for one lifetime.

According to my father, I behaved oddly on that autumn day he and my mom dropped me off at the boarding school, entrusting me to the hands of the great universe (if only they knew the Universe was into Eurotrash music). I insisted they leave as soon as possible so that I could get on with my unpacking and settling down. Hello? What may have instigated such an unromantic, insensitive request on my part? Was that my helpless, tough reaction to an unalterable situation? Did I know that there was no point in postponing the inevitable goodbyes and separations? That the sooner, the better? So Mom, Dad, I love you both, but let's get on with the show?

Who knows what I thought. But the same involuntary coldhearted attitude seemed to have stayed with me as a survival tool. It has become a familiar, unknown part of me, this pattern of "uproot, float, replant."

When it is time to move on from whatever or whoever, imagine you are a tightrope walker balancing hundred feet off the ground. To make it across the wire, you can only concentrate ahead in order to take the next balanced step. Should you be tempted to look back, you will lose balance and fall off. Just remember: Under no circumstances are you to look back. Not until you have settled down in your new environment. Even then, you can merely peek back to make sure no shady characters are following you. This image works best when envisioned in high definition or 3D.

Survival of the coolest. Many roots or ruthlessly rootless? What to do? (With an Indian accent.)

ESMI MAYA = MY NAME MAYA

"To be or not to be." That is *not* the question in the Arabic language. The issue was resolved long ago. The first thing they teach you in an Arabic language class is that there is no "to be."

Incidentally, it is hard to learn any Arabic while going about your everyday chores and life in Dubai. With local Emiratis being a minority, Indians a majority, and Filipinos running the service industry, you would be lucky to remember your English, the unofficial language officially spoken in town.

I decide to learn Arabic just for fun. And to be prepared, in case I got kidnapped by any terrorists or pirates and needed to negotiate my way out. I figure that I speak Farsi already, so I should learn Arabic now, and Korean and Somali later—then I'll be good to go.

❂

It's the first day of class. Here we all are. Eleven students: British, American, Swiss, Indian, Iranian, Turkish, Serbian, Japanese, Spanish, Lithuanian, and German. A mini-representation of the non-Arabic speaking expatriates living in Dubai. I'm not sure where the Russians are; zooming around Sheikh Zayed Road in their Ferraris, perhaps. After all, who needs to speak any language at all when money speaks the first and the last word everywhere.

Looking around the classroom, I feel like I am at a United Nations assembly meeting, gathered to discuss, resolve, or further complicate global issues.

DESERT MOJITO

Our teacher, a sweet Lebanese lady in her sixties, smiles and waits for us to settle down. "*Marhaba*," she says. Then she points to herself. "*Esmi* Amira."

We all know what's coming our way. That finger is going to go around, pointing at each of us to state our names in the same manner. *Esmi* Caroline. *Esmi* Rob. *Esmi* Hamish. *Esmi* Maya, etc.

Naturally, we all assumed we were saying, "My name is so and so." But as it turns out we were just saying, "My name so and so." My name, Maya. I bet Sacha Cohen's Borat would have picked up speaking Arabic faster than the rest of us. When you think about it, "to be" is a redundant verb. A subject *is* the proof of something's existence. And that's that—*khalas*, enough, finished. Once you clarify what you are talking about you can just jump to whatever you want to say about it, without using any form of the verb "to be."

The closest substitute used for "to be" in the Arabic language is the verb "to exist." So the question is not "to be or not to be"; the question is "to exist or not to exist."

✪

I am looking around, wondering about everyone's existence when the classroom door opens. A guy walks in. He's of average height, with wavy dark hair, a long nose, and close-set dark eyes. He looks like he is in his late thirties and is wearing jeans and a white button-down shirt with the sleeves rolled up. He apologizes to the teacher for being late, looks around the room, and walks over to the empty seat next to me. We make eye contact and smile.

We are all waiting for him to get settled down so that the teacher can point her finger at him. He puts down his books on the table and looks up at her. She greets him in Arabic and points to herself and says, "*Esmi* Amira."

She then turns to the Indian guy and he says, "*Esmi* Hamish."

Now she looks back at the newcomer, and waits for him to introduce himself.

"*Esmi* Paolo," he says. "*Ana men Italia.*"

The UN assembly is now complete with an Italian, already talking his head off in Arabic. He turns to the girl from Lithuania to inquire about what the teacher has covered in the fifteen minutes that he was late to class. She is more than willing to help out with a ready smile. I decide to ignore him. I keep my back to him and face the teacher throughout the first half of the class.

After an hour of hellos, how-are-yous, and I-am-froms in Arabic, a tiny headache develops into a full-blown one as my brain adjusts to the new language. The teacher finally announces that it is time for a break—*esteraha*. Everyone leaves for the pantry except for me.

I occupy myself by looking through the book, *Arabic for Businessmen*. I'm thinking, "How about just *Arabic for Business*?" After all, nine out of the twelve students in this class are women. In my head I start planning a full-scale businesswomen's revolution, chanting slogans in Arabic in the streets of Dubai, asking for "R-E-S-P-E-C-T" and demanding equality. I look up and startle when I see the Italian standing right next to me, looking over my shoulder. Sneaky.

"Hi," I say.

"*Marhaba*," he says, showing off his Arabic.

"*Marhabtayn.*"

"Your name is Maya."

"Yes."

"Beautiful name. Where're you from?"

"Oh. Everywhere and nowhere. Here and there."
"You have an American accent."
"Yes."
I keep staring at him, drawn to his gaze.
"Are you okay? I don't bite," he says.
"I'm sorry. I have a little headache, and feel a bit off."
"Hmm. Maya is an international name. It means truth in Japanese."
"Huh! It means illusion in Hindu. Which region are you from in Italy?" I say, pulling myself together.
"Tuscany. Near Florence."
"That's nice."
Right then the students and teacher start walking in the classroom.
"My bites usually don't hurt," he says, smirking as he walks back to his seat.
I give him a fake, no teeth smile and dismiss his cheesy line. There is something both exciting and annoying about him. Who is this guy?
At the end of the class, the teacher makes us exchange numbers with the people sitting next to us, in case we are absent or miss an assignment. Paolo is to my left and Francesca, a sweet Swiss girl, sits to my right. Paolo's business card only has a mobile number and an e-mail address. No job title. His last name is Catelli. I make a mental note to Google him as soon as I get home.
"Please. No crank calls," I say jokingly as I hand him my card.
He looks at me and asks, "What it means? Crank call?"
"It means don't call and hang up, or sing or blow in the phone."
"Ah," he says, happily. "No, signorina. Just biting."

I wonder if his inane flirting lines take away from or add charm to his existence.

Time will tell. *Fiy 'amaani l-laah.* In God's safety, goodbye.

ABU DHABI, BABY!

"Abu Dhabi, watch out. Here we come!" I shout out excitedly, holding on to the handle as Janet swerves the car around the bend, getting on Sheikh Zayed Road, heading down south to the capital, an hour's ride from Dubai.

"Janet, love, our lives are in your hands. Unfortunately," Asif says. "Please get us there in one piece." He straps on his seat belt and clutches the handle above the door.

"We're late. I'm not going that fast. Am I?"

"The speed limit is a hundred here—in kilometers," I inform Janet. "You're going hundred and twenty *miles* per hour. I'm not paying for any traffic tickets."

"I thought it was a hundred and ten out of town."

"We're still in Dubai, love. Please slow down and turn up the AC," Asif says, fanning his face dramatically with his hand.

"All right. All right. I'll slow down. I like Michelle. She's the only one not complaining."

"That's 'cause she's busy texting," Asif leans towards Michelle, trying to peek at her message.

"And, because she usually drives faster than Janet." I look at Michelle in the back seat. She is quietly ignoring us, smirking and texting all the while, working the buttons on her cell phone like there is no tomorrow. "Janet, it's really sweet of you to offer to drive us tonight. Thank you so much," I say.

"Yes. Very sweet. Thanks, love," Asif lets go of the handle to rub Janet's shoulders from the back seat.

"You're most welcome," Janet tilts her head smiling. "My pleasure."

ABU DHABI, BABY!

We are on our way to the Elton John concert. Asif, the key instigator, invited me—but as it turned out, Janet and Michelle were also huge fans of the one and only British Sir Diva.

"I still can't believe they allow such a high-profile gay artist to perform in the capital of an Islamic country," Janet says.

"It's not like he's going to gay out on stage," I say, and immediately hear Asif's screech of disgust from the back seat.

"Maya!" he screams, "what in the world is 'to gay out?'"

"I'm sorry. Not familiar with the lingo. You know what I mean. Anyway, being gay or straight has nothing to do with a person's professional competence."

"I hear all the performers are warned beforehand to dress modestly and comply with the Islamic laws as far as their outfits and the songs they sing and things they say on stage goes," Janet says.

"True. George Michael didn't sing 'I Want Your Sex' at his concert," I say. "That was an awesome concert all the same."

"George Michael—there! Another gay performer here in the UAE," Janet says.

"Honey, we'd have to sit on our asses watching camels perform here if they were to eliminate all the talented, sexy, straight or gay performers and artists," Asif says.

"Talking about risky behavior—hey, Asif, was that ass-groping incident one of your airline's flight attendants?" I ask.

"I heard about that. No it wasn't. But we all think it's a vindictive setup between these two guys."

"Californication" is blasting from the radio. Janet turns down the volume and says, "What's this again? It sounds interesting."

"So, listen…" I begin to recount the hot Dubai gossip-slash-news. "Some Brazilian flight attendant has been accused of, and I quote, 'groping' the bottom of an Arab man at a bar nightclub. The Brazilian says it was an accident, and the victim says it was 'an intentional, hard grope. No doubt about it.'"

Janet and Asif are cracking up.

"I wish I were the victim of an ass-groper," Asif says.

"Listen. There's more. Do you know how much the penalty is for touching someone's 'posterior,' as the news put it?"

"There's a penalty?" Asif asks, in a state of shock. "Honey, then I've been letting a lot of criminals get away."

"Bet you have. It's a serious crime to touch bottoms, posteriors, backs, fronts, and groins in this country. It gets you up to fifteen years of imprisonment." I sit back and let them digest that for a bit.

"That's crazy," Janet says in disbelief. "But Asif, why do you think it was a setup?"

"Because they say that these two guys were colleagues and had problems at work."

"What I want to know is what the Arab was doing at a bar," I say, wondering if the guy was wearing a *kandura* at the time of the incident.

"Good question. I'm confused about the Islamic laws here. There're so many contradictions," Janet says.

"Hello! Religion. It's like questioning why the sky is blue," I say.

"I guess all religions are funny," Janet says. "Last week, one of my Emirati colleagues invited me to her women-only private boat party. She had rented out a beautiful fancy boat and we sailed around Atlantis. We had such a great time. Anyway, I was the only Westerner among all these women in their *abayas* and *sheylas*. I was so shocked to see them all unveil the minute we left shore. As if the captain and the two Filipino caterers didn't count for men."

"Well, did they?" Michelle asks.

"And she speaks," I say, turning to look at Michelle.

"Yes," Janet says. "At least the captain looked straight. Not sure about the Filipino guys, though. But that's not the point. I see women with their heads wrapped in a veil without an *abaya*, in tight jeans and shirts. And then there're some without the *sheyla* covering their heads, wearing an *abaya* like an overcoat with the front open. And to make matters even more confusing, there are those Iranians." Janet sneers at me in frustration. "Maya, maybe you can shed some light on this. I have not met one religious Iranian to this day, and it doesn't make sense because from watching the news, one gets the sense that the Islamic laws are even stricter there than anywhere else in the region, except for perhaps Saudi."

To Janet I am as good as the voice of the Iranian nation. Poor nation.

I tell her what I think. "Traditionally and in general, Iranians are a moderate nation. They all believe in God and they may pray three times…"

"I thought it was five," Janet says.

"Five for Sunnis, three for Shi'as. The majority of Iranians are Shi'as."

"Those lazy ass Iranians," Asif says.

"Whatever. So yeah, as I was saying, they may pray, and may also have their little shot of *araqh* or vodka on the weekends. But I have no idea what the deal is with the Gulf chicks and their *abaya* and *sheylas*."

"If I were a prophet…" Asif says.

Janet and I both turn to look at him. I am wondering how he is planning on finishing that sentence. Michelle also glances up from her phone, raising one eyebrow, before looking back down to continue texting. Imagining Asif as a prophet is both entertaining and scary.

"…I would say: All the ugly, fat people must cover up and all the gorgeous hot ones must bare it all."

"Ha! No comment." Janet smirks at him from the rearview mirror.

"Imagine, a gay prophet. Now that would be the day," I say. "Would that singer Amen fit in your hot people category? He caused quite a riot taking his shirt off on stage during his concert in Dubai last month. Michelle, remember?"

"Hmm?" Michelle mutters from the back seat.

I turn around to see her engrossed, texting away happily again.

"Anyway, it was mad. In the middle of his fourth song, 'Treacherous,' he takes his shirt off. He finishes the song, and immediately all the lights come on. The DJ who had opened for him jumps behind his stand and starts playing some random song. Amen is standing there in the middle of the stage looking all confused. The crowd goes crazy, whistling, shouting, 'Take it off.' He leaves the stage and comes back ten minutes later with his shirt on, apologizing to the crowd, saying he meant no disrespect."

"Sir Elton John is a proper gentleman. He won't take anything off. I love his outfits," Asif says.

"I love his wigs and glasses," Michelle says, finally putting her phone away.

"Who were you texting?" I ask her with a touch of annoyance. I turn around to give her the eye and detect a mischievous look in her eyes.

"You don't know him. I met him last time I was in Beirut."

"I love, love, *love* Beirut," Asif says, placing his hand on his heart, emphasizing the L more strongly each time. "I had so much fun there when I was still single."

"Where's Peter, by the way?" Michelle asks him, trying to dodge answering my question.

Asif frowns, puckers his lips and says, "He's on an assignment in Bahrain. My poor baby."

"Michelle, don't change the subject. Are you keeping secrets? Who's this new secret admirer in Beirut?"

"No secret. His name is Charbel. He's a friend from my NDU days, my university back in Beirut. Last month when I was there I ran into him at Sky Bar. Oh! I almost forgot." She digs in her bag and pulls out a bottle of Absolute Vodka and three plastic cups, and announces, "The Car Bar is open, ladies."

"And what happened at Sky Bar?" Janet inquires this time. We are a nosy crowd.

"Nothing. We just talked and flirted a little. He was always kind of interested in me…So let's see."

Asif looks disappointed at the no-action ending of the story. "You should've just slept with him."

"I did."

"What?!" Janet and I scream out.

"Why didn't you tell us?" I say. "I feel betrayed!"

"I was going to. Really, it was no big deal."

"Good for you," Asif says, happily. "Crazy Lebanese. Please pour me a double shot."

Michelle fills his cup.

"Michelle, please be careful. I don't want to get pulled over." Janet slows down to a hundred and ten, giving Michelle a serious look in the rearview mirror as she hands out our drinks.

"You won't get pulled over. Just don't drive too fast. So sorry, Janet. You can have your drink when we get there. We'll save you some."

"Do you have anything to mix it with?" Asif asks.

"I do," I say. "I was in charge of chips and tonic."

"Love my girls," Asif says. "So is this Charbel cute?"

"Yes. A typical handsome Lebanese guy."

"They *are* hot," Asif says.

"You see, Maya," Janet says, glancing over at me, "I am not the only one into Middle Eastern men." She seems happy to finally find herself among her "Love Middle Eastern Men" support group.

"Whatever. I have a hard time with them," I say.

"Well, fine, I have heard some cheating horror stories," Janet says.

"Oh. Have you now?" I say.

She shrugs one shoulder. "I hear more about disloyalty here, compared to the men back in the States."

"I think it has a lot to do with the upbringing," I say. "Here, married men don't feel it's morally wrong to keep a girlfriend on the side. They do keep their affairs a secret, though. They almost expect a medal if they have been loyal to their partner."

"And what about the women? I wonder how lax and accepting *they* are," Janet asks, sounding puzzled.

"Women are not lax in Lebanon," Michelle says. "We hate all the cheating and…"

"What to do?" I complete her sentence shaking my head from side to side. "Cheers, everyone. Here's to finding us some non-cheating men."

I turn around and raise my cup to Michelle and Asif.

"I got myself one non-cheating jewel," Asif says.

"You are the suspect in this scenario, darling, not him." I turn around and wink at him. He mouths, "Bitch," letting his bottom lip hang lower and longer than necessary.

"So," Janet says, perking up to Michelle, "do you think this new guy from your university has potential? He's all the way in Beirut."

"I don't know. I just saw him that one night. I was with my family the rest of the time."

Janet nods. "Is your whole family back in Beirut?"

"Some. My older sister's in the States, another one's in Doha, and one of my brothers is here."

"Wow! How many brothers and sisters *do* you have?"

"Janet," I say. "This is where you're supposed to first say *mash'allah*—'it's God's will.' Remember? It was one of the first lessons in our Arabic class."

"Oh. Sorry. *Mash'allah, habibti*…Still not clear when to use it. Is it in reply to when someone says something good, like about their health or other stuff?"

"That and whenever you want to express your appreciation and happiness for someone else's fortunes. You say *mash'allah* to protect them from the evil eye," I say. "The closest expression in English I can think of is, 'Knock on wood.'"

"Or scratch your ass," Asif says. "Janet, love, it's already very grand of you to try to understand this Middle Eastern stuff. Nobody expects you to know when to say *mash'allah*, or *al-hamdulillah*, or whatever. Don't let Maya stress you out."

"Asif! You are such a fart. I didn't…"

"All right, kids," Janet intercepts, "Asif, thank you, *habibi*. I'm really trying but it's not easy understanding it all. There're so many unspoken rules and dos and don'ts. I guess it's true for any culture. But I'm intrigued."

"You're doing really well," Michelle reassures her.

"*Shokran*," Janet thanks her. "So how many siblings did you say, Michelle?"

"There are four of us."

Asif and I scratch our asses.

Janet says, "*Mash'allah*, I just have one older brother. *Khalas*."

"I don't have any siblings," Asif says happily.

"That explains why you're so spoiled," I tease him.

"Look who's talking. Miss I'll-Work-When-I-Feel-Like-It!"

"For your information, I've been supporting myself since college. I don't have to explain myself to anyone." I turn around and stick my tongue out at Asif. He does the same.

Janet changes lanes, letting an orange Lamborghini zoom past us and disappear down the freeway. "I love big families. I wish I had a big family," Janet says.

"How old are your parents?" Michelle asks.

"They're in their early seventies. That's another thing—I've lived abroad on and off for about seven years now and I feel that I should be spending more time with them, or at least live on the same continent. But I'm not ready to move back to the States."

Asif holds his cup out to Michelle. "Refill, please. Where else have you lived, Janet?"

"Quite a few places, actually. Japan, India, Spain, Hungary."

"Very nice. I didn't know that. What did you do in all those places?" Michelle says.

"Miscellaneous stuff. Office work, bartending…But teaching English, mostly."

"Hmm. Nice strong drink, Michelle. It's working." Asif takes the packet of chips from me. "Maya please turn up the AC. Janet, what do you do here?"

"I'm a senior soft skills trainer at Dubai Gas and Electricity, Dewa."

"A Dewa diva. Being American, you must make loads of money there," Asif says.

"Can't complain."

Asif squints at the taste of his vodka. "Michelle, how about you? You're in what? Marketing?"

"Human resources."

"Oh. So with all this market crisis what do you do over at Human Resources all day?" Asif asks. "Isn't there a hiring freeze?"

"Not really. I'm busy. The IT telecommunication industry hasn't been hit as hard. Thank God."

"I wish I could say the same for the airline industry. I'm just glad to have a job." Asif checks himself in the rearview mirror, brushing his fingers over his eyebrows with his pinky sticking out.

"You are beautiful, darling,'" I reassure him.

"Tell me something I don't know." He puckers his lips and blows me a kiss.

"Maya told me you're planning on having a big wedding bash in Dubai. So, when's the big day, Asif?" Janet asks.

"Ah." He sighs. "Please. I don't want to talk about it. It stresses me out. It will be sometime in May but we're still looking for a venue. It appears that we ought to be more careful and low key than we'd thought. You just heard all the stories with the gropings and crime. So ridiculous."

"I could just imagine the headline news in the *Khaleej Times*: Dubai Busts Grope Party. Two hundred fabulous men and fifty women arrested," I say, knowing how my joke could well be the actual news.

"Please. Don't joke about it," Asif looks sad and worried. "It's not fair being discriminated against, let alone feeling unsafe for being gay here. I told Peter maybe we should just forget about the party."

"Come on. I'm sure there's really no need to worry, *habibi*," Janet says.

Michelle shakes her head, dwelling on her nail file, and says, "It's just a gathering."

"I also believe that it's not for governments and religions to decide who we should marry," Janet says firmly.

"Or to have sex with. The Middle East is the graveyard of broken hearts," I say, all the joke gone from my voice.

"Ouch," Janet says.

"No, I'm serious. Most people end up doing what their families and tradition expects of them. So everyone has sex with the one they love in secret before marriage, only to end up marrying the one their families approve of in the end. Now here's the catch: A woman breaks up with the boyfriend she loves, and then sews herself up or pretends to be a virgin when marrying a man chosen for her. That husband-to-be has to break up with his girlfriend, or boyfriend in some cases, to marry this revirginized woman whom his family has chosen for him. So everybody's marrying the other person's love in the name of honor and social façades just to keep their families happy. The married couple accepts their circumstances but the woman will always daydream about her true love, who is now married to some other woman, who herself is probably daydreaming about some man." I breathe and take a big gulp of my drink.

"Love, did *you* understand what you just blabbered off?" Asif looks at me with raised eyebrows. "What I heard was man, woman, love, marry, blah, blah, blah."

"That's generally true," Michelle says. "In Lebanon it's not as bad. But families' approval in marriage is still one of the most important things."

"I see what you're saying, Maya. Everyone's married to someone else's love. That's very sad," Janet says. "There seems to be a lot going on behind the scenes that we as Westerners aren't aware of when it comes to this region. I was so surprised when I heard that the hotels aren't allowed to rent rooms to unmarried couples, and that there's a jail penalty for that."

"Yeah, but nobody really checks," Michelle says.

"They won't check," Janet says, "but if these tourists get in any kind of trouble while here, that's the first thing the authorities put their fingers on."

"Especially if they find out you're gay or Muslim," Asif says.

"Poor gays, Muslims, and gay Muslims," I say, finishing off my drink, holding my cup out to Michelle for a refill.

Michelle's phone beeps, breaking the odd heavy silence lingering in the air. We all turn around and give her the look. Asif tries to snatch the phone from Michelle's purse, and Janet turns up the radio.

The radio jockey announces, "To get you started, here's a song for those of you heading down to the Elton John concert in Abu Dhabi. A beautiful evening indeed. Temperature's in the low thirties, a cool breezy night. And a full desert moon. Here he is, Sir Elton John and Kiki Dee."

Janet turns up the volume even more.

Don't go breaking my heart…

Right on cue, Asif starts singing along with Elton John and Janet with Kiki. Michelle grabs her phone back from Asif and starts texting as Janet floors the accelerator.

✪

Abu Dhabi, home of the UAE royal family and government, is the modest capital of the seven emirates and one of the richest cities in the world. The city has a welcoming, traditional, simple texture compared to the flamboyant, boisterously modern neighboring Dubai. The Emiratis outnumber the expatriates and Arabic is in fact the first language spoken.

The concert is at the open-air theatre in the Emirates Palace Hotel. We arrive at eight thirty, well ahead of time and way ahead on our alcohol consumption. Janet refuses to have any of our vodka-tonic at the cozy Car Bar. She parks and drags us to the concert venue, which is already packed with Elton John fans. We make our way to the closest drink stand and get in line. Michelle is in a better state of sobriety than Asif and

DESERT MOJITO

I, who are both giggling like little girls, daring each other to grope someone's "bottom" and get us all in trouble.

❂

I am too restless to stand still in the crowd, and announce that I will meet them back here in ten minutes. I stagger away, feeling good and happy. I look around and see a lot of other people in the same or an even more twisted state of sobriety than mine.

I feel a light tap on my shoulder and turn around. It takes me a while to react to the person standing in front of me. I had totally cleared my memory of him. And according to my clairvoyant consultant, our paths were never to cross again. So, what is he doing here standing in front of me?

"Hi," Kamran says, giving me the crooked smile that used to drive me crazy. He has gained weight, grown a full beard, and has lost the spark in his eyes—gone is the Kamran trademark. Alas. "Surprised to see me here?"

"Hi. Yes…I am…I'm shocked."

"Can you believe I finally managed to get my passport. I paid the penalty for dodging my military service all those years."

"They were probably happy to get rid of a thirty-five-year-old fleeing soldier?" I say, still in disbelief.

"Probably."

"Did you fly in from Tehran just for the concert?"

"Yes."

"You never struck me as an Elton John fan. Who are you here with?" I lose my balance and have to grab on to his arm to keep from falling. He holds me up and keeps his hand on my arm.

"Are you drunk?" he asks, smiling.

"Yes. A little. I hardly drink anymore and when I do…" I burp. "Sorry."

He laughs and lets go of my arm. "We flew in last night. I'm here with my brother and Kasra. Kasra's the Elton John fan. Not me.

"Where's your girlfriend? Rumor has it that she runs a pretty tight ship, not letting you out of her sight," I say maliciously, knowing his Achilles' heel too well. It drives him crazy to have the reputation of being a henpecked man on a tight leash. The leash was our problem. I did not have one. I was way too easygoing and respectful of his space. But in his head, my attitude translated to "enjoy your life without me around but make sure you come home to tell me about how much fun you had at the party, the concert, the ski trip, the road trip," and so on.

He throws his head back and laughs. "I missed you. You haven't changed." He looks me in the eye and says, "It was a guys-only trip."

"I can see you haven't changed, either."

I have a flashback of how I dreaded his "all male" trips to the Caspian Sea and Kish Island, keeping me at arm's length, giving off the impression of being a single available guy whenever he could.

Now I was on the other side. I was no longer the pathetic helpless girlfriend waiting for him at home. I was the girl he met by chance during one of his guy trips.

"Come on, let's have a drink for old time's sake." He takes my hand and leads me to the bar.

❂

My memory of the next hour is blurred and fuzzy. In a nutshell, I remember us kissing in the corner of the bar like teenagers, and being seen by Mark, as in a nightmare, and then being rescued back into reality by Asif.

"Maya!"

I am enjoying myself at the bar when I turn around to see the astonished look on Asif's face with his mouth still open on the "ya."

"What up?" I say, trying to appear as nonchalant as possible as I pull myself away from Kamran's embrace.

Asif is blatantly staring at him, not making the situation any more comfortable.

"This is Kamran. Kamran, this is Asif."

"Nice to meet you, Kamran." He finishes checking Kamran out head to toe, turns and looks at me, with his eyes widened, meaning he does not approve of what he sees, and says, "Sweetie, don't mean to interrupt whatever you have going here. Would you like to join us? We're heading down to the stage."

"Yes. I think we're just about done here." I'm feeling confused, dizzy, and too drunk to measure my embarrassment. "Bye," I say, looking Kamran in the eye knowing the love is gone, even though the chemistry is still there.

"I enjoyed that," Kamran says, curiously looking at Asif who is impatiently waiting for me with his hands on his hips.

Asif grabs my arm as we walk away.

"Oh my God! Asif! He saw me!"

"Honey everybody saw you. You could've gotten seriously arrested for that. He-*who* saw you?"

"Mark saw me! He's here! Crap. What am I going to do?"

"It's okay. It'll probably work to your advantage. Men like whorish more than wholesome."

"I hate you. I'm so drunk. I can't believe I just made out with the ex-love-of-my-life. Why? God why? Why did Mark have to see me? Now he's going to think I've a boyfriend and he won't try anything. Asif!" I'm shouting frantically. "Do something. Let's go find Mark. I want to tell him that Kamran means nothings to me."

Asif puts his arms around me, making me feel even more paranoid. What if Mark sees us now? He does not know that Asif is gay. Great. In Mark's eyes, I will be remembered as Maya, the lady of easy virtue, whore of the Middle East.

"Honey, trust me. Men are turned on by competition. Even though I do think you could've done with a much more charming competition than this Kamran. He was so ordinary looking. I would've never imagined you with his type. Did he have a pot belly when you two were together?"

"No! You are not making me feel any better."

"Are you sure Mark saw you?"

"Yes. That's the only thing I'm sure of in the past hour. Mark seeing me in Kamran's arms. He saw me as he walked past carrying two drinks. Two! Oh my God! He's probably here with his girlfriend, Penelope."

"Shhh. So what? People break up all the time."

There goes my chance of being with a man who vibrates with just the right notes, playing the perfect, most alluring tune to my heart. In my drunken state he is the embodiment of all the conflicting qualities I seek in my ideal mate: good at heart, naughty and good in bed, confident and serious but one who is flexible and makes me laugh. And last but not least, the man who finds me, Maya, all that he has ever dreamt of in a woman.

I look at Asif in despair, hide myself in his embrace, and stumble along.

The lights on the field go off. The bright projectors light up as Sir Elton John walks on stage. Everyone starts clapping. He is dressed in a long black tuxedo with a huge colorful flower embroidered down the front. He sits behind his grand piano and starts playing the ever-so-familiar tune to "Goodbye Yellow Brick Road."

I take that as a bad sign.

A prelude to, "Goodbye, Mark. Goodbye."

THE DIVINE PREJUDICE

"Ramadan Boy"

To eat or not to eat,
To cheat or not to cheat,

To gorge, to bulge,
Perhaps an ice-cream fudge,
Aastagh firullah! (used when asking for forgiveness)
Oh! Dear Allah,

Save me from temptation,
From luster,
From lust,
And the impinging desire to cuss.

Veil me from his kiss
His tender caress,
And those luscious lips.
Ooh! What bliss!
Alas! How must I fast?
When heaven is here,
At my reach,
At last.

I submit my poem, "Ramadan Boy," to a local magazine for their humor writing competition.

✪

It is the first Sunday of Ramadan, the month of fasting for Muslims. I am in Arabic class. It's ten thirty in the morning, break—*esteraha* time. I rush to the pantry to get some water to clear my throat of all the harsh Arabic words I mispronounced during the lesson. Our teacher has informed us that the Ramadan rules also apply to the pantry because it is a public area.

In all Islamic nations, even a liberal multinational one like the UAE, everyone—including the atheist, Taoist, communist, terrorist, and tourist—is expected to respect the rules of this holy month. To clarify the Ramadan dos and don'ts, the newspapers and magazines print a summary of rules for the non-Muslims and the non-observing, "bad" Muslims. The inappropriate behaviors to refrain from in public are: dancing, singing, playing loud music, swearing, wearing revealing clothes, and of course eating, drinking, smoking, and chewing gum between sunrise and sunset. With the exception of fasting, all the aforementioned behaviors are supposed to be observed, *year-round*, in all other conservative Islamic countries. How fun.

Although all the non-Muslim expats respect the laws, many think they should not be penalized for others' choice of religion, and find this month imposing. They believe that eating in the presence of a fasting group can only strengthen their faith in face of temptation. "Isn't that the whole point of this month after all?" they ask.

✦

I head back to the classroom with my water cup in hand.

There is a student back in the class already, sipping a cup of tea. She is from Lithuania, which is somewhere in northern Europe. She seems as harmless and sweet as all the other Lithuanians you meet every day. Except that today, she walked in and shocked everyone first thing in the morning by wearing a red traditional Moroccan outfit—a *kaftan,* a long, hooded robe, just like the one the witches wear in fairy tales. I'm thinking, "Maybe this is her way of showing respect for the holy month."

So here is the Little Red Riding Hood, watching me as I enter, following me around the classroom with her eyes. She waits for me to take a sip of my water, looks down at her outfit, looks back up in surprise, and opens her mouth to speak.

I am thinking, "Thank God. She has just realized she's wearing a *kaftan* and she is about to tell me how she's going through a rough period in her life." Feelings of empathy and compassion are already rushing over me, replacing all my earlier snap judgments.

When all of a sudden she raises her eyebrows and says, "You don't fast?"

Where did that come from? "What's it to you?" is what I would like to say. Plus, can't she see I'm drinking water…ergo, NO! I don't fast.

I remain calm and take another sip of my water. "No," I finally say, firmly.

"But aren't you a Muslim?"

At this point, I'm trying very hard to keep my cool and not make any comments about her nine-a.m., Lithuanian-goes-Moroccan, existential fashion crisis.

"Are you a Christian?" I say.

With a smirk on her face, she says, "Yes. I am. We don't have to fast like you guys."

From her tone, it is apparent that her Christian-since-birth religious righteousness makes her feel superior. I can almost hear her singing, "Nyah-nyah, nyah-nyah, nyah, nyah!" in her head, completed by, "We don't have so many restrictions, because the Creator likes us more. We are his favorites."

DESERT MOJITO

I wonder if the creation scenario goes something like this in her head: The Divine has created all the planets, moons, suns, and stars, then one day he gets bored and decides to create another one, ours. He picks up his creation wand swings it around, and POOF! A rock appears out of thin air. However, much to his dismay, it resembles a ball lightly pressed on two opposite ends rather than the perfect circle he had in mind. He's thinking, 'Hmm, I need to fix my wand. Let's see what I can do with this rock creation as it is.' He then twirls his magic stick a second time and sets the planet on a pivotal tilted orbit. Exhausted from a full day's work he lies down for a nap, letting out a sigh of relief. That is when his breath lightly blows over his lop-sided creation, setting it into the spin of a lifetime. Upon awakening, he checks back up on his rock creation and much to his amazement he notices a fully developed ecosystem with all shapes of life moving around on a now blue, green, white, and brown twirling marble. The human beings are having fun, eating apples, smoking, drinking, and creating. 'If they can create, then they can eventually destroy. Oh, no! Let me fill their hearts with love,' he says to himself. He picks up his trusty wand, completely forgetting its previous malfunction, and once again points and flicks it at his marble planet. POOF! And immediately after that, a big OOPS! The unrepaired wand has made a mess. Human beings can create with love, *and* destroy in the name of love. He then sends all these messengers to straighten things out, but it is of no avail. Their message keeps getting misinterpreted by their followers, who make a bigger mess of matters. At the end, all that is left are different, confusing doctrines making a mockery of the Creator, making him out to be a fashion designer who tells you what to wear, a dietitian who tells you what to eat, and a sex therapist who tells you when, how, and with whom to have intercourse. And the ones who were dealt the laxer rules are under the impression that they are the Creator's favorites.

As I'm about to tell her not to concern herself with these trivialities and that she has bigger issues to worry about, like the Big Bad Wolf shredding her outfit to pieces, the teacher walks in, saving the day.

✺

I wake up in total confusion, open my eyes, and stare at the ceiling. The image lingers in my mind: "Lord's Favorite," written across the label of a half-empty bottle of tequila with a picture of a huge red lily in the front. In the dream I was thinking, "This is a rather odd name for an alcoholic drink." I then wonder if I can be persecuted for having a sacrilegious dream.

I imagine the Creator sobbing in a dark corner somewhere, in total disbelief of the monster-beings that crowd the surface of his planet.

Favorite or not, it is hard to tell if the human race is racing to get closer to or further from divinity.

DESERT MO-HEAT-O AT SAND STORM

HEY, WHERE R YOU? U HAVING SEX?

I press the send button on my phone. Every time Janet is late in replying to my messages, I ask her if she is having sex. It's the fastest way to get a reply, usually to refute the charge and express regret.

HA! HA! GOOD ONE! YES! HAVING SEX ON
THE GOLF COURSE WITH LYAN, MUSTAPHA,
& MARTIN OUR INSTRUCTOR!

I text back, AN ORGY! DIDN'T KNOW THEY HAD SEX INSTRUCTORS IN DUBAI! CALL ME PLZ WHEN DONE.

My phone rings immediately. "Hello, you sex bomb," I say.

"Thank you. How did you know?"

It's a man's voice. Crap! I pull the phone away from my ear to check for the name. No name. I'm embarrassed and silent, desperately hoping that the self-righteous sex bomb has the wrong number.

"You have already forgot me?" he asks.

Then suddenly I recognize the strange English and the accent. It's the Italian from Arabic class. I wanted to kill Janet.

"I'm not calling crank. No whistling, no blowing," he says, chuckling.

"Hi, Paolo. I'm sorry. I was expecting a call from a friend."

"A sex bomb?"

I hear the smile in his voice. I'm feeling awkward. "No. Well. It's a long story. How are you?"

"Good. And you? How's your head?"
"Fine. Thank you."
"Very good. I finished the Arabic homework. You?"
"No. Of course not. It's not due for another four days."
"Lazy."

Whatever, nerd. I find his card in my Arabic notebook pocket and get busy Googling him.

"Well. I like putting things off till the last minute," I say.
"Brava." He chuckles. "I need something, please."
"Sure, shoot."
"Shoot who?"
"I mean. Tell me."
"Ah. Okay. I shoot." He laughs. "Tomorrow, I have to leave for Italy for two weeks. Can you e-mail please the new Arabic homework?"

He is such a geek. He will probably come back from Italy fluent in Arabic.

"Yes. Sure," I say. All of a sudden I am curious to find out why he is going home. "Is everything all right at home?"
"Oh. Yes. Yes. I must go to pick olive trees."
"Are you a farmer?" I blurt out, knowing very well he did not say milk cows, or harvest corn, but what do you call someone who harvests olives?
"Yes. I am an olive and grape farmer."

The guy learns fast. Well, too late now. Let him be the olive farmer. "You have an olive grove and a vineyard?" I say.
"Yes."
"Wow. That's great. What brings you to Dubai?"
"The hot weather."
"Plenty of that here," I say as I click on the only Google link for Paolo Catelli. CCC, the Classic Car Club. He is a member, and a classic Ferrari model is registered next to his name. Nice.

An Italian who drives a Ferrari and owns a vineyard. I'd better be nicer to him.

I hear him clear his throat. "Yes. It's fantastic. I was here for an art auction two months ago. Giuseppe, my friend, has a gallery in Florence. He collects artwork from Middle East. Lucky I was. He couldn't come to the auction and asked me to travel for him."

"Oh. Paolo. How exciting." I hear the immediate effects of the Google search in my voice. "Did you go to the Magic of Persia event and the Christie's auction?"

"Well done. How did you know?"

"I have some artist friends. But tell me, how did you end up staying in Dubai?"

"The weather's nice and Giuseppe's apartment was empty. Why not?"

"Sure. Why not? *Perche no?*" I say, giggling. I am beginning to disgust myself with my Ferrari-infected charm.

"*Brava, brava.* You speak Italian?"

"Not really. I just know the basic words from when I lived in Bellinzona."

"Bellinzona. *Brava*, well done. Tell me later. I go now," he says, just as I'm warming up to find out more about him. "Do you have my business card, my e-mail?"

"Let me see. I should." I say, as I flip his card around in my hand, wondering if I should step up my charm just a notch. "Is it pcatelli at yahoo dot I T?"

"*Brava.* Please no crank e-mails." He chuckles.

I decide that his sense of humor is annoying and there will be plenty of time later for playing the seductive card. "No promises," I say.

"Be careful. I have very good hacker friends," he says.

"No you don't."

He laughs out loud. "I will bring some olive oil for you."

"That'd be nice. *Bon voyage*, Paolo."

I hear him say ciao and hang up.

I have merely hung up as the phone rings again. This time I check before answering. It's Janet the sex bomb.

"Hey, your phone was busy."

"Yes it was. I was talking to an Italian farmer."

"Maya. You do have a very strange sense of humor. How're you doing?"

"I'm great. Michelle and I are meeting at Sand Storm for mojitos in an hour. Want to join?"

"Sure. It's been a while."

"Let's meet at the Starbucks next to Sand Storm in an hour."

"See you there, *habibti*."

✪

Sand Storm is a casual lounge on the promenade next to the beach. The area is called Jumeirah Walk, in the southern section of the city known as New Dubai. Its fancy shops, beauty salons, sidewalk cafes, restaurants, hotels, and a public beach have made it one of the most popular and crowded outdoor venues in Dubai.

Michelle and I are waiting for Janet by one of the two hundred Starbucks cafes on the sidewalk. It is a typical crowded Saturday evening at The Walk; singles, couples, families of locals, expats, and tourists are mingling. The young Emiratis are putting on a show, entertaining the crowd, cruising their Ferraris, Porsches, Maseratis, and Lamborghinis along the narrow cobblestone road that runs between the beach and the sidewalk.

"Do you know how to distinguish between the people from the Gulf countries by their *kanduras*?" I ask Michelle. "They all look the same to me."

"Not really. I just know that the Emirati ones don't have a pocket up in the front."

We are passed by an elderly man in a *kandura,* followed by three children and five women in black face covers—*niqabs*—carrying Fendi, Chanel, and Gucci purses.

"But I know which women are Iranian," Michelle says, nodding in the direction of a couple approaching us.

The young woman is wearing a *chador*—a long black piece of cloth literally meaning "tent" in Farsi. If you have never seen one being worn, the best way to get a feel for this outfit is to drape a cape from your head down instead of from your shoulders down. The women keep the *chador* from falling by holding it shut together with one hand under their chin or biting it tight with their teeth. The ones using their teeth as a tent-clip get their saliva all over the fabric, keeping it moist through the day. There is no scent as memorable as *Eau de Chador*, the dried-up-saliva fragrance on a fabric. A whiff of it can be used as an anesthetic to induce a partial or even major state of unconsciousness. But the woman coming towards us is holding the *chador* loosely with one hand, and carrying a Louis Vuitton purse with the other. She is walking tall and gracefully next to her young and equally elegant husband.

"Very good, Michelle. They're a cute couple. And where is the woman behind her from? Not the one in the *abaya*. The other one."

Confidently weaving her way between the parade of women in masks, tents, shawls, and robes is a six-foot-two blond Russian in blue pumps, white minishorts, and a blue off-shoulder top.

"She is definitely not from Iran," Michelle says.

"You never know," I say, laughing.

We turn around to see Janet making her way to us in her ready red-lips smile, her height dwarfing everyone around her, as usual.

"Well, don't you look all golfy in your white outfit," I say.

"You look like a Ralph Lauren model," Michelle says.

"I suppose that's a compliment. Thank you, but I'm not sure if golf is my thing. Too slow and boring. Especially in this humid weather. Sorry I'm late."

"No problem. I'm hungry. Need some *mezze*."

"Maya. You're always hungry," Michelle says.

"What to do?" I say, shaking my head.

We laugh.

"They have *mezze*. As a matter of fact, their hummus is one of the best I've had," Janet says.

"Then *yallah*," I say, hurrying them toward the Sand Storm.

✪

We place an order of assorted *mezze*, Michelle orders a *shisha*—a water pipe with flavored tobacco—and we settle down on the beanbags facing the Persian Gulf with our Desert Mojitos.

"Long time, no gossip. How's your dating life, Janet? Nabil, Kiyarash, maybe an Abdullah by now?" I say, sarcastically.

"No. No Abdullah. It's been crazy juggling just the two," Janet says, sounding exhausted. "Still not sure what to do. I really like both of them."

"I knew about Nabil," Michelle says, "but who's this Kiyarash?"

"He's a sweet Iranian guy I met at Caribou near my place last month. He's a graphic designer."

"I like Iranians," Michelle says.

"He's such a gentleman. He treats me very well. I feel like a princess when I'm with him. But I've had to go shopping for a whole new wardrobe because the Iranian crowd he hangs out with are always dressed up." Janet looks over at me and says, "Did I tell you he took me out to this really fancy Persian restaurant in Wafi on our first date? I tried the crusty rice. Hum. It's so good."

"Yum, *tadig*. I miss that," I say.

"Is it usual to fight over who pays for the bill or is it just Kiyarash and his friends?"

Michelle and I smile. "It's a Middle Eastern thing," I say.

"It was funny to watch the guys stealing the bill from each other," Janet says. "Interesting. Are women expected to offer, too?"

"Never. Women are almost never expected to pay when there are men around," Michelle says. The Indian waiter sets the *shisha* down next to her beanbag and hands her the pipe.

"I wish all men were like that," Janet grins.

"Yeah, there are many good things about the Middle Eastern ways but it gets tricky and complicated if you have different values," I say. "Even my father said it's hard for Iranian men to deal with a woman with Western values. Maybe it's all that Middle Eastern blood running through their veins. But then you can't generalize."

"Then how come he married an American himself?" Michelle asks.

"Love. Love is blind, they say."

"Maya may be right," Michelle says, puffing on her *shisha*. "It's difficult for a typical Western woman to put up with a typical Middle Eastern man."

"Why would you say that? I've met lots of nice Jordanians, Lebanese, Syrians, and Iranians who I've liked," Janet says.

"Sure. It's one thing meeting them, it's another dating them, and then it's a whole other thing being in a relationship with them. Of course, I repeat, one shouldn't generalize, even though that's generally how I feel," I say.

"I don't understand. Explain, Maya."

Anything I say will just raise more questions. "It's not easy to explain, really." I like to give Janet an accurate portrayal of what I know. "There is all this conflicting stuff going on." I hesitate, uncertain of how to expand on that. "Here is the thing, I think men from this region make very good responsible fathers but not great husbands. At least, that has been my take on the situation."

Janet tilts her head to the side, gives me her contemplative look, and says, "Interesting."

"All right. Forget all that. I can give you a more accurate profile analysis of this Kiyarash guy if I had a chance to meet him. But…On second thought, the best way to find out is to experience it firsthand. Has he lived in Iran all his life?"

"I think so. Up until last year when his father bought him a place in Dubai Marina and he moved here. His apartment is impressive for a twenty-six year old."

"Doesn't sound promising. A spoiled brat. Sorry," I say.

Janet frowns and says, "What? Why?"

"Don't pay attention to Maya—just have fun," Michelle says.

"I really think he's a nice guy. He pays a lot of attention to me and…"

"And shows you around like a trophy," I complete her sentence.

"What do you mean?"

"Iranians love Westerners, and having one as a girlfriend or a boyfriend is a very big deal amongst family and friends. An achievement. It gives them an air of prestige. And you will not be subjected to the same expectations as to your Iranian counterpart."

"I know what she means. It's the same in Lebanon." Michelle says. "Kiyarash will show off with you."

"I'm still not sure I understand why that's bad."

"That's not bad if it lasts."

"But that's true for everyone in a relationship. At the beginning making compromises is easy, but over time it becomes more of an effort," Janet says.

"True." I take a sip of my refreshing mojito. "I love the mojitos here."

"They're called Desert Mojitos," Michelle says, puffing on her *shisha*.

"I wonder why these taste so much fresher than your usual mojitos?" I hold out my glass, staring at its green contents. "No-heato in my mojito," I say, happily.

"I think it's the added sliced cucumbers," Janet says.

"True. But, there is a ting of some other ingredient that makes it familiar-tasting and exotic at the same time."

"The sand, perhaps?" Janet says.

"You should go ask the bartender. He's cute," Michelle says, winking, nodding to the bar.

I turn to check him out but get distracted by the colorful *mezze* plate our waiter has just placed on our table.

"Dig in, girls." I tear off a piece of Arabic bread and dip into the hummus.

Michelle takes away the water pipe from her mouth, turns to Janet and says, "Did you say he's only twenty-six?"

"Oh! No! Not Kiyarash again. Eat." I shake my head as I bite into a juicy dolma.

Janet ignores me, turns to Michelle and says, "Yes." A mischievous smile appears on her face. "Is that bad? A younger guy?"

"I think that's fine." Michelle shrugs her shoulders, places the pipe back in the corner of her mouth, and starts puffing.

I nod. "It's very Hollywood, Janet dear. And this is Holy Dubai filled with younger men. Come on, girls, try some. The *labneh* is delicious."

"Am I considered a cradle-robber?" Janet says, concerned.

"For sure," I say.

"Why? I'm only six years older than him."

"Not because of his age. It's because in this part of the world, guys stay their mother's little boys for most of their adult lives. They're catered to by women—their mothers, sisters, wives, daughters, whatever. The Middle East is a huge cradle for men," I say.

Janet is not listening to my cynical analysis of the cradle issue. She has been distracted by a text message that has just beeped in from her phone on the table. A delighted smile appears on her face. She reads the message out loud: "Hey Janet, long time, no hear. Sorry I was MIA. Had to leave on an unexpected work assignment for Johannesburg the day after we went out. It's a long story. What are you up to this weekend? Smiley face. Nabil."

"I'm going to tell Kiyarash." I wink at Janet.

"Where is this Nabil from again?" asks Michelle.

"British, of Indian descent."

"You're hoarding all the guys," I whine.

"Well, maybe if you weren't so discriminating, I wouldn't have to date them all."

We laugh.

I say, "True. I like all men but…"

"Are you sleeping with both of them?" Michelle asks Janet, interrupting me.

"Of course not. I've hardly seen Nabil. We've been out on a couple of dates. I really like him, but he's busy and not very available. He's always traveling. Here, listen to another one of his messages." She scrolls to find another text message and reads it out loud, "Hi. How are you? Just arrived last night from Mumbai, leaving for London tomorrow. Drinks next weekend? Smiley face."

"I don't like workaholics," Michelle says. "They enjoy work more than spending time with us." Her face is hardly visible behind the white cloud of smoke she has just puffed out.

"There's always something," I say.

I am taking a sip of my mojito when I hear a man's voice say, "Hello," from behind me. Janet and Michelle have already seen him and are looking at me, smiling.

I turn around. It's Mark. My heart begins to hip-hop. He is by himself, holding a bottle of beer, looking at me.

"Oh, hi, Mark." I stand up to greet him.

"Hi, how are you?"

"I'm fine. How are you? Long time, no see. I thought you had probably left Dubai."

"No way. I just got here." He smiles, glancing over at Janet and Michelle, who are looking up at him, smiling.

"Oh. Good."

I point to my mojito sisters who continue to blatantly stare at us. "Mark, meet my friends, Janet and Michelle."

"Hi Mark," Janet says.

Michelle nods and whispers, "Hello."

"Nice to meet you," Mark says, nodding at them, then looks back at me.

"How is it going?" I ask.

"All good. You know…Still getting the hang of things. Been busy setting up at work. Are you still going to the gym?" he asks, grinning.

Oh boy! If only he knew I've practically been camping there.

"Not really. I've been very busy, too," I say.

"What do you do again?"

My natural tendency would be to lie and say something odd and off the wall in response to this seemingly innocent question. One of my favorite responses since moving to Dubai has been, "I play the organ at the Presbyterian church in Deira," the old part of Dubai. The reaction I got to this reply was one of amazement and, "Wow! Dubai is great. Who knew there would be a Presbyterian church in Deira?" At which point I felt like such a loser because apparently the person had no problem taking me at my word. Not that there is anything wrong with being an organ-player; I just don't think I fit the type. My latest is, "I'm the Middle East manager for Hooters International restaurant chain." If they don't already know, once I explain the bodacious requirement for the Hooters employee, the reaction has been the same: guys smiling and women frowning, both saying, "You're kidding!"

But, I do not want to chase Mark away, so I decide to keep my strange sense of humor to myself.

"I'm a freelance commercial photographer. I also write social commentaries and poetry on the side and hope to publish my work someday."

Much to my surprise he smiles and says, "Can't say I've met a poet before."

"There's always a first for everything." That is the tackiest thing I could have ever said, but he keeps smiling.

"How long have you lived in Dubai?" he asks, shifting on one leg, crossing his arms.

"This is my fourth year."

"Are you familiar with the Middle Eastern culture?"

"Sure, why?"

"I've been looking for an artist's point of view on some concepts for my business. I need region-appropriate slogans or catch phrases for a branding type of thing. Have you ever done work like that, or are you interested in trying it out?"

"Yes, I've worked on branding projects," I lie. I would even learn to type in Chinese overnight if that's what it took to spend more time with him.

"Can we get together sometime to discuss what I have in mind? You may be just the person I've been looking for."

And you are definitely the one I've been looking for.

"Sure," I say.

"Do you photographer–poets carry business cards?"

"We sure do."

I turn around to get my purse from the table, and see both Janet and Michelle grinning, making faces at me. I sneak a smile at them for an instant before I get one of my business cards and hand it to Mark.

"Thanks. Nice color. Purple. I'll give you a call soon," he says. "It'll be great if you can help me out."

"Be happy to."

"Thank you. I'll let you get back to your friends," he says, politely. "Talk to you soon."

"Okay. Bye."

I sit back down and stare at Janet and Michelle blankly in a state of shock.

"Way to go, Maya. Finally," Janet says.

"Does he want you to write him a poem?" Michelle asks, picking out a mint leaf from her mojito, putting it in her mouth.

"No, he was vague." I'm in a daze and still need to digest what just happened. "Please let's talk about something else. I don't want to jinx it." There is an odd moment of silence. I'm surprised to hear the serious note in my voice.

Janet glances over at Michelle who is holding the *shisha* pipe in one hand, following Mark with her eyes as he makes his way up the stairs and disappears from our view.

"No jinxing," Janet says, "let's talk about Michelle now."

"Yeah, Michelle," I say, "whatever happened with you and Stephan? Did you dump him?"

"No. He's still around," she says, matter-of-factly. "We wrote on each other's walls on Facebook for a while, then he invited me over to his place to watch a movie, and, you know…" she smiles devilishly.

"That's great news." I raise my glass to drink to her but I'm still thinking of Mark.

"Who's this now?" Janet asks.

"This is my German neighbor," Michelle says.

"A neighbor? That's convenient. I thought you were dating the Lebanese guy in Beirut."

"Not dating, really. I saw Charbel briefly only once last time I was in Beirut."

"Long distance doesn't work. How'd you meet the German guy?" Janet asks.

"You're going to love this story," I say, chuckling.

Michelle sneers at me, then confesses, "It's embarrassing." She takes a puff of her *shisha*, blows out the smoke and says, "I was waiting for the elevator at my apartment complex. I'd just come back from the gym. I hear someone behind me calling out, 'Excuse me.' A blond, good-looking guy in a dark suit walks up to me. He says hi. I say hi. He smiles. I smile back. We get in the elevator. He looks at me and says, 'You dropped this back in the parking lot.' He is holding something up."

"What was it?" Janet asks.

"My black G-string underwear."

The three of us burst out laughing.

Janet says, "How times have changed, from dropping white handkerchiefs to black G-strings. So what happened next?"

"I thought of lying and saying it's not mine, but then I was sure he had seen it fall out of my gym bag. So I took it back and thanked him. He said he's new in Dubai. I gave him my card."

"That's after she got him back for the underwear by telling him she was a devout Muslim when he had asked her about bars in the neighborhood."

"Good one," Janet says.

"Anyway. He added me on Facebook and last week he invited me upstairs to his place to watch a movie…" She raises her eyebrows, smiling. "He's a good guy."

"Hard guys are good to find," I say.

It's a Freudian slip, and Janet screams out, "Maya!"

"I swear that was unintentional."

"Sure it was," Michelle says, smiling.

Janet turns to Michelle. "Those are your lucky black underwear. Take good care of them," she says.

"Yeah. God works in mysterious ways," I say, glancing up to the sky just as the clouds float away, unveiling the beauty of the desert's full moon over the water.

WHEN IT RAINS, IT POURS

I e-mail Paolo his Arabic assignment with a short message asking him about things back home. I joke about the cold weather front hitting Dubai, and the temperature dropping all the way down to seventy-five degrees Fahrenheit.

Of course he can check the weather report to find out that it has actually been raining hard for the past twenty-four hours. As it turns out, this fabulous city has not been designed with rain in mind; there are no gutters, no drainage system. The dry desert land floods immediately—and the picture on today's *Gulf News* of an Indian guy rowing his canoe along Dubai's flooded streets is proof of that.

Last night I was at the gym when it started to rain. By the time I left two hours later, the parking lot was flooded and people were waiting around for the downpour to ease. I got behind the wheel and hoped for the best. As I turned on the main road, I realized that driving my Honda down into what lay before me would be like diving into a swimming pool. I was getting ready to pull aside and wait around with the other stranded *mallers*, when I saw a red Mini Cooper drive past me and swiftly make its way to the slightly higher shoulder path around the mall wall. I decided to follow this confident little thing, praying that it was not planning on pulling any stair-climb stunts. Once out of the flood-zone, I looked at the street-turned-lake behind me, feeling sorry for all the drivers standing on the side of the road, helplessly watching their cars drown right before their eyes. I thanked my Mini Angel and headed home.

It's still raining when I check my e-mails one last time before going to bed, and find a reply from Paolo. Already.

DESERT MOJITO

From: "Paolo Catelli" <PCatelli@yahoo.it>
To: "Maya Williams" <MayaRWilliams@gmail.com>
Subject: Marhaba

Marhaba,

Thank you very very much for homework. It's very cold here. Raining every day. I am jealous of you in sunny Dubai.

We can only take olives when it's not raining. I was in a tree all day yesterday. The olives are nice and big this year. See picture of trees in my back yard. And a picture of the "small" wild boar around the house.

Ma-asalama
Ciao.
Also the homework looks easy.

P.

I click on the picture attachments. His olive grove is a huge field on top of a mountain overlooking a valley. I'm impressed. What was he doing in a tree? He probably meant on top of a tree. The second picture is of a man standing next to a huge black animal hanging upside down in front of a bonfire. I take a closer look. That man, it's him, Paolo. No! Who is this guy? Is he a professional hunter, too? I'm no longer impressed—I'm really curious. I e-mail him back right away.

WHEN IT RAINS, IT POURS

From: "Maya Williams" <MayaRWilliams@gmail.com>
To: "Paolo Catelli" <PCatelli@yahoo.it>
Subject: Marhaba

Marhabtayn Paolo,
You are welcome. The homework looks easy but it's actually a little confusing because of the gender articles. Good luck :)

Thank you for the photos of your olive grove and the wild beast. The olive grove looks very Tuscany and the beast looks very scary. Is that you in the picture? Did you hunt that boar or…!? Are there a lot of these boars around your house?

We will not have Arabic next week because of some religious holiday.

Have fun in the cold. Good luck in the tree with your olives.
Maya

✪

I am being chased by a Ferrari through a thick forest of giant mushrooms. I hear a loud ringing all around me, and look back to find a hairy wild boar hanging upside down from a tree behind me. Then I'm driving the Ferrari chasing the boar with Paolo sitting next to me, smiling. In the dream, I realize this is a dream, and force myself to wake up. I'm breathless. My heart is pounding fast. But I can still hear the loud ringing. It's coming from my mobile. I crack one eye open just enough to find the screaming phone and bring it up close to see the caller's name. It's still a blur. But I can see that it's a local landline number 04…

Contemplating whether to answer the call or not I hear, "Hello? Maya? Hello?"

Crap! My finger has accidentally hit the green button. The guy's voice sounds familiar, too. I decide to speak. "Hello?"

"Hey. Mark here."

Half my brain is still staring at the wild boar and the other half is registering a pleasant, familiar voice. Then it hits me. My eyes and mouth pop wide open. I sit up. I'm tongue-tied.

"Mark from the gym," he says. "I saw you last at Sand Storm. I asked you about commercial slogans and…"

"Of course I remember. I blanked out there for a second. How are you? Sorry, it's been a crazy day."

"Really?" he says, sounding a little surprised. "I always imagined artists and poets working at odd hours through the night and sleeping during the day. That's why I waited till noon to call."

"Not this artist," I lay back down and shut my eyes. "How've you been?"

"Good. Busy. Remember what I briefly talked to you about? The branding slogan thing?"

"Yes, of course."

"If you're still interested, I was wondering if we could meet on Tuesday the fourteenth, so I could show you what I have in mind and if you can help out."

"Tuesday, Tuesday…"

"That'll be in ten days. I hope to finalize a lot of the boring, time-consuming bureaucratic stuff by then and get down to the fun stuff."

"Sure. I'll make time. Where's your office?"

"In Deira next to the Russian Hotel. Do you know the area?"

"Not really," I say, wondering if he gets lots of Russian action.

"Do you want to write down the directions?"

"Actually I'm driving now. Do you mind texting it to me?"

"I'll do that," he says, calmly.

"Tuesday, what time?"

"How does eleven sound?"

"Eleven is good."

"All right then. I'll text you the address and will see you soon."

"Yeah. Sounds good."

"Bye."

"Bye," I say.

I hear him hang up but I keep the phone held up to my ear. My eyes are still closed. I have a huge smile on my face. My phone beeps.

SEE YOU AT 11, TUESDAY THE 14TH.

We are textually connected. Text me up, baby.

I open my eyes to a beautiful sunny day.

LET US DISCRIMINATE, PRETEND, FIT IN

I am at Ramin and Parisa's villa on the B "frond" in Jumierah Palm. They are an Iranian couple who have lived in the States for the past twenty years, and have just moved to Dubai from Seattle with their son Sam and daughter Nasim, eight and six years old. Parisa is my cousin's childhood friend, who I came to know during her frequent visits to Tehran during my time working there. She is a financial strategic planner and her husband, Ramin, is a neurologist. Ramin was offered a job in Dubai and they both relocated after Parisa had also secured herself a position at the Swiss National Bank.

Parisa and I are sitting outside, facing a body of water: once part of the Persian Gulf and now part of an Arabian Bluff. Ramin is checking his e-mails on his laptop station set up at the bar, and their children are playing tennis on the Wii. I'm reviewing the babysitter profiles sent to Parisa by one of the many giant Filipino employment companies in Dubai. Having a Filipino nanny–housekeeper is one of the major perks of moving to Dubai for families. The children get an entourage of Filipino babysitters, all busy chatting with each other, running after the kids, blurting out words in Filipino which probably translate to *little spoiled brat, rascal, fatty*, and so on.

I'm looking through the finalists Parisa has scrupulously short-listed.

"What were the criteria exactly for these lucky five women to have made your illustrious list?" I ask.

"My assessment was made on the basis of age, looks, education, and of course, experience."

"Looks? Why would that matter?" I lower my voice and whisper, "Are you worried about Ramin?"

She cracks up. "Oh! God no! I've asked around and it's a well-known fact that the pretty ones end up either pregnant or married the first year."

"So these five are the oldest, ugliest ones?" I look at the pictures on the forms.

"Not ugly, but not pretty or naughty-looking either. I also needed someone who can cook and help with the housework."

"Why can't you take care of your own kids?"

"Oh! Maya. You obviously have no idea what you're talking about. I can't quit my job. We still have our house back in Seattle and we just bought this villa. Plus I enjoy working and there's just not enough time to do it all. It's nice to have help."

"Whatever. Are you going to make her wear a pink uniform?"

Parisa laughs out, puts out her cigarette and says, "Of course not. I hate those uniforms. I want her to be part of the family. You know?"

I really don't know. I always assumed that when I had kids and if I were rich, I would just hire someone to cook and help around the house, so I could spend time raising my children. But this theory still remains to be tested.

"This one looks good." I read out the qualifications off the form: "Speaks fluent English, cooks, has five years of babysitting experience, twenty-eight years old…She's not too good-looking. And she's a Pisces."

"Let me see that." She takes the form from me. "Not bad. Why is Pisces good?"

"I like that sign. For most part they are level-headed people who mean well. I enjoy their company. But then it all depends on your sign, too. What's yours?"

"Scorpio."

"Perfect. You two will get along just fine."

"Can you check the others astrological signs, too, please? I'm so glad you're here." She hands me four more forms. "So, how's your work going?"

"It's all right."

"I don't know how you can afford living here by doing freelance work."

"It's easy. I don't do all the stuff you guys do—no Sunday champagne brunches, weekend trips, eating out at five-star hotels, shopping, massage parlors, beauty salons, tennis lessons, horseback riding lessons…What else?"

She chuckles, and in all honesty and wonder, asks, "What do you *do* then?"

"The usual," I say, "observe, *savoir*, savor."

"Hmm. Too profound for me. But seriously, how do you make ends meet here?"

I lean close and whisper, "I'm also living off renting my body on the side, if you know what I mean," and give her a wink.

"Really?" she says, smiling. "And how's that working out for you?"

"Must you ask?" I sit up, sticking out my chest.

"You have it so easy. No kids, no husband, no in-laws, no nine-to-five job."

"I do have a pretty good life. Thank you. But I can't take credit for it. It hasn't been by choice for most part. It has just happened this way so far."

"Lucky you," she says with wonder in her eyes.

"Lucky Maya," Ramin says, coming towards us with a bottle of wine, three glasses, and a smile. "So, how are you? Where've you been? We hardly see you."

"Busy chasing after a bite of bread," I say with a tired voice, imitating a typical Iranian response.

"Is that right?" he says.

"How do you guys like it here?" I ask. "Bet you don't miss the freezing, drab Seattle weather."

"We love Dubai," Ramin says as he uncorks the wine. "We love the sun, and how everything's simple, safe, and convenient. How many years have you been here now?"

"Four."

"You're practically a local. By the way, how come houses don't have mailboxes here? How are we supposed to receive mail?"

"I know, weird not to have a mailman. The streets aren't marked yet. I'm sure you've noticed that the city's still in the making. You must get a PO box at the post office. You can use your home address for courier service only."

"Okay. Now my next question. Where can we buy alcohol in town?"

"Technically, you can't if you're a Muslim. Get it at the airport. There're also a few designated stores that sell alcohol to foreigners who have a liquor card."

"How will they know if I'm a Muslim?" Ramin asks, pouring wine in our glasses.

"Honey. Your features scream Muslim," Parisa reminds Ramin.

We all laugh. "A few years ago, they used to be strict with the Muslim thing, even at the airport," I say. "Customs stopped my friend's uncle who had just flown in from Tehran. Supposedly he had stocked up on bottles of whiskey and vodka, and the customs officer told him that Muslims aren't allowed to buy alcohol. He said he was Zoroastrian. He was then asked to show his passport. Guess what his last name was?"

"Mohammadi?" Ramin suggests.

"Close. It was Haji Rahmani!"

We burst out laughing.

"Imagine. Haji. He could not be any more Muslim," I say.

"Mom, what is a haji?" Sam asks. He must have just sneaked up behind us.

"Where'd you come from?" Parisa turns around and gives him a kiss. "It's too complicated, my love. Good Muslims who go visit God's house in Mecca are called Haji."

"Are we haji?" Sam asks as he wraps his arms tight around Parisa's neck.

"No, sweetie. We're not," Parisa says.

"So we are bad Muslims?"

"No. We are not. Where's Nasim? Go play with your sister." She kisses him again and sends him off inside.

Parisa rolls her eyes and says, "That Muslim thing is going to be a headache. Can you believe taking Islamic studies classes is mandatory for all the Muslim students at all the schools here? We tried to get them out of it but it was too late. They know we're Muslim."

I chuckle. "Hey, that'll inspire Sam to become a haji."

"That'll be the day," Parisa says, rolling her eyes.

"So, Maya…Do you really like living here?" Ramin asks, sipping his wine.

"It's all right. It gets really boring and hot as hell in the summer. It's a very safe country, though. There's hardly any theft and crime. And everyone goes about doing their own thing without bothering one another."

"We've noticed that," he says. "Who're your friends?"

"I have a lot of friends. American, Lebanese, British, Pakistani…"

"Where's your boyfriend from?" He is trying to sound innocent, asking an obviously nosy question.

"Which one?"

"Oh! How many are there?" He raises his eyebrows, smirking.

"Sweetie, she's got one from each country. That's the real reason why she moved to Dubai," Parisa says, winking at me.

"I wanted to introduce you to a really nice colleague of mine," Ramin says. "He's an oncologist, half-Iraqi, half-Palestinian, he—"

"Wow! A double whammy!" I blurt out.

Parisa presses her lips together. "Maya! That's mean."

I shrug my shoulders. "Yeah, sorry."

Undeterred, Ramin continues his pitch. "He's a good man. And quite handsome, too."

"I don't like good men. I like bad boys. Why else do you think I'm still single?"

"Are you serious? Why?" Ramin asks surprised. "Bad boys don't want to settle down. Don't you want to settle down?"

"I do. But…Parisa knows. I've washed my hands clean of the Middle Eastern men."

"But why? We're the best. Handsome. Strong. The most manly men you can find on Earth." He rolls the tip of his invisible handlebar moustache.

"Trust me, Ramin, I know all the good attributes but my experience with Kamran was sufficient for a lifetime. And for your information, he actually did have the real moustache."

"How long were you guys together?" Parisa asks.

"Too long. But at least I cleared all karma with him. According to my clairvoyant, our paths will supposedly never cross in any future lives." That is, if I stay on my intended path and not wander off of it like I did at the Elton John concert. I feel a passing pang in my chest as I recall the incident.

"Ha! You're weird," Parisa says, lighting up another cigarette.

"Maya, you can't generalize." Ramin swirls the wine in his glass and says, "Just meet this guy. His name is Ziyad."

"Ramin *joon*. She has to consult with her clairvoyant first," Parisa says, coming to my rescue.

"Yeah, that's right." I nod to Ramin. I hand back the babysitter forms to Parisa and say, "And the Pisces is still my favorite."

"Okay. Thanks. What are you doing this weekend? Do you want to come to Nasim's birthday party at Ski Dubai?"

"You've invited all the kids to Ski Dubai?" I say surprised. "Doesn't that cost a lot?"

"It's the easiest option. They have birthday packages. The kids play in the snow, go sledging, play games, get fed…"

"Funny," I say. "Your kids escape the beautiful Seattle snow, only to end up in the mall playing with fake snow. How many kids are there?"

"Around fifteen. Everybody goes all-out on birthdays here. It's way more overdone than in the States."

"I hear birthday parties here cost as much as a mini-wedding. Don't buy into it, Parisa," I say, even though I know the reason they moved to Dubai was that they actually like to buy into it all.

"We have to," Parisa says. "We don't want our kids to feel left out."

I wonder if by "kids" she actually means herself and Ramin. Then I remind myself that single, childless people have no right to judge the group on the other side of the fence.

BOOGIE WOOGIE ART

"Well, well. Look who's back from the dead," I say quite audibly as I make my way to Mona. A few other apparently back-from-the-dead martyrs turn around to look at me, making sure I am not talking to them.

Mona is Kuwaiti–British. We became art gallery buddies after running into each other at a few exhibitions. We usually meet up at the opening night, look at the art, mingle with the artists, check out the crowd, have a bit of champagne and hors-d'oeuvres, catch up on the Dubai gossip, hug, kiss, and go home till we meet again at the next event.

"Where have you been?" I say as we hug.

"In a relationship."

"And?"

"And it's over. And I'm back." She raises an eyebrow.

"Should I congratulate or comfort you?" I ask carefully.

"A congratulations would be comforting. Are you still mental, you little toad? I've missed you."

I congratulate Mona, as we settle down a bit awkwardly on the red and black *Cadillac* beanbags made specially for this event.

We are at Maverick, one of the über-active art galleries in Al Quoz Industrial Area. Prior to the city's mega-expansion, this area was considered the periphery of Dubai, but now it is smack in the middle of everything. It faces the sail of the Burj al Arab Hotel across the freeway and the ski slopes of the mall just a few streets down. However, it still remains unpretentiously barren and pristine—an area to avoid at night for the faint-hearted, who do not care to be reminded that they are living in the middle of the desert in the Middle East. Among warehouses and storage spaces, huge trucks and high loaders roam the dusty streets, and laborers on foot or on dinky bikes weave in and out of traffic in their colorful sarongs. And I will never forget my fright the first time I lost my way to the Front Line Gallery and found myself at the Al Quoz cemetery gates instead.

The art galleries are all tucked away in the sandy alleys and dark backstreets of this industrial area. The art scene is dominated by mostly Middle Eastern artists, including ones whose works are censored and banned in their own countries—namely, Iran. Although there's still censorship in compliance with the UAE's Islamic laws and political stance, these venues serve as quasi-independent, intellectual oases amid this vast desert of flamboyance and philistines.

This month Maverick is holding a special music-related film series on Wednesday nights. Last week we were happy to watch Metallica get semi-cured through group therapy, and tonight we may get depressed as Chet Baker croons and trumpets his way through addiction.

The seats are filling up fast and the salon has become jam-packed in a blink of an eye. People stand in the back. I take a quick look around for familiar faces and Mark. No luck. He is too fresh off the boat to know about this place. Oh well. What to do? Mona and I squeeze deeper into our beanbags as the lights go off and the movie starts.

We are halfway through it, watching one of Chet's rare happy moments—he is poised to kiss his girlfriend on the lips—when all of a sudden the image on the screen goes blank and the salon sinks into complete darkness. For an instant nobody talks and there is complete silence.

Then we hear: "Sorry for the censorship. But we have to do this…" It's the gallery owner—she is standing next to a young guy who is struggling to hold a black piece of cardboard in place over the projector lens. "Otherwise we will be banned from showing any more films," she continues. We can still hear Chet and his girlfriend make kissing noises.

The room bursts out into chuckles and laughter, momentarily reminded of the very Islamic state of affairs here. Finally the "obscene" scene is over and we can watch the rest of the movie uninterrupted.

The movie ends and the lights are switched on. I stretch and look around, checking out the crowd.

"How depressing. Poor Chet. Drugs have taken away so many legends," I say.

"Yeah," Mona says, sounding unmoved. "Any cute guys around here?" she says, scanning the gallery.

"So you're back on the prowl already? I really missed you," I say. "Seriously, what happened to you? Where have you been the past few months?"

"Sweetie. Trust me. It was intense." She brings her head close and whispers, "I almost married an undercover secret service guy of some sort, or maybe a hit man, for all I know!"

"What? Secret service? Like James Bond? How'd you manage that? Or rather…not manage that?"

"Right. To be honest, I rather not talk about it in detail. It still literally freaks me out." She pauses. "He said he loved me and that I was the one he had been dreaming of all his life. He even introduced me to his parents on Skype."

"The spy who loved you," I say, giggling.

"You suck."

"Oh, come on. Do tell. This is too good." I'm genuinely shocked. "Did he come right out and tell you he was MI5 or 6 or whatever?"

"Of course not. He claimed to be a tactical commercial agent for a South American transport company." She sighs. "All right, here's the story in a nutshell. We met at a networking event and things got serious, fast. We were practically living together in under a month. Two weeks before leaving for our first trip together to Musandam, Oman, I was over at his place. He was working on his computer and I was watching the telly. His building security guy rings up to let him know his car alarm has gone off. He runs down to the parking lot. I get up to quickly check my e-mails. That's when I see he has forgotten to log off his instant messenger. So naturally, I first check out his contact list. No one interesting there. Then I dare to click on his mail."

She stops talking. Scans the area with her eyes. Bends down and whispers in my ears "I find the page carpeted with e-mails from Federal Bureau of Investigation."

"FBI? *Holy cow*! What'd you do?"

"Shush," she says, checking over her shoulder. "I open one and can't make sense of it."

"Nooo! You didn't!"

"Yes I did. I had to know what I had got myself into. But then all of a sudden I got scared, wondering if these messages have special detectors identifying the reader."

"What? Like, 'Hi Mona, we can see you' type of thing?'" I say, laughing.

"Not funny, you nutter. Anyway, I confronted him when he came back up, and asked for an explanation of the FBI e-mails. He told me he used to cooperate with Interpol for a while and that's why they have his name on file, blah, blah, blah. I broke up with him that night."

"Why? Maybe he was one of the good guys. You should've stuck around with the spy who loved you."

"Are you kidding? I can't stand anyone remotely connected to undercover operations of any kind."

"Unless you're under the covers with them?" I tease her. "Not sure what that means, coming from someone who goes into hiding for three months."

"I'm sorry, sweetie. I'll make it up to you."

"Where was he from?"

"He claimed to be American–Argentinean, but who knows. Now, enough about me. What about you? Anyone special in your life?"

"Yeah. No. Not really. I sort of really like this one guy, Mark. But nothing has happened yet."

"Hmm. *Inshallah*, soon. Wait for me here. I need to use the loo."

She walks down the hall to stand in the long bathroom line. I see someone waving to me from afar. It's none other than naughty Asif. He turns around, whispers something to the tall guy standing next to him and they both head my way.

He gives me a warm hug, gently kisses me on one cheek, and says, "Peter, this is Maya. The one I've been telling you about. The crazy one."

I shake Peter's hand. "Thanks for that great introduction. Hi, Peter. So glad to finally meet you."

"Likewise. I've heard so much about you."

"All good I hope."

"Oh, yes," Peter says, smiling. "Asif loves you."

Asif looks happier than I have ever seen him. "Maya. Guess what?" Just like Mona, he checks over his shoulders before he whispers, "We finally set our Dubai wedding party date."

I clap my hands and hug him. "I am so happy for you. When is it?"

"May fifteenth."

"I can't wait, Asif. That's great."

"We will send you the official invitation soon. It'll be at our friend's mansion in Jumeirah."

"I'll be there."

"You better. Please find a man by then." He winks. "We have to dash out to pick up a friend from the airport. I'll call you." He blows me a kiss, and the happy couple prance away, their pinkies brushing against each other.

Mona is back in time to see them walk out of the gallery.

"Are they together?" she asks, while searching her bag to check the text message that has just beeped in.

"They are more than together. They got married a while back."

"*Wallah?*"

"*Wallah.* They got married in Boston."

She is not listening. She is preoccupied reading her text message.

"Is the text from Money Penny?"

She grins. "Do you think it's funny being James Bond's ex-fiancée?" She hands me her phone and says, "Here, read this."

Obligingly, I read the message out loud: "How are you, hon? I'm in Doha. Back on Tuesday. How about dinner on Wednesday? Smiley."

"*Hon?* Who is this guy?" I hand the phone back to her.

"No one, really. Just some chap. I don't much fancy him. He's around."

"Is that right? He must fancy your fanciness," I say with a horrible imitation of her crisp British accent.

"Jealous?" She smirks at me, raising an eyebrow.

"So very jealous."

"When's our next art event?" she asks, half her attention on a text message.

"Let's see. Art Dubai is coming up soon."

"Oh, that's right." She stops texting. "How does this sound: 'Wednesday is a good night at the Cavalli Club. Have a safe trip. See you soon.'"

"Cavalli, eh? Poor guy. Pricey."

"I'm worth it. Should I put a smiley at the end?"

"Sure, why not. Smile it up." I say as I make my way to my car. "Let's stay in touch. Don't go missing on me again."

"Promise. Great seeing you, love."

"Same here. Stay out of trouble, Pussy Galore."

WATER, FISHY MEN, AND CLUB CHURCH

It's two in the afternoon on a Friday, the prime-time weekend pool hour in Dubai. I make my way to the elevator with a towel, a water bottle, a copy of the *Time Out* magazine, and of course, my mobile.

The elevator door opens and I see four guys staring back at me. They make room for me as I smile sweetly and step inside. The elevator door closes, goes down one and half floors, and then stops. Ten seconds pass and it is still not moving, and neither are any of the men around me.

I am wondering how long before somebody reacts. That's when I hear, "Shit," uttered by one of them.

As I look at the four faces around me, I have to force myself to hide a mischievous smile. I am immediately reminded of one of those ethnic jokes, which starts off like this: "An Indian, a Chinese, a British, and a Russian are stuck in an elevator. The British says, 'Shit'…"

Another few seconds goes by before the Asian guy dressed in work clothes, who is hauling a huge leather shoulder bag, pushes the red emergency button. The alarm goes off, and miraculously the elevator starts moving.

"Phew. That was close," the British guy says.

Close to what, I wonder.

The muscular Russian, who is wearing a pair of baggy grey sweats and a tight navel-revealing t-shirt, has kept a straight face this whole time, and is staring straight at the door. The Indian guy is busy reading a text message that has just beeped in.

WATER, FISHY MEN, AND CLUB CHURCH

I'm disappointed in the eventless affair, thinking, Where's the joke in that? What an international group of duds.

I make my way to the only available poolside lounge chairs, next to three Lebanese guys who could pass for triplets. They are in their twenties with gym-built, tan bodies, oiled head to toe, reflecting the sunlight brighter than a mirror. One is texting. The other is moving his feet and head, tapping his fingers, singing under his breath to an Arabic song. And the third one answers his phone as it rings.

"*Bonjour yaa habibi, kifik?*" he says, as he tilts his head back, laughs and continues talking. "*Wallaheh?...Quand?... Demain?...A...A...*Okay...No! *Semaine prochaine* I will be in Beirut." He then bursts into laughter and whispers, "*Erfik... Yallah*, bye."

I was so proud of myself for understanding the Arabic/English/French combo. Some Lebanese do insist on speaking French. To an outsider they just look like French-speaking Lebanese, and not Lebanese-looking French. Somebody needs to tell them that.

As I'm judging and demolishing the polyglot Lebanese in my head, I hear a text message beep in. It's from Janet. LET'S GO DANCING TONIGHT.

DISCO?! I text back.

HEHE. DO THEY STILL CALL IT THAT?

THEY CALL IT THAT IF THEY WANT TO GIVE THEIR AGE AWAY. LET ME CHECK OUT VENUES IN TIME OUT.

K.

I lie back to flip through this week's *Time Out*. "Fifty Reasons Why Everyone Loves Dubai" is written on the cover, with a picture of two index fingers and thumbs shaping a heart around

"Loves." There is an entire week's worth of nightlife events to choose from at venues with virtuous, scientific names: Chi, Spirit, Quantum, Sanctuary, Alpha, Pure, etc.

I lie back. My thoughts wander off to Mark and our upcoming meeting. Again, I wonder if the girl I saw him with is his girlfriend. Probably. I doubt a man of his stature and looks will be left alone for long around here.

An unsettling feeling of confusion sweeps over me. What am I doing here? I should be married with children, checking out the "Kids" section of *Time Out* instead. After all, I was around when these places were still called discos, as opposed to these misleading holy names. This city and this lifestyle are ridiculous. This place feels like a huge sorority/fraternity house. How did I manage to avoid that scene all those years back in college, only to land in the epicenter of its real-life version years later? What a waste my life has been…

✪

"MAYA!" someone shouts from a distance.

It takes me a few seconds to find my way out of the dark crevices of my mind. I hear a woman's voice again, and sit up to see someone waving to me from inside the pool.

It's none other than Susan, my next-door neighbor, standing in the water. "Come on. Get in. The water feels nice."

Susan is a career woman in media, in her mid-forties and last I heard, still single. She gets attracted to high-profile politicians and businessmen who wear power suits, use Powerpoints, take power lunches, enjoy power naps, and date power-loving women like her.

She was in love with one of these power creatures for five years, but unfortunately, this powerman proved to be disempowered when it came to committing.

I disembark the morbid train of my thoughts and step in the cool, clear water. It does not take long for Susan to update me on Mr. Power's status; he ended up marrying a chick who, according to Susan, had *forced* him into marriage by getting herself pregnant. I'm thinking, now that's POWER.

I ask her, "Where do you think the problem is when it comes to settling down?"

"It's obvious, darling. Mature men who want to commit are as scarce as the water in this desert we are living in."

I'm thinking, Single men: mature, immature, and premature, do not move to Dubai to settle down.

"Do you think we're in the age of instant, effortless satisfaction?" I ask her.

"Huh? Not sure what you mean, but who knows what's going on? It just seems like they don't make them like they used to anymore," Susan says as she bends back, dipping her hair in the water.

"Men are slippery like fish," I say.

"And, have the memory of a goldfish," Susan adds, smiling.

I giggle and say, "Funny you mention that. Lately I've been wondering how having a short attention span may actually be an evolutionary leap forward—a survival of the fittest kind of thing, you know?"

"I don't know what to think. But I've been meeting a lot of people, both men and women, who gladly diagnose themselves as suffering from ADD to justify their fickle attitude." Susan rolls her eyes.

"Yeah," I say as I watch the Lebanese triplet dive in the water.

Water, water everywhere...

✦

DESERT MOJITO

I get out of the pool to find two text messages waiting for me.

One is from Janet. DJ OLD SOUL PLAYING AT TRINITY. HOUSE MUSIC. NICE VENUE. OK WITH YOU?

The other text message is from Caroline, one of the girls in my Arabic class. WATCH EURONEWS NOW! OUR CLASSMATE IS FAMOUS.

Curiosity is killing me. I pack up in haste, say goodbye to Susan, and head back to my apartment. The elevator is out of order again. I sprint up four flights of stairs as I run down the list of the people in our Arabic class. None of them seem newsworthy.

I turn the TV on. I have this nagging feeling I am not going to like what I see. The weather report is on Euronews. I flick through the other news channels—no famous classmates are anywhere to be seen. I switch back to Euronews and wait. Finally the headline news comes on: global warming…bomb explosion…largest artifact bust of the decade.

"OH! MY! GOD!" I scream out.

There he is! Paolo's picture splashed across the screen, staring straight into the camera. Standing next to him is a burly guy in a black suit, grinning.

I turn up the volume: "Giuseppe Brutto and his head of operations, Paolo Catelli, better known as CAT, have been arrested after three cargos of smuggled priceless artifacts were seized in Dubai. The prospective buyer is said to have been a Russian. Following their arrest, over one hundred million dollars worth of precious stones, art masterpieces, and artifacts were further seized in four warehouses outside Florence, Italy. The *carabinieri* and Dubai customs police are tight-lipped about the details of the arrest."

I am stunned. A chill runs down my veins. This is my closest encounter with a high-profile criminal. Come to think of it, there was something fishy about Paolo all along.

WATER, FISHY MEN, AND CLUB CHURCH

My excitement is too overwhelming for me to handle all alone. I call Caroline.

"Italian mafia right under our nose," I blurt out as soon as she picks up.

I hear Caroline laugh out loud.

"Hi, Maya. That's some news. Wasn't he your friend?" she asks.

"OH! God no! We exchanged numbers in class and he asked me to e-mail him our Arabic homework—which I did!" I begin to get worried now. "Oh, no! Do you think they'll check his e-mails to investigate the ones connected to him here in Dubai?"

"They might," Caroline says in a serious tone.

"Are you for real? Crap! Should I keep a low profile or leave town? But I haven't done anything. I'm a law-abiding Dubaian."

I hear her crack up. "Come on, Maya. Why would anyone suspect you? Do you know any Russian millionaires in the art scene here?"

"As a matter of fact I do," I reply, firmly.

"Are you serious?" She is not laughing anymore.

"I met him when he came to pick Paolo up from Arabic class one time."

"You're joking! What was his name?"

"Mikhail Gorbachev," I say and burst out into laughter.

"Ah! MAYA!" she shouts out.

"I'm sorry. You had it coming." I notice a small piece of paper slipped under my apartment door.

"Hey. I need to go. Mikhail is at the door to negotiate my hush money."

"See you in class," she says, and hangs up.

I walk to the door to pick up the paper. The message is handwritten in blue ink pen: "I am a housemaid looking job part-time to working. If you need plz call me. Thank you," signed, Rana and a mobile number.

I hear a message beep in. It's from Janet.

WHERE R U?!! TRINITY AT MIDNIGHT OK?

SOUNDS GOOD, I text back, looking forward to telling her about my close brush with the mafioso.

○

Trinity is on the thirty-third floor of Gulf Hilton hotel. Janet and I meet in the lobby. I fill her in on the Paolo breaking news as we are walking to the elevator.

"There is no reason to worry about being under suspicion just because you knew him," Janet says, dwarfing me in her high heels.

I look up at her. "I'm not so sure." I nod in the direction of the two guys coming towards us from the far end of the hall. "Here we go. The mafia are here. Janet, should anything happen to me, my Facebook password is jazzylullaby. Log on with my Yahoo account and inform everyone."

Janet laughs out loud. "Status report: Maya kidnapped by mafia. Help!"

"I'm serious. And if you run into Mark tell him that I was falling in love with him even though I hardly knew him."

"And do you want me to donate your clothes to charity?"

The look on her face is priceless when the two guys I had pointed out earlier walk up to us as we get in line at the entrance of the club elevator.

"Excuse us, ladies," the taller guy says, looking straight at me. Meanwhile, the stocky but better-looking one starts checking Janet out. "Are you going to Trinity?"

WATER, FISHY MEN, AND CLUB CHURCH

"Why do you ask?" I say, trying to look calm.

He looks at me intensely. "Can you please…"

…Follow us without making a scene. There's a gun pointed at you from the balcony, I finish in my head.

"…do us a favor. They don't allow single men in. Do you mind if we say we're with you?"

I'm staring at him blankly when Janet says, "Phew! You scared us. That would be fine." She turns to me giving me the I-told-you-they-were-not-from-the-mafia look.

We stand in line with our new male companions, Tariq and Firaz. Stocky Tariq cannot take his eyes off Janet, and Firaz is a multitasker; he is holding a conversation with us while texting, and non-discretely checking out every woman who passes by.

We escort the men in, and much to our surprise they do not offer to pay for our entrance fees. The two bouncers at the door have pumped enough iron to bounce any troublemakers off the walls with a flick of their pinkies. One of them asks to check our purses.

I joke, saying, "If you tell me exactly what you're looking for, I'll bring it next time."

He frowns and says, "So-ree?"

"Nothing," I say, as I put on a sweet smile, batting my lashes. I look away to see the sign, *Club dress policy: no national clothes, no shorts, hats, sandals.*

We pass inspection and make it inside the club. The music is loud. It is *very* loud. Once again I wonder if I am too old for this scene.

Janet is already in front of the line at the bar ordering our drinks. There is a lively mix of under-thirty-fives in all shapes and shades dancing, standing around drinking, and checking each other out on the dance floor. Scanning the area, I spot Amer, my Emirati friend from the gym. He is lounging comfortably in one of the VIP areas with a bottle of seltzer water in an ice bucket on the table. He is in the company of three other guys, who also appear to be from one of the Gulf countries.

I wonder if there are also any Emirati women here, incognito.

Janet comes back with two drinks, and we go up to the third floor to check out the scene.

"It's crowded," Janet shouts out as she looks down on the dance floor.

"Yup. Very," I shout back.

"It's too loud," Janet shouts over the music, which seems to be stuck on a sharp screech. It sounds like a shuttle getting ready for takeoff.

"Yup, Very," I shout back. I shake my head and say, "What to do?" The Indian accent gets lost in the music, which is thumping even louder now.

Just then I see Tariq making his way towards us. I nudge Janet. "Here comes your boyfriend."

"What?" she shouts out. She bends down and brings her ear close. But Tariq is already standing next to her before I get a chance to repeat myself. She turns around, sees him, then looks back at me, rolling her eyes.

I give her a reassuring smirk, meaning, "Good luck with that."

As Tariq starts talking to her, I look away, now appreciative of the loud music as the perfect buffer between their conversation and me.

I look back down at the clubbers on the dance floor below. All of them have one arm raised and are facing the DJ stand, which is high up on a platform to the side. With the green laser beam shining from behind, lighting his bald head, the DJ is nothing short of a preacher with a halo, perched in his pulpit. He is mixing, spinning, chopping, draining, slicing, cooking up songs from his altar, all to entertain the congregation facing him from the dance nave. His head is tilted to one side, pinching a huge headphone between his ear and his shoulder. He is building up the tempo, energizing the crowd with every beat he adds on. The dancers have their heads turned towards their raised arm, as if sniffing their armpits. The DJ is manipulating the dancers, making them more ecstatic, more eager for the climax. Finally a millisecond lapse of silence in the music signals the moment is upon them…and…there it goes—BOOM! BOOM! BOOM!—the dance floor pulsates with dancers popping up and down, with now both arms raised up high, cheering the DJ on.

Amen. Hallelujah.

I look over to see Janet's frustrated face, begging me with her eyes to be rescued from Mr. Tariq. I interrupt their conversation and employ the good old bathroom-escape plan. She says goodbye to Tariq and thanks me as we make our way back down to the ground floor.

I turn around to ask Janet if she wants to dance, when I see her talking to a guy. And from the look on her face I can tell she does not need to be rescued this time around.

"Maya, this is Bill," she shouts out as she nudges me lightly, letting me know something is up.

"Hi Bill, nice to meet you," I shout out, extending my arm to shake this guy's hand. With his strong Indian or Pakistani features, he looks like everything but a Bill.

"It's Nabil," he shouts out in my ear.

"I'm sorry. It's too loud in here," I shout back, once again reminded of the old people who are hard of hearing and mispronounce names when introduced to new people.

"No worries. Full blast, ain't it?" he says with the British accent coming through loud and clear.

DESERT MOJITO

I'm now certain that this is the infamous workaholic Nabil. Janet looks at me with misty eyes, smiling, double-ticking her eyebrows.

"I like this song. I want to dance," I say.

I wink at Janet and make my way to the dance floor.

As I turn to face the community dance partner, Mr. DJ, I see Amer coming towards me and waving. He makes it right in time for us to join in raising our arms with the crowd, jumping up and down to BOOM, BOOM, BOOM.

Shake it. Shake it. Yeah *habibi*.

CROSSING BRIDGES

"Good morning. Russian Hotel." The voice on the line is a woman's, a Filipino.

"Hi. Could you please give me directions how to get there?"

"Ma'am? Speak to who?"

"I need directions to your hotel, please," I repeat, using fewer words this time.

"Room number 280?"

"Connect. Reception, please," I say, hoping to get someone more helpful. The line clicks over.

"Hallo? Reception."

Great. A nice English-speaking Indian guy.

"Hi. Could you please tell me how to get there coming from south?"

"Madam? Is he a guest?" At this point I am ready to tear my hair out and realize the situation is not going to get any better.

"*Need address*," I say, slowly.

"Yes, madam. Where you come from?"

"From south. Marina area."

"Okay, madam. You go straight, straight, straight. Come to Deira. Al Maktoum Bridge. Turn right. Left at roundabout. Near clock tower. Russian Hotel opposite Rak Bank, between Air India and Pakistan Airline." He stops talking.

There is a moment of complete silence. My jaw has dropped and I'm staring into oblivion, in a state of disbelief—go straight, straight, straight? Where? Come to Deira! Daah?! How? Where in Deira? Which exit do I get off on? It's useless. I should have known better by now than to call and ask for directions. I have no idea what he is talking about, so I thank him, hang up, and call for a cab instead.

DESERT MOJITO

✦

I'm meeting Mark at eleven in his office to discuss the project. This is the first time we are seeing each other non-coincidentally. I have my professional outfit on, or at least what I imagine a photographer–poet posing as a PR agent would wear to a meeting: a basic pair of tight black leather pants, a black long-sleeve button down linen shirt, and a leather choker with an enormous silver peace pendant dangling down the front.

I'm excited. My heart jingles every time I think of him. I'm also nervous because I'd like to impress him, but I have no idea what his project is about and I feel unprepared. Why didn't I ask? Why didn't I get more information? Too late now. I just have to wing it.

The taxi driver, a Pakistani man in his late thirties, is not happy to be driving to Deira, the epicenter of Dubai traffic. In an attempt to distract him from where we are heading, I start asking him questions about his life. He has a wife and four children who he visits once a year in Islamabad. And he has yet to see his newborn son. He has a bachelor's degree in economics and has been living in Dubai for nine years.

When he finds out my father is Iranian, a smile immediately spreads across his face and he says, "Pakistani people like Irani president. He is brave man. Strong man, saying no to America." At which point he raises a clenched fist. "May Allah keep him safe." He looks in the mirror to check my reaction.

I nod back, raise my fist and say, "God is good."

Long ago I decided that any reaction to comments on controversial issues when living in a controversial area is pointless, especially when it comes to discussing religion and politics.

The rest of the way he keeps me entertained by analyzing the socio-political situation in the Middle East. His awareness and intelligence are amusing. He should be the region's specialist on CNN, BBC, or Al Jazeera. He just needs to refine his accent a little.

At five to eleven, we arrive at an ugly commercial building that is glazed in green glass, where Mark's office is supposed to be. I thank Karim and wish him well as I get out of the cab.

I'm standing in front of the building, admiring its hideous color, when I hear Karim's voice: "Madam. Madam…" I turn around. He leans out of the window and says, "Say hi to your president." He then laughs out loud.

Even though I have a feeling Karim is being mischievous and has figured out my tongue-biting stance on issues, I play along and assure him that next time the president comes over for lunch I'll wish him well. Karim laughs, waves goodbye, and drives off.

✣

A tiny Filipino woman greets me with a sweet smile and directs me to Mark's office in the corner of a long corridor. He is on the phone when I walk in. He smiles at me, nods, and waves me over.

My heart skips a beat at the sight of him. He looks even better in his semi-formal work clothes. He is wearing a blue dress shirt, loose black pants, and black leather sports shoes. I fight the strong urge to run over and hold him tight in my arms. I manage to control myself and calmly walk over to the huge window overlooking the busy Dubai Creek, the commercial transit port for vessels in the region. Crates and cartons are being loaded on boats, while dhows, dinghies, and dilapidated wooden boats—a*bras*—are transporting people across the water. I let myself get carried away by a vision: Mark and I renting an *abra*…He has his arms around me…My head is resting on his shoulder…The sun is setting over the Dubai Creek when all of a sudden we find ourselves surrounded by ten ships with diamond-studded Jolly Roger flags flying overhead.

"A penny for your thoughts." His voice snaps me out of my Bolly-Holly scenario, and I turn around to find him standing right behind me.

"My thoughts cost a lot more than that," I say. I can actually feel my eyes sparkling as I extend my hand to greet him.

"I'm sure they do," he says. He takes my hand and leans over to give me a kiss on the cheek. I'm pleasantly surprised, thinking, "How cultured of him—he's so with the program."

"Thank you so much for coming down. Sorry to drag you all the way to this part of town."

"That's all right. As much as I prefer the authenticity of this older part, please don't tell anyone I crossed."

"Crossed what?" he asks curiously.

I smile and say, "You know how if you are a posh city-dweller living in Manhattan, you say, 'I don't cross,' meaning you don't leave the island for New Jersey, Brooklyn…?" I am hoping he knows what in the world I'm talking about. He nods, smirking, and I continue. "Well, being a posh New Dubai city girl, I say, 'I don't cross,' meaning I don't cross Makhtoum or Garhoud Bridge to Deira."

I immediately regret what I've said, thinking I could have totally done without that explanation. I hope he does not perceive me as a conceited snob, who thinks less of him because his office is in Deira.

"I lived in New Jersey for two years," he says, with a straight face.

Oh, no! I feel like an arrogant worm.

He cracks up and says, "Just kidding, Maya. I've never lived in Jersey, or New York for that matter. Unfortunately here, I have to cross every day, and yes, you're right…It's a pain. The traffic's horrible."

"On the bright side," I say, still feeling awkward, "you get to watch all the action here on the bay when you get bored."

"I actually prefer this area if it weren't for the traffic. When I'm in this older part of Dubai, it feels like I'm actually in the Middle East as opposed to Vegas."

"The new part does have a Vegas feel to it, doesn't it?"

"Vegas without the sin," he says as we walk back to the seating area.

I look at him wondering if he is putting me on again or if he is serious. He raises his eyebrows in surprise and says, "You don't seem to agree."

"Well. Let's just say that there's more to Dubai than meets the eye. And that's generally true for all over the Middle East."

"I knew you were the person I'd been looking for. That's exactly why I need your help. Someone with insight into the ways of the region. I need to catch up fast. I feel a bit paranoid about saying or doing the wrong thing, unknowingly insulting the locals I work with."

"I'm a novice myself when it comes to the Emirates and the Gulf."

"I'm sure you're way ahead of me," he says, as he walks over to his desk to get his laptop. "Do you live by yourself?"

"Yes. Don't you?" I say as I take a seat on the black leather couch.

"I sure do. It's kind of hard to live with other people when you're past your twenties."

There is a bowl of chocolate and peanut M&Ms in a round glass bowl on the coffee table—a man after my heart. I'm making myself comfortable on the couch when I hear him say, "The couch matches your outfit."

"Who knew? I blend right in," I say, feeling self-conscious. Who wants to match a couch? Even though it's better than matching a curtain. "So, where're you from?" I ask.

DESERT MOJITO

"I was born in New Haven and brought up all over. Both my parents were in academia and we moved around a lot."

"Nice. Did you go to Yale?"

"I wish. My older brother did, though. My father taught economics there."

"Wow!" I'm now more impressed and nervous than before. It's not everyday you meet someone whose father has taught at Yale. "How'd you end up in Dubai?"

His look is one of thoughtful consideration, as if wondering how much of the truth he should divulge. He takes a deep breath and says, "I needed a change, really. I work for a marketing company based in Miami. We set up theme restaurants. We're in charge of everything from finding the venue, to setting up, to training and opening. There was a position for an overseas project manager—I applied and got it...It hasn't been easy. Things get done very *very* slowly around here." He presses his lips together and flicks his eyebrows. He is too much of a gentleman to say what's on his mind. He has no idea what he has got himself into. Progress here is not made at the pace he is used to, back in the States. Moving at the Middle Eastern pace for a productive American is like a samba dancer trying to move with the rhythm of a tai chi form.

"Welcome to the Middle East. Is this your first time here?"

"It is." He hands me his card. His last name is Clover. Mark Clover.

"Thanks." I look back up at him and say, "Things run at a completely different pace here—very inefficient and slow compared to the let's-get-down-to-business American attitude. You'll get used to it. It's got its own peculiar charms, too, once you adjust." I take a red M&M from the bowl. "If you want to keep sane, it's best to accept the way things are right from the start." I pop the M&M in my mouth.

"I'm beginning to realize that. They say *inshallah* to everything. 'So we'll meet tomorrow at two to discuss the budget?' *Inshallah*. 'Will you be able to close the deal by next week?' *Inshallah*," he says, chuckling. "It's taking me a while to get used to this *inshallah* attitude."

I laugh and say, "Welcome to the *Inshallah* region of the world. Yes. There's always the reminder that, at the end of the day, God is the decision maker and *inshallah*, God willing, it will all go as we planned."

"I get it. And on some level it's true that we don't have control over it all, no matter what we like to believe." He sighs. "But do we need to be reminded of it in the middle of a business deal?"

"Hey, but it sounds like you've learned the correct use of *inshallah* already," I say.

"What'd you mean? It's obvious."

"You'd think. Right? I heard this Asian guy use it for past events, which totally defeats the purpose, not mentioning sounding funny. He'd say stuff like, 'I got a promotion last week, *inshallah*.'"

We laugh out loud. I am happy to make him laugh.

He looks at me. "On the other hand, what I really find pleasing is all the hospitality. And how at every business meeting there's a plate of dates and sweets on the table. And sweetened tea is served in tiny Moroccan tea glasses, which is way more than I can offer you here." He points to his colorful bowl of M&Ms.

"I love M&Ms," I say. "How about when you meet a business partner for the first time and you spend at least the first twenty minutes discussing the weather, Burj Khalifa, how you like Dubai, the economy…Camels and gazelles…"

He smiles. "I actually do enjoy that part, too—all that extra chatter to weigh out the other person. You know, building trust, getting to know your opponent before you get down to discussing the serious stuff," he says. "But the business part is still too vague and *inshallah*-ish for me…Anyway. How about you? I've been wondering where you're from. It's hard to tell."

Nice. He has been thinking about me.

"Born in the States. My dad's Iranian, mom was American."

"Was?"

"She passed away when I was fifteen."

"Sorry to hear that."

"That's all right. It was a long time ago."

"You sound very American."

"I'm sorry," I say.

We laugh.

"Were you brought up in the States?"

"Kind of, but not really. We moved to Tehran when I was four. Then I was sent abroad for high school and have been a drifter pretty much ever since."

"Wow! I thought *I* was the nomad. It'll be interesting to share stories sometime. Shall we move on to the serious section of the program?"

I nod.

"Oh. Sorry. I almost forgot. Can I get you some tea or coffee?"

"A cup of tea would be nice," I say.

He leaves the room and comes back with two blue mugs and sits down next to me on the couch.

"Here's the thing," he says. "This is my first time in the Middle East, as you already know. I've gotten a good feel for Dubai during the past few months—the culture, rules, and most important, as you already pointed out, the unspoken rules. But I have to make sure that culturally, the final restaurant concepts I am to propose are well-suited for the area. I was hoping you could help me fine-tune my Western ideas to fit the Middle Eastern ones. You can be my personal regional cultural advisor. That is, if you have some free time, of course. I've made some local connections but I don't feel that they're one hundred percent open with me."

My heart is pacing fast. I feel dizzy. I calmly say, "I know what you mean. The locals don't easily open up to any outsiders. It's tough getting the real scoop. They seem unapproachable, but they're really nice people. And I do have time for a little consulting. Sure."

"Good," he says and takes a sip of his tea. "Do you like it here?"

"Not really sure how I feel. Both yes and no. I like the country's semi-liberal, pro-Western attitude mixed in with the Middle Eastern flair. And it's for sure the safest place I've ever lived."

"Dubai *is* a very safe place. But as an artist, hasn't it been hard for you to get inspired for your poetry here?" He glances at me, gently smiling.

I smile back. "Not really. I have written a few about Dubai. The series is called Dubaiology." I pause. His eyes are smiling, but he doesn't say anything. So I continue. "You know, nothing deep, just for fun. There is a rap song in the series, too. A spin off Grand Master Flash's 'New York, New York.'" All of a sudden I'm feeling embarrassed and I shrug my shoulders.

"Do you know that one by heart?" he asks.

"Not completely. Do you want to hear it?"

"Of course I do."

"This isn't one to judge my style by, but it's a funny one," I say, as I dig into my purse for my notebook.

"I'd like to hear them all." He chuckles. "Let's hear Maya featuring Grand Master Flash." He pauses then says, "You carry your poetry around?"

"Have to. You never know when the inspiration will hit you." I start flipping through my notebook. *He wants to hear them all* echoes in my heart. "All right," I say.

I find my "Dubai, Dubai" song and start reading it out loud to him.

> *Dubai, Dubai, small city of big dreams,*
> *And everything in Dubai, ain't always what it seems,*
> *You might get fooled if you come from out of town,*
> *But I'm in the mall and I know my way around,*
>
> *Too much, too many people, too much (aha-ha-ha).*
> *Too much, too many people, too much.*
>
> *Glass castles in the sky, rise up high,*
> *Built to shelter the rich and greedy,*
> *Rows of hotels and malls, decorated in lights,*
> *Disguised in Madinat, Pyramids, and Festival City.*
>
> *Miles of mighty people,*
> *Where sand is plenty and Indians many.*
>
> *I'm living on dry desert land with shiny green glass,*
> *Where I get to ski in a mall,*
> *Before I head to the beach, to tan my ass...*

I hear him laughing out loud. I look up to check if he is amused or bemused.

"I'm sorry. Please don't stop. This is funny. You're good Maya!" he says.

So I continue.

> *Salesman, businessman, banker, and realtor*
> *Run all the dirham action,*
> *legal, illegal, and Sharia transaction.*

At the end of the day, they head to Bur Dubai
To cool down and get some hot Russian satisfaction.

I got a bad habit and I just can't break it,
Villas and cars on mind, and I just can't shake it,
I make tax-free dirhams and I want my space,
A villa on Jumeirah Palm or Island,
Woom woom, zoom my Ferrari off to a camel race.

New York, Paris, London, Berlin, your days are gone
Dubai is IT, global city number one.

Russian, Iranian, Brit, Filipino, Lebanese, and Bahraini,
we all call each other habibi, baby, in the U.A.E.

From four corners of the world we all get along,
Have our pink resident visa, and smoke sheesha,
Who knows, we may even be safe from Hezbollah, al-Qaeda,
And…the nuclear bomb…Inshallah!

Too much, too many people, too much (aha-ha-ha).
Too much, too many people, too much.

I close my notebook and look up, feeling embarrassed and stupid.

He starts clapping. "Good job, Maya. Very witty, and true. Do you think I can have a copy?"

"Only if you promise not to publish it under your own name."

"As tempting as that does sound, I promise I won't." He stares at me pensively, making me feel more uncomfortable. "Can I hear another one?"

I'm feeling uneasy and say, "Shouldn't we get some work done first?"

"Sure. Sure. You're right. Enough playing around. But I do want to hear more of them. I love reading books and poetry."

"Me, too," I say.

"Okay now. Let's see, business, business... Themed restaurants." He punches away on his laptop, making a *tsk*, *tsk* sound with his mouth. "Have you been to Beirut?" he asks.

"Yes. A few times. Why?"

"I hear there was a military themed bar–lounge there, decorated with sandbags, weapons, bullets... Sounds of machine guns blasting from the speakers..." He sounds and looks serious all of a sudden. "Their slogan is 'A Drink Can't Kill Ya.' And drink names are Terrorist, M16, Suicide Bomber, Kalashnikov, and so on."

"I've heard of the place. Not sure if it's still open, though," I say, still uncertain what he is getting at.

"I don't find the concept entertaining by any means," he says, shuffling around on the leather couch.

"I agree. We must draw the line somewhere," I say, sounding as serious as he does now.

"Crazy world," he says. "Anyhow... First let me show you some clips and pictures of the restaurant projects I've been involved in, then I'll tell you what I have in mind for Dubai."

He then proceeds to tell me about Ghetto Pepper, a popular restaurant in Los Angeles with the motto "No Respect." It has graffiti-covered walls, serves ghetto food, and plays obscene rap songs. The waitresses are called ghetto chicks and have hair dyed blue, red, or purple, wear gold-plated teeth, and have long curly nails. These "chicks" are obliged to be politically wrong and have an attitude with the customers, rolling their eyes impatiently, sighing, huffing, and puffing. The customer is never right in Ghetto Pepper.

"I'm assuming this concept is not appropriate for this region at all," he says.

"Definitely not," I say.

He then shows me a clip of a restaurant in Tokyo targeting young single Japanese. It is called Singles' Appetite, and according to Mark, it has been a huge success. At the entrance there is a sign reading, *No mobiles allowed—please check in your mobiles at the phone-park counter.*

"This alone will pose problems here," I say.

"You may be surprised. The Japanese are just as addicted to their cell phones, but it worked with them. Here, watch the rest," he says as he pushes play on the video. The restaurant is divided by gender; women on one side marked X, guys on the side marked Y. There is a party-of-four minimum rule at each booth. Each table has embedded electronic screens in the middle. You can view others by selecting their table number, and exchange text messages with them on the screen. The X and the Y sides can also treat each other to drinks and appetizers with suggestive names such as Meet Me, Hot Beef, Sexiyaki, Too Hot For You, Am Shy. And as a token of appreciation, the customers are offered condoms on their way out.

"How fun," I say. "This would've been a good one for Dubai, since it has the separate male and female sections. But the underlying sexual intentions of singles meeting, and condoms being handed out, would not be in line with the culture here."

"I didn't think so, either," he says.

He moves on to Vegabands, a vegetarian restaurant set in a dark, high-ceilinged space filled with giant trees, exotic flowers and plants, and streams with real fish swimming around. Speakers play ambient sounds of wildlife, rain, birds, and what have you. Tables are set around wet tree trunks and some are even set up high on top of the trees, accessible through bridged platforms. The food is served on large banana leaves instead of plates.

"And here are the two restaurants in San Francisco," he says as he shows me Willy Wonka Desserts, a house-shaped cake structure in the middle of a fenced-garden. And there's also Gothic Wrath, set in a reportedly haunted nineteenth century building.

"So? What do you think?" he asks, leaning back in his chair folding his hands behind his head.

"No Hooters?" I say teasingly.

"Unfortunately not." He frowns and pretends to sound disappointed.

"I'm very, *very* impressed. How many restaurants are you planning on opening here?"

"Two. I'm pretty sure we're doing the Vegabands one but I want you to look at a couple of other new concepts I have."

He lays down a blue folder on the table. I pop a green peanut M&M in my mouth as he unveils his new concept—"For your eyes only," he adds.

❂

I leave his office two hours later feeling high and happy, but emotionally disoriented. Before this encounter I could have blamed my attraction purely on the invisible pheromones, hypnotizing me into thinking he is the most extraordinary man on my planet. And now, after actually spending time with him, my attraction has been enhanced tenfold; his mannerisms, his voice, his comments, his kind eyes, his sense of humor, his interest in the new, his love of books, his laughter, the *tsk, tsk* sound he makes, his choice of words—they are all like a dream come to life.

The bad news is that other than his interest in hearing more of my poetry, I did not pick up on any signals indicative of anything more than a purely business relationship.

I cannot allow myself be drawn into an imaginary, one-sided love. I know better at this age—those flings only end in frustration. I'm a level-headed, logical woman who knows where to lay her eggs (what's left of them). Mark is just a friendly business acquaintance, and that's that, *khalas*. Eggs are not being laid here.

I update my Facebook status when I get home: "Floating across bridges."

AT THE PERSIAN GULF

Janet's text beeps in early in the morning, at nine on Friday. HAPPY PROPHET'S DAY. I'M AT THE BEACH. ARE YOU UP? IT'S A BEAUTIFUL DAY. CARE TO JOIN ME?

I text her back. HAPPY PROPHET'S DAY TO YOU, TOO! WHICH BEACH? ANY HOTTIES AROUND?

Janet replies immediately. JBR BEACH. NEXT TO THE HILTON. MANY HOTTIES. HURRY.

VAMOS AL BAHAR. THE PROPHET BETTER NOT FIND OUT ABOUT MY BIKINI AND THE BEACH ACTIVITIES!! I text as I walk to the closet to look for my flip-flops.

> HEHE. YOU'RE BEYOND REDEMPTION MY
> DEAR. HURRY UP AND GET HERE.

✪

Janet has been going through what she calls a dry spell, even though she has been dating like there is no tomorrow. She never heard back from Nabil after our evening out at Trinity, after which she had ended up spending the night at his place. And her relationship with Kiyarash ended abruptly one day when he called her to say that he was not able to renew his residency visa and had to return to Iran for a while. She was not too devastated and even admitted to being relieved. She said even though Kiyarash was a gentleman and took great care of her, she could not see their relationship going anywhere and that they did not have much in common. He called her once in a while from Tehran to see how she was doing.

AT THE PERSIAN GULF

Today is a clear sunny day. I have been up for a half an hour looking through all the major local magazines and papers, catching up on news around town. Both the *Time Out* and *7 Days* remind me that I'm missing out on Dinner in the Sky, where I can dine comfortably strapped in a chair, suspended fifty meters in the air. The platform is right next to where I am heading. I must check it out and tell Mark about it.

❂

As I drive up over the ramp to get on Sheikh Zayed Road, I pass a group of Indian construction workers in blue and orange overalls who are napping under the bridge, taking refuge from the heat. For newcomers the sight of countless Indian laborers around the city is at first shocking, then heart-wrenching and emotionally stirring, and finally, accepted as the way of things in Dubai. The Indian laborers, who are said to be underpaid and overworked, become part of the city in the making. The foundation of every structure built on this hot desert plain is drenched in the sweat of their round-the-clock labor. They are Dubai. The residents become numb to their presence, just like they do to all its other oddities. And, if you have lived here long enough, you do not see them as a separate entity; as someone once sadly remarked, "they become part of the scenery."

Feeling guilty and ashamed of my comfortable life, I drive past these invisible hard workers, and head for the gas station.

I pull up to the pump. A skinny, tall Indian attendant walks up to my window. I roll the window down just enough for him to hear me say, "Special full, please." He gives me his best smile and heads to the gas pump.

I hear a knock on the passenger side window and look over to see a burly Filipino guy with huge and chubby cheeks. He holds up a menu and keeps smiling. I roll down the window. The hot, humid air blows in immediately. Mr. Smile says, "How about a nice cup of coffee while you wait, ma'am?" Smile. Smile. Smile.

Simple pleasures of life right at my doorstep, with a smile. Who can say no to that smile?

"Sure. I'll have your Costa Gulf special, please."

His smile stretches even wider, so much that his eyes shrink to two thin slits. He runs to the coffee shop to get my order.

All the while another attendant has been busy wiping my windshield.

I feel spoiled and embarrassed to be on the receiving end of this system. I am not going out of my way to receive this kind of service. It is forced on me. It is part of the unavoidable perks of living in Dubai. I ask myself if so much convenience is really necessary. What have I done to deserve it? Nothing. I am just one of the lucky ones. The only comforting thought I have is that at least the system is providing jobs for a lot of people.

I tip everyone in sight to compensate for my guilt, and head out to the beach.

❂

I park between a red convertible Ferrari and a silver Bentley—a typical parking lot scene in Dubai. I check out the plate numbers. The Ferrari's plate number is 24, which is considered high up on the Emirati car-plate hierarchy. There is an inversely proportional relationship between the number of digits on a plate and status; the lower the digits, the higher your status, or at least the more money you paid to buy status. You can buy and sell your plate numbers in the Distinguished Number Plate Auction: plate number Z 60 just sold for 1.4 million dirhams, around $380,000. Plate number 1 belongs to the sheikh. My five-digit plate number is at the bottom of the hierarchy, categorizing me as a peasant.

The beach is unusually crowded today, vibrating with lots of bare energy. Tanned, fit men and women are sprinkled around, posing, flashing skin, abs, ass, and more. This would have been too good to miss. I immediately text Michelle and tell her to join us.

I spot Janet's chalk white, SPF 50–covered body right away. She is not too hard to miss among the pinks and the browns. She sees me and waves. It is awfully tempting to walk past her and spread my towel in the space between the two handsome men lying near her.

"*Sabah al kheyr*. What in the world is going on?" I say as I lay my towel down. "Where did all these Adonises come from all of a sudden? I don't know which way to look."

"*Sabah al nour*." Janet looks up, grinning. "I know. It's a good day, isn't it?"

"A good day to be bad," I say.

"I have to be good. I have a dinner date tonight." She hands me the SPF 50 spray and turns her back to me.

"Oh. With who?" I start spraying her back.

"This Lebanese guy I met in my pottery class. Ramzy."

"You deserve a medal. You just don't seem to give up, do you?"

"Actually, if this doesn't work out then that's it for me and Middle Eastern men. I finally figured out why I find them attractive and why I keep getting sucked into these dead-end dates," she says.

"I meant give up on laying off your 'speed-dating' track in general. But go ahead, tell me why."

"I love being wooed. I love being asked out. I enjoy getting dressed up to go out on a dinner date and be charmed. And the Middle Eastern men know how to do all this very well. They behave in the classical courteous, chivalrous way I love. I feel taken care of and safe in their presence. That's why it's hard for me to say no when I'm asked out by them."

"Ha! So, this Ramzy is really your last attempt to make it work with a Middle Eastern man?" I ask her in disbelief.

"Yeah," she says, unconvinced.

"You never know. Times have changed and the new generation is very different. My cousins are really good with their girlfriends and the married ones are fully involved in doing house chores, raising their children, or whatever."

"Oh. My, my, Maya. Why do I get the feeling you have a soft spot for the Middle Eastern men no matter what you preach?" she says, pushing her sun glasses down to give me the look, with a raised eyebrow.

I cannot help but smirk back at her. "I might."

"I knew it," Janet screams out.

"Shh. Janet. Come on." I lie back down on my towel and add, "That is the end of this conversation."

"All right, all right. But you can't let one bad experience ruin it for the rest of them."

"Yeah, yeah," I whimper.

"Anyway. As for me, from now on, I'll try to give other nationalities a chance, too. That's my Prophet Day resolution."

"Lovely. Good luck."

"Thanks." She smiles. "I really like this Ramzy guy. He was the only one who appreciated my awkward slanted flower pot in class. He called it the Tower of Pisa. I thought that was sweet."

"For dinner, you guys should try the sky restaurant thingy, which should be dangling somewhere around here." I sit up and look around for the contraption. And, as promised, there it is, a raised platform hanging fifty meters high from a crane, with a long oval dining table in the middle and twenty-something seats attached around. Janet follows my stare, and by the sight of her eyebrows, raised way above her round, oversized Jackie O sunglasses, I can tell she is just as impressed.

"Why would anyone want to eat while dangling, strapped in a seat?" Janet says.

"Why not? Dubai has to be on the cutting edge of all the '-ests' in the world: best, tallest, first, biggest, strangest." I look back up. "What if you have to use the washroom?"

"Ha! Good question. And more important, where would we do our mid-dinner makeup touch up?" Janet says in utter disbelief.

"Will they have flying waiters flapping around taking orders?" I say.

Janet frowns and says, "This is too weird even for Dubai. Anyway, I think he said something about going to Ras al Khaymah. I've never been there. It should be fun."

"I remember Ras al Khaymah being the hub of some shady characters in Fredrick Forsyth's *The Afghan*."

Janet chuckles and lies back down on her towel. "I remember when I had first moved here it took me a while to get used to being surrounded by the Middle Eastern men. Now I can't seem to wean myself off them."

"Whatever," I say rolling my eyes.

"Oh, come on. Those dark features and the way they carry themselves...You can't deny that there's something very manly about them. It's hard to describe."

"We will never get in a fight over men," I say, right when a shadow falls across me. It's Michelle, smiling naughtily. She is all decked out in her straw cattleman cowboy hat, Dolce & Gabana shades, and a yellow sundress, which looks like it's painted on.

"Hello, girls." She says, looking around. "Oh! Is this Dubai or Beirut?"

"Dubai the one and only. You got here fast!" I say.

"I was about to go to the pool when I got your text. I took the elevator down instead of up. And, *voila*. Thanks for calling me. How long you've been here? Did I miss anything?"

"No. Perfect timing. I just got here, too," I say.

"How've you been? How's your neighbor? What was his name?" Janet asks her.

"I'm good. Stephan lost his job." Michelle says, pouting. "He's moving back to Germany this weekend."

"Oh! Sorry. It's scary how many people are still being made redundant," Janet says.

"I really hate that expression, *to be made redundant,*" I say, shaking my head. "Here you are, going through life trying to believe you are one of a kind, then WHAM! They tell you, 'Sorry, but contrary to your belief, you are actually not all that special. In fact, you are redundant and therefore unnecessary." My serious annoyed tone surprises me. "Redundant! How can a person be called redundant? That is wack."

Michelle and Janet are looking at me with their eyebrows raised, in silence.

"Ooh, Maya…Guess you really don't like that word," Michelle says.

"I don't."

"Wack? Who uses *that* word?" Janet says, laughing.

"Better than using 'made redundant,' which by the…"

"Girls. Girls. Look, six o'clock," Michelle interrupts me.

Janet and I turn to look in two opposite directions. I see a line of Indian construction workers in blue overalls, sitting crouched on the sand dunes a few feet away from us, checking out the women. It's their favorite happy-hour activity. They sneak off to the beach every chance they get during their lunch

AT THE PERSIAN GULF

and afternoon breaks to watch women in bathing suits. A live show. Nobody can really blame them. After all, part of the reason the rest of us are here, too, is to check each other out. So what difference does it make who the audience is? But, I know for a fact that being checked out by a construction worker makes all women feel uncomfortable. Being checked out by the Spanish guy who just walked by, however, would've been flattering. Do our prejudices extend as far as choosing whose fantasies we like to fulfill?

"Maya, you are looking in the wrong direction. That's twelve o'clock. Look the other way," Janet says, interrupting another series of guilt-ridden realizations about life.

"I can never get the right clock directions." Once I turn to six, I see who is capturing every woman's imagination at the beach. There he is, in orange shorts, wearing classic brown Ray-Ban Wayfarers. He is the full package: long muscular legs, ripped abs, a wide chest, well-shaped biceps, dirty blond hair, an angular jaw, and a finely carved nose. He is well aware that everyone—except for the Indian construction workers, or maybe even they, too—is enjoying his presence. He makes his way to the water and dives in.

There is a moment of absolute silence around. Then, as if hypnotized, at least five women catwalk their way into the water and dive in after him. Michelle included.

Janet and I start to giggle.

Shortly a string of women of all shapes and shades are swimming around him like sharks.

"He's got an aqua-harem going there," Janet says, amazed.

"Eh...He's probably gay." I shrug my shoulders.

"What's going on with us women these days? Are we supposed to start chasing men now? Whatever happened with men pursuing women?" Janet is obviously irritated with the gender role reversal issue.

"Seems like those days are long gone," I say, "but I also believe that men are reacting and adapting to the way women are treating them."

"What do you mean?"

"Women nowadays are too opinionated and independent. Perhaps genetically and biologically, men know how to court the classical, quiet, coy women of a few words. So, they don't know what to do with us wild creatures."

Right then, Michelle reaches out to examine the harem guy's biceps. She frowns, pretending to be unimpressed by the obviously immaculate work of art, before she throws her head back, laughing.

"Hmm! Interesting. So does that mean that submissive, shy women are getting pursued, as opposed to our kind?" Janet asks.

"Who knows? There are also some women who want to have fun without getting involved in a relationship, further confusing the situation."

"That's true. But then even that backfires. You know my friend Luise? She had a crush on her colleague. Finally they go on a business trip together. She was looking forward to having some innocent fun with him…" Janet trails off and points to Michelle, who is now putting her cowboy hat on the harem guy's head. "But he tells her, 'I know you're not the kind of girl who's looking for a one-night-stand, and I respect that.'"

"Poor Luise," I say.

"She said that she was so close to telling him, 'But that's exactly what I'm looking for. Please, I want a one-night-stand.'" Janet lies back down on her towel, laughing.

"That's funny. What's a woman to do? Men saying no to sex is more proof that the end of the world is approaching," I say.

"Right up there with global warming, earthquakes, floods and wars, *habibti*," Janet says.

"But come on. I don't buy that for one second. The guys saying no to sex, or not pursuing us, must be getting it somewhere."

"Russian girls. Beautiful, easy, and uncomplicated," Janet suggests.

"Oh, those Russians." I look around to spot quite a few around. "And Chinese and Filipinos, too," I say, nodding in the direction of a Westerner in his sixties walking hand-in-hand with a twenty-something-year-old Asian woman on the beach.

"Do you think it's a Dubai thing, or that we're just keeping pace with the rest of the world? Are women supposed to start asking guys out?" Janet says, sounding seriously concerned.

"That's a very good question. I've been in this region far too long to know the trend elsewhere. You were just in the States. Did you pick up on the vibes there?"

"Not really. I think it's a Dubai thing," Janet says. "People are here to make fast money, drive fast cars, and have fast fun. None of the guys seem to be looking for anything serious. Everything has a temporary feel to it. It's like the Wild West."

"I like that. Dubai: The Wild, Wild East."

"Maya. Look! Michelle is heading our way with that guy. Good job, *habibti*!"

"When in Rome, do the Romans," I say.

As Michelle and her catch of the day make their way towards us, two camels meant for the tourists are slowly making their way across the beach. A woman in a red bikini is riding one. Astride the other is the proud camel owner in a white *kandura* and designer sunglasses, his legs dangling over to one side, talking away on his mobile.

The Wild, Wild East indeed.

BEEP BEEP! TEXT ME

JANET: FINALLY HEARD FROM RAMZY AFTER TWO WEEKS. IMAGINE! HERE'S HIS TEXT: "HEY, HOW R U? SORRY I'VE BEEN OUT OF TOUCH. CRAZY WORK AND A FRIEND DROPPED IN UNEXPECTEDLY LAST WEEKEND. HOPE ALL IS WELL WITH YOU. ENJOYED THE BOOK YOU LENT ME." SHOULD I REPLY?

ME: HE'S GOT BALLS!!! SAY: "ALL'S WELL. THANK YOU. CRAZY WORK HERE, TOO. FUNNY I DIDN'T NOTICE YOUR ABSENCE, AT ALL!" TONE DOWN THE LAST LINE IF U MUST.

JANET: HOW ABOUT SOMETHING LIKE THIS: "HEY, I'M VERY WELL. THANKS. GLAD YOU ENJOYED THE BOOK—YOU CAN KEEP IT."

ME: NO. THAT SOUNDS LIKE U R ANGRY. U WANT TO SOUND UNMOVED BY HIS ABSENCE. JUST SEND HIM THE REPLY I SENT U.

JANET: WHAT REPLY?!! I DID NOT GET YOUR MESSAGE. IT DIDN'T SOMEHOW GO TO HIM!! DID IT? SINCE I FORWARDED HIS MESSAGE TO U. CAN U IMAGINE...WOOPS.

ME: THAT'S NOT POSSIBLE. IS IT??!

JANET: PHEW. YR REPLY JUST CAME IN...HEHE. IT WOULD HAVE SERVED HIM WELL. I LIKE YOURS BETTER. LET'S SEE WHAT HE DOES WITH IT. WILL WAIT HALF HOUR BEFORE REPLYING. LET HIM SWEAT IT OUT.

ME: GOOD PLAN.

JANET: HEHE. SHOULD I PUT A SMILEY FACE? OR A WINK?

ME: NO. NOTHING.

JANET: HOW ABOUT A DOT DOT DOT AFTER CRAZY WORK. SO IT WILL BE: "ALL IS WELL. THANK YOU. CRAZY WORK..."

ME: I LIKE THAT. HE WON'T KNOW WHAT TO MAKE OF IT.

JANET: HOW WE LOVE TORTURING MEN :)

ME: THEY NEED IT. IT ENHANCES THEIR VIRILITY.

JANET: I'M GOING TO THE MOVIES WITH ROLLING ROCK TOMORROW. CAN'T DECIDE WHAT TO WEAR. WHAT DO YOU THINK, SPICY LITTLE PINK DRESS OR SEXY JEANS AND HEELS COMBO?

ME: IT DEPENDS WHAT'S ON YOUR AGENDA? WINK! WINK!

JANET: JUST PLAYING AT THIS POINT. NO DEFINED AGENDA.

ME: THEN, SEE HOW U FEEL TOMORROW.

JANET: AN ORGANIC APPROACH. IT ALWAYS WORKS.

ME: BTW. U THINK YOU'VE GOT ENOUGH SATELLITES THERE?

JANET: HEHE. WHAT TO DO? ANY NEWS OF MR. CLOVER?

ME: NOPE :(

JANET: DHL GUY HERE. MUST GO, TA-TA.

My thumbs are numb from texting. We should have just called each other. But, there are elements of gameplay and suspense that make texting more fun.

I lie down on my bed. I close my eyes, wondering what Mark might be doing right now at three in the afternoon. We have been meeting once a week for work and we are well set on the friendship route. Lovely. I am feeling frustrated, drained, and strange. As if I have been running all my life but not going anywhere. Like, on a treadmill.

Maybe if I had a family, a husband, and kids I would have something to show for all this time. But show how, and why? As proof of my existence? Do I need to get married to make sense of it all?

I do not have the heart for the game of love anymore, the eternal search for a partner, the eternal search for the right guy, the eternal ending up with the wrong guys, or the eternal figuring out answers to the questions, what now? Who next? What next? And, now I am full of excitement about having met someone who has stirred my deepest interest, yet we are only ending up as friends.

I need to get over the Clover crush. Move on.

I feel a sudden urge to talk to my father, the one reliable, loving man in my life.

I dial his number. He picks up on the third ring.

"Hello, my daughter," I hear him say on the other end of the line.

"Hi, *baba*. How're you?"

"I'm great. I just got back from my voice lesson. We learned a really nice variation of the song, 'Since the Dawn of Time.'" His kind, warm voice is already comforting me.

"How does that song go again?"

"'Since the dawn of time, I was crazy...'" He starts singing his heart out over the phone. "I was crazy about your face, lost in..."

"Oh, right, right. I actually do know this song, and it's one I like. You're a good singer. Good job."

"Thank you. I must learn to control my inflections better. I'm still not sure why you don't like the traditional Iranian songs. They're beautiful," he says, and then continues to sing, "I was crazy about…" But he stops and says, "I used to change the lyrics and sing, 'Crazy about your hair,' when I sang to your mom."

"Ahh. That's sweet. Baba…Is that how you felt? Were you really crazy about her?" I whisper, hoping not to have ruined his jovial mood.

There is a long pause before he says softly, "Yes. Especially when it came to her beautiful hair."

He gets quiet again.

"How do you think people end up with each other? Is it some random thing—the right timing, right place? How do you know who's the right person for you? Did you know?"

"Right person? Hmm. Your mom and I fell in love. We really didn't think about the right or wrong of it. At least I didn't."

"You guys were lucky. Things are so much more complicated these days."

"How so? People still fall in love, darling."

"Easier said than done."

"You've been in love more than I have, haven't you?" He chuckles, knowing the answer to his question.

"You know I have," I say, "but none of them have worked out."

"What's bothering you? Have you met someone?"

"No. Not really. Not sure."

He hesitates and says, "Did you hear about Lili's daughter? Arezoo?"

"No."

"She met someone over the Internet and they're getting married in the summer." He sounds amazed.

"Really? Good for her," I say.

"I don't know…This Internet meeting is all too strange for my generation."

"Yeah, but it's quite usual these days," I say.

"I think you're too real to meet people in the virtual world."

"Thanks. And don't worry. I've tried the Internet dating and it's just not my cup of tea. I'm just not that photogenic, or maybe it's the too-real thing. But…" I pause, wondering whether this is the right time to confide in him about Mark. "There is actually someone, in real life…This guy, Mark. I've been doing freelance kind of creative consulting work for him. He's the exact type of guy I'd like to end up with. But I don't think he's interested in me."

"How dare he? Do you want me to come there and beat him up?" he says. We both laugh out loud. "Where's he from?"

"He's American."

I hear a sigh from the other end. "They're good men, good people in general."

"I'm just tired of putting myself out there. I thought I'd be married with children by now."

"But you've had a very interesting, colorful life. You've seen and done so much more than all your married friends. You'll be married and happy when it's time."

"Anytime now would be nice."

"You'll meet him—someone like yourself," he says, reassuringly.

"When? It's already getting too late for me to have kids."

"My dear. There're more things you can do with your life than having children. It's very hard raising kids in this world nowadays, anyway."

"Maybe…" I am wondering if he is right. Am I a lucky one who does not have to follow the herd? Am I really? "Baba, I'll tell you this New-Age baby kid story, and then I have to run off to my haircut appointment."

BEEP BEEP! TEXT ME

"Okay."

"This is what I heard eavesdropping on two five or six year olds at the beach," I say, and then act out the dialogue. It went something like this.

Girl: Hey Dave, I have a business that sells rocks and loose sand.

Boy: Ok. I want to buy some loose sand.

Girl: You have to order it online.

Boy: Ok, www.loosesand.com/now. I ordered it rush delivery.

Girl: I am shipping it now…

I hear my father laugh out loud on the other side.

"Oh. Funny. You see. Gone are the days of buckets and shovels," he says.

We say bye and I hang up just in time to answer the buzzer.

"Hiya, sista." I see my Chinese DVD pirate, Shishi, smiling into the camera at the door.

"Hi, Shishi. Come in." I buzz her in.

When you live in "the middle of the East," home deliveries of all sorts are one of the area's perks. You make one phone call and items legal and illegal are delivered to your door: groceries, cigarettes, food, pirated DVDs, music CDs, alcohol, pornography magazines…You name it.

I see Shishi walking down the corridor, her gaunt body tilted to one side as she hauls her blue beach bag full of at least three hundred DVDs. She takes her shoes off at the door, even though I have told her many times that it's not necessary. Some other customers must have given her a hard time. Or maybe at their bootleg distribution training they are told to observe this Middle Eastern custom. A faint smell of nicotine follows her in the room as she makes her way to the couch. The cigarette stench is probably from driving around all day in a car with black-tinted windows, from one neighborhood to another, with her other Chinese pirate buddies who smoke like chimneys in between deliveries. Her long wavy hair is pined to the side with a shiny butterfly hairpin. And her manicured and pedicured nails are a joyous reminder of how women the world over, of all creed and breed, pirate or president, in times of war or peace, value and celebrate their femininity.

"Nice nail polish, Shishi," I say.

She is busy taking out the DVDs from her beach bag. "Tank yo," she laughs and hands me the first batch of films. "You no have boyfriend?"

Here we go again. Every time, that is the first thing she asks me and quietly waits for my response, which is always the same: "No, Shishi. Do you have anyone for me?"

"You want marry Chinese? I know good Chinese man. You marry him," she says, throwing her head back, laughing. She grabs my arm and says, "You nice lady. Must have boyfriend."

Yeah, yeah.

I always have to return or exchange a few movies. Some because the quality was bad and they were manually filmed with the camera hidden under some guy's jacket in the movie theatre (as opposed to properly pirated off the original version in the studio). Then there are ones where the voices are out of synch with the scene. Also, it is not uncommon for an actor or actress to switch to speaking a few lines in Russian during the most crucial scenes right in the middle of the film.

Yes, there is a lot you have to endure when watching films for ten dirhams (about $2.70) a disc in the comfort of your home. Not that watching a movie in the theatre is any less cumbersome. Moviegoers are encouraged to use their own imagination when it comes to any kind of physically intimate scenes. We see a lot of couples "almost kissing" on screen. As we get ready for that long-anticipated first kiss between two people, we see a pair of puckered lips getting close—and all of a sudden cut to moving away. Sometime the film has been so severely mutilated that the audience cannot make sense of the plot. Too bad in the digital age the operator cannot collect the censored cuts like Alfredo did in Tonatore's *Cinema Paradiso*.

Shishi's phone beeps a message. She checks it, dials a number, and hands me the phone. "You talk," she says.

I look at her in surprise, trying to figure out what just happened, when I hear a guy's voice on the other side of the phone. I'm just hoping Shishi is not playing matchmaker.

"Hello?" I say, still looking at Shishi waiting for any clues about her unexpected behavior.

"Hi. Who is this?" the guy asks in perfect British English.

"This is Shishi's friend," I say, still shocked.

"Could you please tell her I think I left my keys in her car at the gas station."

I breathe a sigh of relief and tell him to hold on while I try to help Shishi understand what he has just said, using sign language and only the necessary words, "His key, you have? Your car, in gas station?"

"Okay, okay," Shishi says smiling, probably more relieved than I that he is not saying something like the police have just caught him with the films and asked him to turn in his pirate. "I coming five minute," she says to tell him.

I relay the message and he says he will be waiting for her at the same place in front of Burger King.

I hear another message beep in, this time coming from my phone instead.

It's from Mona.

DESERT MOJITO

HEY HON HOW ARE YOU? THE AUSSIE TEXTED: "YOU STILL ALIVE?" WHAT DO I DO?

I pick out twelve movies and bid Shishi farewell for two weeks as I get busy with my second job as the text-consultant.

Mona's Aussie is an obnoxious, pushy guy named Richard, who has been playing hide and seek with her. I have never met him but I did not like the sound of him from the word go, so this is my chance to get him back.

Do men realize that there is an army of women behind each text? Women who know them well even though they have never met? Our texts to men are cumulative best effort of several women—one in the foreground, and her best friends in the background. A guy really has to outsmart many women before getting to the one he wants. And the scary part is that they still manage to leave us baffled and confused.

Under sensitive texting situations, we almost never dare to reply to a guy's text without consulting with at least two girlfriends: one conservative and tough, one liberal and easy-going. We either call to read his message or forward it to our girlfriend or friends, and wait for suggestions before replying. If we are already among our girlfriends, we read the message out loud to them and we compose a group response. Then we add the smiley most appropriate for the occasion to set the right tone. My favorite is the dot dot dot; it's the most ambiguous, ambivalent, vague symbol. It gives the person on the other end the liberty of completing the sentence as he pleases.

I crack my fingers and get to work.

ME: HI DAALIN.' U STILL INTERESTED IN THE AUSSIE?!!

MONA: NOT REALLY. HE HANGS OUT WITH THE GROUP. CAN'T SNUB HIM. DON'T WANT TO BE RUDE.

BEEP BEEP! TEXT ME

ME: HE'S THE RUDE ONE. ASKING IF YOU'RE STILL ALIVE. HE'S BAD NEWS. IGNORE HIM.

MONA: SHOULD I SAY: 'BEEN BUSY, HOW R U?'

ME: NO. JUST SAY: 'ALIVE AND KICKING.'

MONA: I LIKE THAT BUT HE MAY TAKE IT THE WRONG WAY.

ME: WRONG WAY?! HOW?! WHATEVER! FINE. BE POLITE.

My phone rings. It's Mona.

"Hello, Miss Congeniality," I say, secretly glad to be relieved of a long round of texting.

"Sweetie. I can't just blow him off," Mona says.

"Why not? Wasn't he the one who accused you of playing hard to get when you refused his invitation to wine and cheese at ten in the evening on a Monday night?"

"That was mental. Wasn't it? Honestly, what was he thinking?" she says.

"He was thinking he's God's gift to women and you're ready to cater to him at a snap of his fingers."

"So what do I do? He does come across a bit aggressive, doesn't he?"

"Totally. You want a man who treats you well, and doesn't say, 'Are you alive?' after his already inappropriate wine invitation."

"Inappropriate!" she says, making fun of me. "He's a bit of a minger, I suppose."

"Minger! You Brits use the weirdest words."

"You nutter. 'Yeah, man. That's so, like, not cool, man, totally man,'" she says, slurring her words to imitate my American accent.

DESERT MOJITO

"Listen. Got to dash off now. No time for chinwagging," I come back at her, hoping she finds my British slang impressive.

"That was seriously appalling," she say. "Back to Richard. Can I just be polite and say, 'Hi. I'm doing well. How're you doing?'"

"Fine. Be polite. Darling, I got to go. I'm late for my haircut," I say.

"*Yallah*, bye," she says.

We hang up.

❂

As I grab my purse and head out the door, I hear another message beep in.

> MICHELLE: JBR AHMED IS GAY!!!
>
> ME: YOU MEAN, THE HAREM/BICEPS AHMED?
>
> MICHELLE: YES :(

I get in my car and call her. "Hi. Don't say I didn't warn you."

"Can't hear you. Where are you?" Michelle says.

"I'm in the parking lot. And late for my haircut. Tell me what happened?"

"Last night I invited him to come to the ladies' night out at Forbidden Fruit, the Lebanese club. It was me, Nadia, and Latifa. When we—"

I laugh out loud. "Perfect, Michelle. He was one of the ladies!"

She chuckles and says, "True. So when—"

"Why would you invite a hot Canadian guy to a ladies' night at a wild Lebanese club?"

"I thought it'd be fun. He's been texting me from Riyadh saying we must go out when he gets back. *Khalas*, I invited him. Everyone at the club was checking him out. Both guys and girls. He loved the Arabic songs. He was shaking his hips better than all the Lebanese around!"

"That should've been your first clue, a belly-shaking Canadian!" I say, laughing, imagining the spectacular scene he must have made.

"True. I leave him alone for a few minutes to go to the bathroom. And when I come back, I can't find him. I finally see him in the corner with Foad!"

"Who is Foad?"

"Foad Z. is Lebanon's gayest, hottest singer."

"Oops. Sorry, babe. Tough competition there. But still that doesn't make Ahmed gay. What was Ahmed's real name?"

"Alan. No that doesn't make him gay. Not until Foad kissed him on the lips and he kissed him back!"

"You're kidding!" I scream out. "That is very brave of them."

"True, but it was a quick kiss. I finally get his attention. He winks at me and gives me the 'call me' thumb-pinky sign."

"Maybe he's bi?" I say, trying to be comforting.

"Maya. He's gay," she says, sounding frustrated and hopeless.

"Don't you wish there was a gay identification sign so they would not waste straight people's time and energy? You know, like the wedding ring married people wear to announce their unavailability. Maybe gays can have something more permanent, like a tattoo, a tiny G, or an angel with rainbow color wings, or…I don't know, anything to let us know they're gay."

"Oh! That would've been really nice," Michelle says. "Okay, Maya. I should get back to work. Did I tell you I'm going to Beirut this weekend for my nephew's baptism?"

"You didn't. Have fun. Sorry about Alan. There's a lot of fish in the sea."

"Gay fish!" Michelle says, laughing.

She hangs up abruptly, right as I'm about to wish her a *bon voyage*.

My phone rings again. I press the green button. "Calling to say bye?" I say.

"How'd you know? That's crazy." I hear Mark's voice on the other end.

"Oh. Hi. It's you. No. No. I thought it was…" I stop talking. His words hit me with some delay. He has called to say goodbye! Is he leaving Dubai? I knew it was all too good to be true. Why? Why? Why are you leaving me?

"Hello? Maya? You still there?"

"Sorry. Yes. Sorry. I dropped the phone."

"I'm at the airport, leaving for the States in an hour," he says.

My heart sinks. "You've given up too fast. We could've made it work if you had stayed." The words jump out of my mouth before I even realized that they were there.

"I'm sorry? Give what up? What do you mean?"

"You know. Give up on the region, Middle East, Dubai, Deira."

He starts laughing. "I'm going for a mini-family reunion. Coming back to good old Deira in ten days."

I hear a loud honk from behind. The light has turned green and I'm not moving. Relieved and over my shock, I start driving and say happily, "Oh. Okay."

"I was flipping through this local magazine, *Ahlan*, at the duty free shop and saw your picture."

Oh, no! Keep calm, Maya.

"Really? Where am I? What event?"

"Dubai Film Festival. It's a picture of you with two guys. Let me see their names," he says, "Asif Sands and Peter Quist."

"They're married," I say quickly.

"Oh. Okay," he says, sounding confused.

"To each other," I clarify.

"Huh."

"Yes. How do I look in the picture?"

"It's a nice shot."

Come on. Give me something to work with here, Mark. How about, "You look awesome *as always*?" Instead, I ask, "Are you going to Miami?"

"No. I'm going to my parents'. They live in Pasadena. It's my mom's seventieth birthday. We're throwing her a surprise party."

"How fun. Is she expecting you?"

"No. My brother and sister think it'll be fun to keep me part of the surprise. But I'm not so sure it's a good idea. Don't want to shock her."

"She'll be fine. She'll love it."

"You think?"

"Sure. It's not like she thinks you're dead and all of a sudden you show up at her doorstep. Will your whole family be there—uncles, aunts, cousins?"

"My brother and sister will be there with their spouses." He pauses for an instant. "I have a small family. I think my mom's brother, Uncle Phil, will be there, too. I doubt my cousins will make it. They all live far away. How about you?"

"Well. A bit short notice there, otherwise I would've loved to join you."

He chuckles and says, "Do you have a big family?"

"Just me. But I have a big extended family—four uncles and five aunts on my dad's side, and two uncles on my mom's, and of course many cousins."

"Wow! *Mashallah*."

"Impressive, Mark. You know when to use *mashallah*."

"*Alhamdullilah*," he says.

I giggle.

"What? Was that wrong?"

"No. Yes. Well…I'm not sure, to be honest. We'll discuss it when you get back," I say, still laughing silently, adoring his attempts to learn the Middle Eastern culture.

"I've been meaning to call you all this week but was swamped," he says, making my heart skip a beat. This guy is bad for my heart. "I wanted to know if you can join me for a business dinner on the twenty-fifth. It's with Probel, the advertising company I'm working with. I'd like you to be there, if you could."

"Sure. I'll mark my calendar."

"Thank you. I'll let you know the details later. How's your poetry going?"

"I'm working on a new one."

"Maya featuring Lady Gaga?" he says.

Finally! He teases me.

"No. It's all my own, Maya featuring Maya."

"I'd like to read it. Maybe you can e-mail it to me."

"It's not finished yet. I can send you some of my old ones if you like."

"Yes. Of course. I look forward to reading them." He is silent, then says, "Before I forget, do you know where Kish is?"

"Of course I do. It's one of Iran's free zone islands across the Persian Gulf. Why?"

"I'd really like to visit Iran while I'm on this part of the world. But my travel agent tells me Iran is a high-risk country. Not sure exactly what that means, but getting a visa may be next to impossible for an American, and he suggested visiting one of the free zone islands which doesn't require a visa yet."

"That's right. High-risk baby." I laugh. "I think you're allowed to stay for two weeks on Kish Island without a visa. But, Kish Island will not give you a feel for Iran."

"Why?"

"Well. Let's just say there's a reason why it's called the 'free' zone, aside for the commercial reasons. People go there to shop and enjoy the more relaxed atmosphere of the island without the Islamic police breathing down their necks. It's like a resort really."

"Have you been there?"

"Oh, yeah. Many times. The five years I lived and worked in Tehran, Kish was the easiest place to get away to when I needed to keep sane. Plus, it's got great coral reefs if you're into snorkeling and diving."

"Really?" he says, surprised. "I have my open-water diving certificate, but haven't dived for a few years now. I like to check it out when I come back. Maybe you can be my tour guide?"

I am doing one of those silent girly screams, with my mouth wide open. I unhinge my jaws, get the cool in my voice, and say, "Hmm. I haven't been there for a while. We'll talk about it when you get back."

"Do you need anything from the States?" he says.

I'm thinking "you" but say, "An In-N-Out burger."

He chuckles and says, "I love that place."

"Me, too. I'm a closet fan. I don't care much for red meat in general, but love In-N-Out."

"Huh," he says. "It'll be our secret."

My phone starts beeping.

"What was that?"

"I think my phone's running out of battery," I say.

"Hey, sorry there," he says.

"No. It's not your fault. Have a safe trip," I say.

"Thanks. See you in a couple of weeks."

DESERT MOJITO

My phone goes dead.

Good phone, hanging in there for that last call. I cannot wipe the smile off my face as my brain replays every single word we just exchanged.

From: "Mark Clover" <MarkC@restset.com>
To: "Maya Williams" <MayaRWilliams @gmail.com>
Subject: Hi from California

Hi Maya,

It's hard to believe I'm all the way on this side of the world. Have already hit In-N-Out a couple of times. I took a couple of days off from family and did a solo hike. The weather was pristine and birds and desert life were out. Good stuff.

From the news over here, it looks like Dubai is moving from rich and pretentious to just pretentious these days. Our business dinner has been confirmed for next Wednesday (I get back late Tuesday night) at Nobu on the Palm. Hope you can still make it.

Picked up "The Collected Poems" by Sylvia Plath. What do you think of her work? I'm still hoping to read some of your poems.

Take care,
Mark

From: "Maya Williams" <MayaRWilliams@gmail.com>
To: "Mark Clover" <MarkC@restset.com>
Subject: Hi from Dubai

Hi Mark,

Glad to hear you're enjoying yourself.

Sylvia Plath, eh? A bit drab but some beautiful poetry, even though I'm not sure how to feel about her choosing death over life. But, then again, it's hard to judge how powerful pain can be and to what extremes it can push a person.

Nobu! Fancy. Do I need to be updated on anything before the meeting?

As promised I'm attaching one of my poems. It's part of my "Moon" series, one of my favorites. I wrote it in the earlier part of this millennium.

Have a safe trip back.

Maya

P.S. Have a burger for me.

From: "Mark Clover" <MarkC@restset.com>
To: "Maya Williams" <MayaRWilliams@gmail.com>
Subject: No poetry!!!

Nobu was Probel's suggestion. Never been. You are my assistant as far as they're concerned. Probel is owned by an Emirati guy. I'll be meeting him for the first time that night.

There was no poetry attachment!
Mark

From: "Maya Williams" <MayaRWilliams@gmail.com>

To: "Mark Clover" <MarkC@restset.com>
Subject: No poetry!!!

Okay. I am your assistant.

Oops! Sorry forgot to attach the poetry. Here you go:

Moon #1

Last night I was dreaming,
Of you and me

Chasing each other in the sky
Between the stars,
Singing, "Twinkle, twinkle little star,
Now I wonder where you are."

We reach the moon,
And I see your face,
Light up,
"Come on,
Jump up!" you say to me,
"This is our chance to break free."

You reach down to pull me up
On the full moon,
On our beloved La Lune,

I reach to you with both hands,
Thinking of the story "Le Petit Prince,"

Blue moon, you saw me standing on you,
Without a dream,
'Cause they had all come true,

You never know,

You never know,
You never know,

Tears of joy,
Tears of joy,
Tears of joy.

Moon #2

An angel was caught in the spider web,
Next to my bed,
With wings so fine,
With a voice so high,
She says to me,
"Could you help me please?"

I think to myself,
"Oh! God!
Even angels can't run free!"
Being only human,
And greedy,
I ask her,
"What's in it for me?"

She smiles at me,
Looks at me,
In a dreamy glance and says,
"The dream of La Lune,
And the Little Prince."

My heart skips a hundred beats,
Ready to fly off into a million bits,

She is speaking of my
raison d'être
And not the dismal Eid Fitr!

So in disbelief,
I set her free,
Thinking whatever will be, will be.

I hear a hum,
From the walls around,
I see a light,
Shining,
From the ground,
I see the angel talk to the moon,
Knowing I'll be all right soon.

Maya

From: "Mark Clover" <MarkC@restset.com>
To: "Maya Williams" <MayaRWilliams@gmail.com>
Subject: Poetry

Wow. Interesting poetry. Not what I was expecting. So does the story have a good ending? Isn't Eid Fitr the happy occasion marking the end of Ramadan? The dismal threw me off. Why dismal?

Mark

From: "Maya Williams" <MayaRWilliams@gmail.com>
To: "Mark Clover" <MarkC@restset.com>
Subject: Poetry

Haha! Shocked you did I? The end is not clear. There is an eclipse of the moon by the end of the series. Gets very dark.

You are right, Eid Fitr is a happy occasion, and so is Ramadan—in the Arab world, that is. I must have written the poem sometime near Eid Fitr in Tehran and may have been ticked off by all the pretend-fasting and other lies and deceptions there. That would explain the "dismal."

Maya

From: "Mark Clover" <MarkC@restset.com>
To: "Maya Williams" <MayaRWilliams@gmail.com
Subject: Poetry

Hi there,

Thanks for the explanation. I guess all religions are pretty much the same. I'm not much of a believer, an agnostic.

It must've been hard for you living in Tehran.

See you in a few days.

Take care,
Mark

HOMO SAPIENS BOTHERING HOMO SAPIENS

A message from Maurice beeps in: MISS YOU. ON THE PLANE TAKING OFF FOR TOKYO FOR WORK. LET'S MEET SOMEWHERE IN EUROPE NEXT MONTH. I DON'T WANT TO COME TO DUBAI.

MISS YOU, TOO, I reply. AM BROKE. CAN MEET YOU ANYWHERE IN WALKING DISTANCE.

> MY TREAT. HOW ABOUT MADRID, MEMORIAL DAY WEEKEND?

> WOW! THANKS FOR THE OFFER. WHAT'S UP? ANY NEW MEN IN YOUR LIFE? I text back.

> NO! MAY BECOME A LESBIAN SOON. HOW ABOUT YOU?

> STAYING STRAIGHT :)

> CUTE.

> COME TO DUBAI. PLEEESE. I MISS YOU.

> WILL CALL YOU. LOVE YOU. He finishes the conversation.

✪

Michelle will take comfort in Maurice's lesbian joke. She has a knack for getting attracted to gay men and once she said, "Lately it seems like in order to be with a man I need to get a sex change and become gay."

Either way, heteros are getting gypped.

DESERT MOJITO

Maurice, whom I have known since elementary school, jokes with everyone about how he turned gay after I broke his heart when we were nine years old.

We became friends in fourth grade in Tehran. The teacher made us sit by order of height; shortest in the front, tallest in the back. Maurice asked to be seated in the front row because he was a nerd, and I was forced to sit next to him on the third day because I talked too much in the back.

He still sits in the front row—the front row of a Fortune 400 American corporation. And I still talk a lot.

Our lifelong love of chocolate played a very crucial role in our elementary school friendship. After school I would spend a lot of time at his house. We would first have a snack, and then do our homework, and finally get to the entertainment section of our program: I would lounge on his bed munching on chocolate and he would play the latest song by Googoosh, the Iranian diva, and show me all the new dance moves he had picked up from a music show called *Rang-a-Rang*—colorful—on pre-Islamic Iranian TV.

Even though I was young, I knew he didn't feel like a typical guy. He did not walk, talk, eat, and definitely did not dance like other boys at school. The last day of class I confided in him about being in love with Omid, the tallest and blondest guy in our class. I had a camera with me and made Maurice pretend it was his, so that he could take a picture of Omid and I together for my diary. When we were done with our last final, waiting for our parents to pick us up, Maurice was unusually quiet. He asked to write in my diary.

To this day I have not seen teardrops as round and as big as I saw that day, rolling down Maurice's cheeks as he wrote in my tiny flower-patterned notebook. I remember feeling confused when he started to cry but didn't know how to react. I stood by him quietly and waited for him to finish writing.

He was avoiding my presence. He finally looked up at me with bloodshot eyes, handed the diary back and said, "Don't read it now, please."

Maurice had confessed his love for me and had expressed his sorrow over my not loving him back the same way. I felt horrible and confused.

Looking back on my rocky start on the path to love, I can draw three definite conclusions: (1) Love knows no sexual orientation boundaries, even at an early age; (2) being rejected is painful at all ages; (3) the feminine instinct never lies. Maurice felt gay, even at that age.

✪

Another text message beeps in. It's Alia, saying she is outside waiting for me.

I met Alia teaching a business writing workshop designed for Emirati bank employees. She was one of the most ambitious and inquisitive students in class. She works part-time, and is finishing up her MBA at the American University in Dubai. It's eight fifteen on a Wednesday morning and we are heading to MOE to do a mall-walk, which in Dubai is the equivalent of an early morning walk in a park.

"*Marhaba.* I can't believe I agreed to do this," I say as I get in Alia's car.

"Hi, *habibti*," she says. "How are you?" She sounds too energetic and perked up for such early hour of the morning.

"Last time I woke up this early to do sports was...aaah... never!" I say.

She looks over at me and laughs. There is not a trace of sleep on her perfectly made-up face. Her morning makeup looks better than my best makeup attempts for a wedding.

"It will be fun. You will feel good," she assures me.

"Nice car," I say, slipping a little forward on the plastic cover each time she puts on her brake.

"It's my mom's. My car's at the mechanics. Put on your seat belt, *habibti*."

"What's up with the plastic cover? You know you're supposed to take it off once you start using the car."

"My parents like to keep it on. I don't like it, either, but they say it will stay clean this way."

"Clean and slippery," I utter, sounding annoyed. "I'm sorry. I'm still waking up. I've seen how some people keep the plastic cover on the TV remote control, too."

"My parents do that, too," she says. She looks over at me, smiling. "You know how parents are."

"Sure."

Feeling doubly worse, I try to find something nice to say. "But your parents seem to be quite liberal if they're not putting pressure on you to wear the *abaya* and the *sheyla*."

She glances over and says, "Actually, they don't like it when I don't wear it. But I have convinced them that it's hard to do sports in them."

"Smart girl. You look very nice with or without the *abaya*," I say, hoping to have made up for the earlier damage induced. "So, how's life? How's your job?"

"*Alhamdulillah*, everything's good. A lot of people are losing their jobs but we are safe as Emiratis. The law protects us."

"You do have some great laws here for the locals. Just the other day I heard that when an Emirati gets married the government gives him a piece of land or a house. Is that true?"

"Yes. It's true. The laws are good. But it's good for Westerners, too. They are all overpaid here."

"True. Their salaries are ridiculously high. That's why they come here—to make money." I'm already feeling exhausted from having to both think and talk this early in the morning, wondering how I can make it through the entire mall-walk.

"I know this Canadian lady who works as a trainer for our bank. Her salary's twenty eight thousand dirhams a month," Alia says, looking at me with raised eyebrows.

"That's a lot. That's—what?—like eight thousand dollars. It seems like everybody has a clear understanding of what is going on here as far as the favoritisms and prejudices go. But… What to do?"

"That's true." She checks her face in the mirror.

"Even when it comes to socializing, for the most part everyone stays with his own clan. I read somewhere that the toughest countries for foreigners to integrate with the locals are Britain and the United Arab Emirates." We pass under the grey concrete of Ski Dubai structure, which protrudes out in the sky like a giant freak of anti-nature. "Which is interesting and ironic in a sense since Dubai is filled with British expats."

"Not true. We are very friendly," she says. "The British may not be friendly, but we are. Look how many guests we have in our country." She glances over and smiles.

"That's right," I smile back at her, reminding myself that this *is* her country I'm living in, after all, and I'd better shut up.

"Are you ready to mall-walk?" she says as she parks, taking up two spaces.

"Ready as I can ever be," I say, still wondering why I consented to taking part in this ridiculous ordeal.

✸

The mall feels ominous at eight in the morning. All the stores are closed. The only people around are the Indian cleaning staff, the security guards, and us, the lady mall-walkers. We are a colorful bunch: Indian, Syrian, German, Canadian, Italian, French, you name it. There are around thirty of us ladies gathered in front of the Nike store. Alia and I sign in and join everyone else standing around in a circle, stretching. The organizer informs us about the reporter from *Gulf News* doing a piece on mall-walking for the special weekend edition on active ladies. She gives us a heads-up on the photographer who will be snapping pictures as we make our rounds.

Before we get started, I am welcomed by the mall-walk trainer, Lucy, who shows me the complicated back and forth arm movements, and the proper heel-first technique.

Alia wishes me luck and we start walking. Before I know it, one by one, I am overtaken by all the mall-walkers, zooming by me, leaving me to my easy strides. These women are serious and crazy, I'm thinking. I have to walk at least twenty times faster than I am now if I am to avoid the embarrassment of them passing me on their second lap around.

Lucy turns around, sees me lagging behind, and shouts out, "Come on. This's no time for window shopping! Use your arms. Your heels. Like this," she says, exaggerating her own movements. "Come on. Faster. MOVE IT!"

I start using the arm-leg mall-walk technique as instructed, and much to my surprise, begin to pick up speed. I manage to catch up to a Syrian girl at Harvey Nichols. We introduce ourselves in between breaths. Holding a conversation while strutting soon proves to be pretty strenuous. We pass a couple of other mall-walkers by Ski Dubai, and my Syrian partner falls behind near the food court.

As I pass Louis Vuitton, approaching Debenhams, I notice the *Gulf News* photographer kneeling on the floor, waiting to snap some shots of the next person: me. Great. Crap.

I can just imagine the "Active Ladies of Dubai" article; there I am with my beautiful puffy eyes, a messy ponytail, and sweat-soaked shirt, walking by the green projector-lit Debenhams window as a stunned mannequin in a red raincoat looks on. And, of course my picture will be next to the other Dubai active lady; a tan and toned twenty year old running on the beach with wind-blown hair, her face lit poetically by the gentle sunset hues.

I snap out of these horrifying mental images, and comfort myself with the adage that even bad publicity is good publicity. As I approach the photographer, I put on my sweetest smile, moving my arms back and forth with all my might, showing off my mall-walk expertise, when I hear the *click-click-click* firing of his camera.

I am sweating profusely and breathing hard as I start my second lap around the mall. I still cannot get over the strange sensation of speed walking around an empty mall. I'm experiencing the equivalent mall experience of jogging outdoors in the early morning; the rest of the world is still asleep. I'm taken in by the silence and the serenity as I tread on the freshly washed floors, past the perfect window displays, taking in the intoxicating heady scent of disinfectants in the air. Oh, what joy.

Alia is waiting for me next to the escalator by Home Centre, clapping as I finish my third lap drenched in sweat.

"How was it? You did good," she says, handing me a bottle of water.

"It's not as easy as it sounds," I say, panting. "You were right."

"I knew you'd like it."

I laugh and say, "Well, yeah, but…No, not really. It's actually a combination of everything I dread: early morning, well, eight o'clock, exercise, mall, stores, only women, being photographed…Not my kind of scene."

Alia starts laughing and much to my dismay says, "Mr. Suleiman, the photographer, asked for your name and copied it off the sign-in sheet. You're lucky. Your picture will be in the *Gulf News*."

"Lovely. Got to find Mr. Suleiman and steal his camera," I say, wondering what it is with me and my picture, ending up in all these random publications around town.

I dry off my face, feeling relieved to be done with the mall-walk chapter of my life. "So are we done here?" I say.

"No," Alia says excitedly. "The best part is now. We all meet down at Barista to have our morning coffee."

"That is indeed the best part. That's where we should have started." I smile and grab Alia's arm, dragging myself to the coffee shop. I feel my phone vibrate in my pocket just as I throw myself down on the chair at the coffee shop. I'm surprised to see that the text message is from Asif, saying to call him.

I order my breakfast and excuse myself from the table to make the call.

"You're awake!" he says, not sounding like his usual spunky self.

"Please don't tell anyone," I say. "I have a reputation to keep. Is everything all right?"

"I'm not sure. I'm really worried and needed to talk to you," he says.

"Sure. What's up?"

I don't hear a sound. "Helloooo," I say. The line was probably cut off.

"I'm here," he says. I hear him sniffling.

"Asif? What's wrong? Are you crying?"

"Oh! I'm just so tired of having to pretend I'm not gay in this city. I'm sick of it. I'm sick of lying. I'm sick of being scared. And for what? For being myself. Maya. Just being myself," he says, as his voice fades and I can hear him cry into the phone. "I want to live in a place where being gay is my right—not a crime. My right as a human being. And to be with the partner I love, openly."

"I know, I know, darling. It's okay. Calm down. It'll be okay. We all have to pretend one way or another here," I say. I can hear him trying to catch his breath as I continue, "Sweetheart, this is an Islamic country. With Islamic rules."

"I'm so tired," he says.

"Why all of a sudden, though? You've been dealing with this issue all these years, living here."

"Things have changed since Peter and I got married. I've been feeling differently. I want us to be recognized and respected as a couple. As a married couple."

"I understand. Soon, one day soon. It's in the horizon," I say trying to sound hopeful and comforting.

"Not in our lifetime," he says, hopelessly.

"Well, not in the Middle East for sure. But, darling…You know how gays are fighting for their rights all over the world. The same-sex marriage, gays in military, all of that." He has stopped crying and I can tell he is listening intently. "I even heard that gays in India are getting legal rights and had their first ever selection of gay Valentine's cards."

"That's cute. But it'll take a lot more than gay cards. We want to adopt a child or two and have a family, Maya. We want the full package."

"You can have all that. But not here. What does Peter think?"

"We've both been thinking about leaving Dubai. I mean, Jesus! We can't even celebrate our marriage publically. Last night we…" He chokes on his words again. "We could not even research gay marriages on the Internet 'cause of the censorship."

187

"What do you mean?"

"When we Googled countries where gay marriage is legal, we got the censorship page with the cross-eyed cartoon character from that Emirati animation series. You know, the four old women in burkas." He sighs and shouts, "SURF SAFELY! THIS WEBSITE IS NOT ACCESSIBLE IN THE U.A.E." The message pops up on the screen with one of these grandma cartoon characters, pointing her finger at me, standing next to a black, lit bomb. Can you believe this?"

"What do you mean? Like flipping you off?" I say, chuckling.

"Maya. No. This is not a good time to joke," he says, chuckling in spite of himself. "Her index finger, you know, like you do when someone has…"

"I know, Asif. I know. It's okay. Darling. This is an Islamic country. You know how it is."

"Yeah. I know. There are no gay Muslims. Right! What a joke. Half of these guys…"

"Shh. Listen to me. You know the way of life around this region. Not exactly known for its gay-friendly ways, darling. And, you know, Dubai is probably one of your best bets if you have to live in the Middle East. Well, maybe aside from Lebanon."

"I know. Peter and I love it here, otherwise. Anyway. I'm sorry. Didn't mean to ruin your day. But I do feel a little better now that I've vented off."

"Glad to be of service. That's what friends are for. Dump on me, baby. But I thought you guys were throwing your commitment ceremony party at a villa in Jumeirah."

"Our friend is a local and he backed out last week. He's scared, too. We understand. But the good news is," Asif says with the zing back in his voice, "that's why I called you to begin with before I lost it."

"Love good news. *Yallah*. Let's hear it."

"Yesterday we booked the Flying Carpet lounge."

"Yay," I scream out. "That's great, Asif. That's such a beautiful venue. Right overlooking the water."

"Glad you approve. But, we couldn't sleep last night after booking the place. We are worried sick that someone might blow the whistle on us."

"Everything will be just fine," I say, when I hear Alia shouting my name, waving me over.

"Where are you?" Asif asks in a suspicious tone.

"At the mall. Check out the weekend edition of *Gulf News*. You'll know."

"Oh! Can't wait. Maya. I wanted to ask you for a favor."

"Sure. Anything."

"We're asking people close to us to speak at our reception. And the topic is elements of a good relationship in their opinion. I'd like you to say something, too. It'll mean a lot to me. Please say yes."

"I'll be honored. What a great idea. But I really don't think you've thought this through, Asif. I'm single. Someone needs to tell *me* about those elements."

"You know the elements. You just need to settle your ass down." He giggles and says, "Write a poem about the importance of oral sex in a relationship."

We both laugh out loud.

"Fine. I'll think of something," I say.

"Thanks, Maya. Again, sorry if I lost it."

"Love you. Glad you called. It'll be an amazing party. You'll see."

As I push the little red button and walk back to the mall-walkers' table, I start to get worried. What if they actually do get in trouble for throwing this party? I sit down, feeling sad for Asif. I take a sip of my lukewarm coffee and a bite of my chocolate croissant, and hear a voice from behind say,

"Bad girl. *Tsch*. *Tsch*. You really shouldn't be eating that. A mall-walker has fruit for breakfast."

I stop mid-chew and look up to see Lucy staring down at me. I feel like a child caught with her hands, head, and feet in the cookie jar.

I smile at her thinking, You mall-walkers *are* fruitcakes. "I'm sorry. I didn't know the rules. Next time," I say.

✺

Homo sapiens. Our rules, our bad and good, our dos and don'ts, our or-else-we'll-make-your-lives-hell ultimatums. What is up with this hypocritical world? It bothers me that we love to bother each other so much, and that is just the way it is. I can't enjoy the rest of my chocolate croissant.

LADIES' FIGHT CLUB

I am at a hospital somewhere in the middle of Bur Dubai, keeping Janet company. She has been diagnosed with some sexually transmitted disease and was kept overnight at the hospital for additional tests. She is certain she caught it from Ramzy, the Tower of Pisa sweet-talker in her pottery class.

She had gone out with him exclusively for two months, and her joy had filled our conversations, texts, and calls. They connected intellectually, emotionally, and sexually. Her unintentional infatuation with exotic, macho Middle Eastern men had finally paid off with him. Or so it seemed. We had laughed about how lucky she was to hit the jackpot on her last try. The only thing she did not like about him was how he refrained from holding her hand, and in general, showing any form of affection in public. Giving him the benefit of doubt, I suggested that he had a shy nature, which she vetoed right away. Then I came up with a more solid justification—he probably had a religious upbringing, which she also strongly vetoed, saying he had a secular upbringing, and had spent most of his life living in Canada, away from his family.

That left the "no benefits and lots of doubts" option. But, I kept my thoughts to myself since the only remaining, logical explanation was the presence of a significant other abroad, and friends or family members around in Dubai, ready to blow the whistle on him should he be seen cuddling up to a pretty Western woman.

As it turns out, Mr. Ramzy's refined, multi-faceted interest in women had driven him to having it all: a wife in Canada (from whom he claimed to be separated), a girlfriend (Janet), and paid ladies to fill up the lonely, late hours of his Arabian nights.

Poor Janet. She is despairingly quiet. Her insurance will not cover the hospital charges given the nature of the disease. All sexually transmitted issues must first prove to have been caused through a legitimate intimate encounter. And there is nothing legal about having sex with a man who is not your husband, let alone someone else's husband.

I am sprawled out on a white leather loveseat, my arms crossed behind my head. "Come on, look at the bright side; at least your hospital room qualifies as a suite at a five-star hotel."

Janet is playing around with buttons; raising, lowering, twisting, and elevating her state-of-the-art hospital bed.

"Yes. I'm paying for each and every star," she says, rolling her eyes. "I should've known better. I should've known when all of a sudden he said he had to go on a two-week business trip to Canada."

"How could you've known? He was very good at playing his role. You really can't blame yourself."

"How about when he said, 'I really don't like holding hands in public?' I just assumed he was strange that way. You know how some guys are."

"I know the type, they're like, 'I'll only hold hands if I have to.' So unromantic." I realize I am not making her feel any better. "Janet, this could've happened to any of us with any guy. It's hard to trust someone you've known for a short time. 'What to do?'" I say, with an Indian accent, shaking my head.

She smiles and says, "What to do? Should I call him and let him know about this mess?" She sounds helpless in her flower-studded five star hospital robe.

"Like he'd care! No! Absolutely not!" I say, firmly. "When did you hear from him last?"

"It's been a while. We had a text exchange. He wanted to stop by to return the book I had lent him."

"Oh my God! That was eons ago. What an ass. I'm really mad at him. I hate lying cowards. Poor excuse of a man. He can stick the book…"

Right then, Divine, the cheerful Filipino nurse, walks in smiling and carrying a folder. "How are you feeling, Miss Janet?" she says.

"I'm fine. When can I leave?"

Divine smiles and hands Janet the folder and says, "You are ready. You pay your bill and go home."

Janet takes a look at her bill and flushes. "I can't believe this. Can I put it on my credit card?"

"Sorry, Miss Janet. Cash only."

"This is ridiculous. Why?"

The nurse looks at Janet, obviously not knowing the reason why herself. Janet looks at me and throws her arms up in the air and says, "Can you believe this?"

"It's okay. Let's pay and get out of here." I get up and go over to her bedside.

"I don't have any cash," she says.

"I do," I say, "Just got paid. It's in dollars, though. Hold on a sec. I'll go exchange it. I saw a Dubai Islamic bank downstairs. I'll be right back."

✲

There are lots of people waiting around the bank. I take a number and find a seat.

About five minutes has gone by when I hear, "*Psst. Psst.*" The sound is coming from the guy sitting next to me. He is an Indian guy in his early twenties. He is looking ahead, pretending he wasn't the one who had just made that barely audible, hideous sound. He knows he has my attention. He continues to hold onto to his inconspicuous pose, staring into the oblivion ahead, and starts tapping his pen on a pile of papers that is tilted in my direction. As I look down on the pile, he unfolds the corner of the top paper to expose his scribbled mobile number. I had to gather all the strength in my jaw to keep myself from exploding into laughter. I press down hard on my teeth, forcing my mouth shut, and slowly turn my head away.

I am not sure how to make sense of what I am feeling. On one hand I feel defenseless and vulnerable as the weaker gender, but on the other hand, I feel powerful and dominant. The world appears to be ruled by men all over, but are the women, the seemingly vulnerable ones, the invisible driving force? We are just like gravity, the most negligible force in particle physics, the one that holds us all on the Earth. A woman is the force that:

Always attracts, never repels.

Cannot be absorbed, transformed, or shielded against.

Has an infinite range.

Or is the world ruled by the power that a man *and* a woman create together? The power that is capable of creating new life? But where does love fit into this formula?

✦

Janet is still irritated and quiet as we get in my car. My attempt to lighten her mood by telling her about the *psst* guy at the bank backfires completely.

"Men are scum. Seriously. Is that all they want?" Janet says, as she tears off her hospital wristband. "I understand the Indian guy, but how can a well-educated, well-read businessman have the same desires?"

"It's all as nature intended," I say. "What's important is that you are healthy now and Ramzy's out of the picture."

"The doctor said that I have to take it easy on my body for a while." She looks at me and sighs. "Did you know that right from the start, my mom didn't have a good feeling about Ramzy? I should've followed her instincts."

"What?" I look over at her, surprised. "You told your mom? She knows about all this? Hospital and everything?"

"Of course. I tell her everything. She's my best advisor."

"That's so cool," I say, wondering if that would have been the case with me if my mom were to be still around.

"I guess that does it for me and dating for a while," Janet says, giving me a sideways glance.

"Is that right? Time to kick the habit?" I say, grinning.

"Yes. I need to get away from Dubai."

"Why don't you take one of your trips?"

"I plan to. As soon as I'm one hundred percent again. I'm planning a short visit to Moscow and St. Petersburg," she says, glancing over, smiling.

"That would definitely take your mind away from all this."

Right then a text message beeps in on my mobile.

"Could you check that for me please," I say.

She takes my phone out of my purse, lets out a squeak and says, "It's from Clover."

"Yay. He's back. What does he say? It's probably about tonight."

"What?" she says surprised. "Maya? You guys have a date?"

"It's not a date," I say, disappointed. "It's a business dinner with his PR people."

"When did this happen? Why didn't you tell me?"

"Well, I didn't have a chance to tell you with all the stuff you had going on. I'll fill you in. Please, read the message to me first."

"I'm sorry. Okay," she looks down on my phone and reads out loud. "He says 'Hi there. Hope you're well. I'm back. Very jet-lagged. See you tonight?'" Janet screams, "Oh my God! So tell me. Wasn't he in the States for a family thing?"

"Yes he was. We had a little e-mail exchange while he was there," I say.

"I guess I've missed out on a lot."

"It's okay. You had a lot on your mind. Could you please text him back and say, 'Welcome back. See you tonight.'"

She starts texting. "Smiley at the end?"

"Sure, why not."

"Done. Sent to dear Clover. Let's see what our American boy is made of. Good stuff, hopefully. Where is this business dinner taking place?"

"Nobu, on the Palm, at seven thirty."

"And here you are taking care of me when you should be out getting ready for tonight. Thank you so much, Maya. Are you excited to see him?"

"Not sure how I feel. I'm kind of nervous. All along I've been trying not to be attracted to him, because he seems to be taking the friendship route." I breathe out a loud sigh and continue to say, "He insisted I e-mail him one of my poems which I finally did. Two poems from my 'Moon' series."

"You actually have a series? I've known you for how long now? Three years going on four, and not once have you read any of your poetry to me. I always thought you were sort of kidding around about being a poet."

"Unfortunately, I was not kidding."

"So what was his reaction? Did he comment?"

"I'll forward his e-mails to you when I get home. Not sure what to make of them. Now I regret sending that special series. I had written them many years ago when Kamran and I had gotten back together."

"Oh! So it's a romantic one?" Janet glances at me.

"In a way. But since I didn't want to give Mark the wrong idea…"

"You mean, the right idea," Janet says, smirking.

"Well, yes, whatever. I did mention that the series was written in the early years of the new millennium."

"I can't wait to read the poems and his comments," Janet says. "Just have fun, *habibti*. Remember what you always tell me. Get to know him. Only time will tell. Before I forget…" She takes her mobile out of her purse, and with an air of vengeance starts pressing buttons. "I'm deleting Ramzy's number and all his messages."

"Good for you."

❂

I drop Janet off, go home, change, and beautify just in time for my dinner with Mark. Driving over to the Palm I see the blue and white metro train snake its way down Sheikh Zayed Road. It's been exciting being part of this once-in-a-lifetime chance to live amid a city in the making. I have borne witness to half of these high rises, bridges, roads, islands, and now the metro coming to life in the past four years. All the while, the world was busy watching in amazement, eagerly waiting for Dubai's bubble to burst. Then suddenly WHAM! There goes the surprise global bubble instead; hitting not only this high-profile Eden of the Middle East, but everyone the world over.

I'm fifteen minutes late, and extremely nervous. I make my way to Nobu, through the fancy lobby at the Atlantis Hotel, passing shops, restaurants, and a huge aquarium. As I enter the restaurant, I spot Mark seated at a round corner table next to the window with two other guys. As I approach his table my heart begins racing, pounding faster and harder as I get closer, just like a homing device beeping louder and faster as it closes in on its target.

He sees me, smiles, and gets up to greet me.

"Hi there," he says, as he kisses me lightly on the cheek. "I want you to meet Martin and Thomas from our Miami office. This is Maya, the area expert I was telling you about."

"Nice to meet you, Maya," the Martin guy says.

"Maya, our Middle East correspondent," Thomas says, and we all laugh.

"Yeah, right. Hi. Pleased to meet you, and sorry I'm late."

"We just got here, too. Sofia called and said that they're on their way with Mr. Morshed," Mark says.

I feel sick in my stomach at the sound of the name, Sofia. I did not have to wait long to find out why.

"Oh! There they are," Marks says.

I turn around. There she is, walking gracefully between the tables in a classic black cocktail dress, followed by three Emiratis: a forty-something-year-old gentleman in a beautiful navy blue *kandura*, who I presume to be Mr. Morshed, Probel's owner, and two other tall men in white *kanduras* walking behind him.

Sofia is none other than "Penelope," the petite, pretty girl I had seen Mark with at the World Cup.

I feel an eclipse of my short-lived, moonlit heart. Mark was like a shooting star, brightening my sky momentarily, only to disappear leaving me with a pitch black night.

"Maya, Martin, Thomas…Mr. Morshed and Sofia, his assistant," Mark introduces us.

Mr. Morshed introduces Mr. Akkad and Mr. Shaban as they all take their seats.

Sofia does not waste any time and has me under surveillance from the moment she sits down. I can feel her stare, and am feeling disturbed by her presence. The men are completely oblivious of this loud, silent dialogue between the two women at the table. I can feel her feminine-assessment turbine rolling at full speed, measuring, scanning, adding, subtracting, and deducing on the competitive female scale. She finally sits back with a content smile on her pretty face, which could only mean she has no worries and can kick my ass if I should have any kind of interest, other than professional, in her Mark.

I decide right then and there that although Mark does not seem romantically interested in me, Ms. Penelope over here cannot have him without a fight. I am determined to throw her off her comfortable monopoly over Mark as soon as the moment presents itself. The fight begins. Bring it on, chicky.

❂

The dinner passes in a very typical Middle Eastern/Western manner: a lot of blah blah blahs, ha ha has, ho ho hos, to-be-honest-with-yous, pats on the back, exchanges of appreciation for work well done, and complaints about delays in documentation preparation, permit acquisition, health, safety clearance, site construction issues, and *inshallahs, mashallahs, wallahs,* and *alhamdulillahs.*

Finally, right before dessert is served, the much-anticipated moment presents itself—that is to say, Penelope excuses herself from the table to go to the powder room. It is time to mess with Penelope's peace of mind by giving her a piece of my mind.

"Great idea. I think I'll join you," I say, which in a woman's world is the equivalent of, "Let's take this outside."

I get up and follow her.

The instant we are out of the boys' earshot, she asks, "How long have you been working for Mark?"

Nice preemptive strike.

"I'm not sure if you can call it that. We're more like friends than colleagues. I do freelance research for him every once in a while," I say, sounding breezy, hoping to tickle her imagination.

"Where're you from?" she asks.

"My dad's from Brooklyn and my mom's from Pachaka," I say, fully aware that she had not asked about my heritage.

She gives me a suspicious sideways glance and says, "Hmm, I've never heard of Pachaka."

"I know. I get that a lot," I say, comforting her misguided ignorance. "It's a small island off the Ivory Coast. You should check it out. It's beautiful."

She gives me the "whatever" look and says, "How did you end up in Dubai?"

"I was here visiting a friend, liked it, and moved."

"Was it easy for you to find a job?"

"I can work out of anywhere," I say. "I'm an art collector. Actually Dubai has opened up a whole new area to me. The Middle East is an untapped market—just emerging. I love it."

From the look on her face I can tell I've won the first round. Wham! Knock down.

We get to the ladies' room just in time for the next round. I chuckle to myself behind the closed bathroom door, taking pleasure in my award-winning, wicked-witch performance. We meet back up at the sink.

"And you? Where are *you* from?" I ask her before she gets a chance to set herself up for another series of shots at my background.

"I'm half Swiss, half Spanish."

"Hmm." But I'm thinking that her reality is already sounding better than my fictional past. I say, "I can see the Spanish."

"Yes. From my mother's side. I was born in Zurich, though."

"Nice. I love Swiss chocolate," I say. I figure one honest word out of my mouth will not hurt.

She then looks at me in the mirror and says, "You look familiar. Not sure where I've seen you before."

"Yeah. I have one of those familiar faces. I'm pretty sure this is the first time we've met."

"Maybe." She stares into my eyes and looks like she is flipping through her mental memory chart. "Wasn't your picture in the *Gulf News*? The lady mall-walkers?"

So. She cannot remember seeing me at the World Cup, but why? Why? Why out of all the people, does *she* have to be the one to see that appalling picture?

"No, must've been someone else. I don't do that kind of stuff," I say in a serious tone, frowning. I go for the knock out blow right before we make it to the table, and ask her, "Are you coming to the beach party tomorrow night?"

"What beach party?" she sounds and looks surprised.

"Oh. Then I guess it's just Mark and his Miami colleagues." Knock out.

Mark looks at us as we each take our seats. Whether he will ever figure out why my face displays ultimate contentment, and Penelope's one of distorted confusion, remains to be seen. He must know something has gone on since now Penelope is giving him the you-have-it-coming deadly stare.

"So, *inshallah*, next month this time we'll be having dinner at our own restaurant, Peace Time," Mr. Morshed says, smiling as he looks at Mark.

"*Inshallah*," Mark says immediately, nodding.

Thomas raises his wine glass and says, "*Inshallah*. Here's to Peace Time."

"Cheers to Peace Time," Martin says, also raising his wine glass.

There is an odd moment of silence. The rest of us at the table know that cheers with wine and *inshallah* do not exactly go together. Mark glances over at me. I'm not sure what to do.

Sofia who looks like she is still squirming out from under the rubble of our verbal sparring match, is avoiding eye contact with everyone. And the Emiratis are not sure how to react.

Come on Maya, do something. After all, you're the one Mark counts on for resolving uncomfortable cultural gaps.

I raise my water glass and cheerfully say, "Peace Time."

Mark, who looks like he was holding his breath for the very long few seconds, follows my lead as Mr. Morshed smiles back at us, taking a sip of his water.

✦

We are all waiting for our cars at the valet in front of the restaurant. I notice that Sofia is avoiding both Mark and I, standing quietly next to Mr. Morshed. I had not realized I could be so good at making another person feel so bad. Never before have I let my vicious side shine as brightly as it just did in that short trip to the bathroom. I'm not proud of my behavior, but I am enjoying the sweet taste of wickedness. I get in my car and wave goodbye to everyone.

HE'S WITH US. I'M WITH HIM. WHO'S WITH ME?

"I can't believe you're leaving. I just got back!" Michelle says, helping me put my hand luggage in the trunk.

"Please don't even get me started. You're never around these days. It's like you work in Dubai but live in Beirut," I say.

Michelle grins as we get in her car. "We have all the way to the airport to catch up. You first," she says as she starts the car and takes off before I have a chance to put on my seat belt.

"All right. Here's mine in a nutshell: My freelance job as Mark's advisor, or whatever, has been really hectic this past month. I've been helping him out with miscellaneous stuff—finalizing their restaurant's slogan, preparing their press releases, and so on. It's been fun, but frustrating because I've fallen for him and I don't think he's interested." I look over at her, pouting.

"But you're just about to leave on a trip together."

"Yay. Kish, here we come," I say, lifting my arms in triumph.

"How do you know he's not interested in you?" Michelle says, raising one well-groomed eyebrow.

"Because I just know. You can tell when a guy is interested. Plus I suspect he's dating this one chick, Sofia."

"So! Make him interested. You have him all to yourself for two days. Seduce him, Maya. *Yallah*!"

"I don't know. Let's see. How about you? What's up with all these weekend trips to Beirut?" I glance over and add, "I can see the obvious reasons." I suck in my cheeks and pucker my lips.

She laughs and says, "No. The lips and cheeks are mine. Original."

I check her out head to toe and say, "Then, what is it? You're glowing. You seem different. Don't tell me you got a boob job."

"I'd like to one day soon. But no, original boobs," she says happily.

"You're the Lebanese black sheep," I say, teasingly.

"I'm offended." She glances over at me, takes in a deep breath and says, "Remember Charbel? My classmate from Notre Dame University?"

"Yes. Oh! Michelle. Naughty. Naughty. Now that explains the glow."

She continues to smile. "He really likes me. He says he's been trying to go out with me ever since college. I never thought of him that way back then."

"And now?"

"Well, now yes. He's caring and responsible. He wants to have a family, and he wants me to move to Beirut to look for a job."

"NO!" I scream out. "When were you planning on telling me all this? That's great. But you can't move. I won't miss you, but you know…All the gay guys will. Who's going to attract them now?"

"There are plenty to attract in Beirut," she says, laughing. "I don't mind moving. I'm getting bored in Dubai. I like to be close to my family. And Charbel seems serious. We Skype every night. I think he really loves me. "

"Seriously? You're really moving?"

"I'm thinking about it. I've already started looking for jobs there."

"It all happened so fast."

"True. I don't want to tell anybody until I'm sure," she says. "Now back to you. Why are you going to Kish with Mark when there're all these other fun places around? Why not Istanbul or Maldives? Why Kish?"

"Oh. I wish. You need to ask him that. He's just curious about Iran. And now that he's in the area he wants to have a feel for it, even if it means just visiting Kish. He wants to go diving, too."

"Hmm. Where are you guys staying?"

"At my father's apartment." I glance over naughtily, flicking my eyebrows.

"Good. Does your father know?"

"Of course he does. Michelle, darling, I don't think he worries about preserving my virginity at this point."

"True," she chuckles, "If we were still virgins…"

"Bite your tongue." I interrupt her, cringing at the thought.

"…we could've put it up for bidding on the Internet," Michelle says, laughing.

"Lovely. I wonder how much mine would've auctioned off for. I'd say half a million."

"Dollars?"

"Of course not. British pounds."

We burst out laughing.

"Wooh. Seriously, tell me. What does your father know about Mark?"

"There's not much to know except that I have a thing for him."

"I admire your relationship with your father. He sounds really cool and open-minded for a Middle Eastern man."

"Thanks. Yes, he's great. I love him. I've lucked out."

✦

It's no secret that in this region premarital sex can threaten a woman's marital desirability, therefore lowering her chances of marrying her clan's Prince Charming. Naturally, it is not only logical, but appropriate for an otherwise law-abiding female citizen to lie to everyone about slip-ups and extracurricular, experimental activities—which, God forbid, may have taken place prior to her white wedding day. And the men play along, happily singing, "I see trees of green, red roses, too, I see them bloom for me and for you, and I think to myself, what a wonderful world…" as they imagine an untouched red cherry dangling to be picked, a flower waiting to be cut on their wedding night.

Right!

✸

Mark is already at the check-in counter when I arrive. We get our boarding passes and make our way to the waiting area at our departure gate, which is packed with Filipinos and Romanians.

"I'd heard about the people making visa-change runs to Kish from Dubai. What exactly does that mean?" Mark asks.

"To renew their work visa they need to leave the country. Kish is just a half hour's plane-ride away and the companies have a contract with travel agencies for just this purpose. Airfare and accommodation included."

"Is that right?" he says, before he gets distracted by two bearded men joining us at the gate. One of them is in a brown suit, twirling a black rosary bead around his middle and index fingers, scrupulously scanning the people around him. "Will we get in trouble for traveling together?" Mark looks at me with obvious concern.

"We'll be fine as long as no one's given too much information. Here's your story: You're my cousin's friend. You're meeting my cousin in Kish to go diving. But I wouldn't worry about it. Nobody's going to question you."

"I hope not. I haven't told my family I'm going to Iran. Imagine if I'm suspected of being an American spy and I make headline news," he says, excitedly.

Now he has me worried. "You're not connected to any fishy humanitarian, peace, or political activist groups are you?" I realize I should have asked him this prior to making our travel arrangements.

He laughs and says, "Since when is being a humanitarian fishy?"

"Since there are fishy people around abusing human rights."

"No. None of that. I'm clean of all selfless, philanthropist activities."

"Good for you. Then you'll be fine," I say, cheerfully.

The gate opens, and we get ready for boarding. I get up to put a loose-fitting knee-length linen robe over my clothes. "Remember this," I say. "Iranians love foreigners and they ask a lot of questions. Don't feel obliged to share too much information. Just follow my lead."

Mark is watching me as I button up my robe and says, "Do you have to cover up from here?"

"Not really. But since we're flying an Iranian airliner, I like to. Out of respect, and also to draw less attention to myself. If we were taking Emirates Airlines or some other non-Iranian airliner, I would've covered up once we landed in Iran, before leaving the plane."

He points at my ensemble and grins, "Is this an Islamic *hijab*?"

I nod.

"You just look like someone who's wearing a long robe over her jeans." He says, sounding disappointed.

DESERT MOJITO

"No kidding!" I wear a white shawl over my head, tuck the sides behind my ears to keep it from falling, and flick the rest over my shoulders. "Now I look like someone with a robe and a head scarf over her head." I say, teasingly.

"I'm sorry. What I meant was that, what you have on looks like ordinary street clothes." He hesitates, and scans me over, head to toe. "I had this idea of women wrapped in heavy black cloths and cloaks, all covered up. Not this. I like it. You look good in this."

Well, so much for that. My unrecognizable *hijab* is serving its exact opposite intended purpose, inviting more attention.

"You may not have liked it as much if you had to cover up yourself," I say.

"Probably not."

"You're going to see a clear difference between the women forced to cover as opposed to the ones who do it by choice, from women wrapped in black *chadors*—although not many of them here in Kish—to ones with dyed blond hair and bouffants sticking out from under sheer thin scarves."

"So you're a happy medium?" He smiles.

"I'm the best."

"I'm sure you are."

And you are all talk and no action. Whatever, I'm thinking.

✪

As our transfer bus approaches the plane on the runway, I see Mark's eyes sparkle at the sight of the aircraft. "No way! This is a beautiful plane. What is it?"

Before I have a chance to give him the wrong, albeit creative background story on the plane, one of the huge Romanian guys standing next to us says, "It's a Fokker 50. Made in the Netherlands. Turbo plane. Six bladed propellers."

"Thank you," Mark says appreciatively. "You must travel this route frequently."

"I work on the oil-rig on the Persian Gulf, off of Kish Island," Mr. Fokker says and abruptly turns his back to Mark.

The plane cabin is small with two seats on each side of the twenty-odd rows. We are welcomed and directed to our seats at the back of the plane by a well-groomed flight attendant, who is dressed in a long navy blue overcoat, matching pants and pumps. Her round face is framed by a veil wrapped around her head, tucked inside her overcoat. We pass the two bearded Iranian passengers we saw earlier; the conspicuous one with the black rosary beads is sitting in the aisle seat, staring ahead into space, avoiding all eye contact, which, judging by his type, could only mean one thing: He is seeing everything and not a single living creature in sight is getting past him unnoticed. He is the embodiment of the Big Brother who is supposedly *not* watching you.

Mark and I take our seats and buckle-up as the flight announcement welcomes the passengers on board, first in Persian and then in English: "In the name of God, the compassionate, the merciful. Hail to the martyrs and the Supreme Leader. We ask God for a safe flight and journey for all the passengers aboard. We…"

A twenty-something-year-old flight attendant in a white, short-sleeve shirt and navy blue pants starts distributing candy down the aisle. And, shortly after, we are airborne.

✡

Mark gets busy reading an article in the flight magazine on Iran's tourist sites. There are colorful pictures of men skiing, men diving, families visiting the historical sites in Isfahan,

Persepolis in Shiraz, and other inviting destinations in the desert, mountains, and forests of Iran.

I am enjoying my physical vicinity to Mark. His knees are touching the seat in front of him, and his left arm is lightly brushing against mine, each time setting off a cascade of chemical reactions.

He looks up from the magazine and says, "Too bad I can't see all this," pointing at the pictures.

"I know," I say. "The advertisements should read, 'Visit the ancient mystical land of Persia,' and then in fine print, 'Good luck getting a visa,' next to a winking smiley."

He laughs. "A pity. These ski slopes look amazing. Do you ski?"

"A little. And you?" All of a sudden I have a vivid flashback of how well he skied and how hard I had slammed into the metal post while checking him out.

"I used to race in my younger days. I miss it," he says.

"Really! Have you won any prizes?"

"Yeah. A couple. How're the slopes in Iran? According to this article there's actually one slope in the city. In Tehran! And, a few others around."

"That's right. They're not bad. Especially if there's a lot of snow and..." I lower my voice, "few religious police."

"What does skiing have to do with religion?"

"Mark...Darling...The police are there to protect the people from temptation, under all circumstances. Skiing, walking, talking—it's all the same." Seeing his confused look, I continue, "Sometimes they are stricter on people than other times. The so-called climate of the day—which mostly depends on politics—is the deciding factor in the extent of their permissiveness, and how much you will be allowed to enjoy leisure activities and interactions with other people." I pause, sigh and say, "Nowadays, it's not that bad."

"So we couldn't ski together in Tehran?" he asks, still sounding confused.

"Are you kidding? Of course we could. You can do anything as long as you're in tune with the climate of the week and the flavor of the day."

"It all sounds very complex and confusing, but I'll take your word for it. How about having parties or gatherings? Are they allowed?"

"Not really. But you know what they say: 'You can take an Iranian out of a party, but you can't take the party out of an Iranian.'"

He laughs and says, "Is that right?"

"Yeah. For centuries Iranians have enjoyed and lived on gatherings, having a good time, eating, drinking, chatting, gossiping, singing, dancing, playing backgammon, discussing the political climate, what have you…" I say. "But since thirty years ago, people have had to keep all the gatherings in line with the Islamic codes."

"How do they manage that?"

I smirk and say, "Oh, gosh. Where do I begin? It's complicated. Let's say there's a wedding. The police may stop by to wish the bride and the groom well, and more importantly, to remind them that they are there for their protection. Hint. Hint. And, they get paid for their services. If you don't want trouble when times are tough, then avoid high-profile parties. Feel the climate and behave accordingly."

"It sounds like keeping an eye out for the weather report is very important in Iran." He smirks then pauses and says, "I've taken a lot for granted living in complete freedom all my life."

"Freedom is nice, but if you don't have that luxury…" I hesitate, uncertain as to how to finish my sentence. "You will learn how to get around freedom hurdles, and hurdlers."

"What do you mean?"

"It's hard to explain. People in Iran, and probably all other repressed societies, become very alert and aware individuals. They evolve with the system and find ways to get around restrictions."

"Like how?"

"Like how I just taught you to lie about being my cousin's friend if you were to be questioned as to the nature of our relationship." He nods and I continue, "As simple as that. And you know—you just learn to edit and censor yourself to conceal the truth, and blatantly lie so that you can do the things you like, to avoid getting in trouble. This duality has been woven into the fabric of society. Kids grow up knowing it's wrong to lie, but it's just the way it is: a survival skill."

"You seem to have it all figured out."

"Huh. Well, I didn't really have much choice. I didn't want to be singled out as the stupid girl who told the truth. I had to learn it the hard way, by trial and error, when I was working there."

"I can't imagine wasting all that energy on pretending. And over such silly things, like lying about being friends."

"I couldn't, either. But believe it. Naivety won't get you anywhere except in trouble."

We stop our conversation as the flight attendants pass out refreshment trays of cake, peanuts and juice.

"It just sounds very unnatural to lead a double life," Mark says, sipping on his orange juice.

"Exactly. But nature has nothing to do with anything here," I say.

"So people pretend to be religious but they really aren't. Is that it?"

"Not exactly. Iranians are a faithful nation, and in general, faith in God is a strong characteristic of people in this region regardless of how closely or loosely they observe whatever religion they follow—be it Islam, Zoroastrianism, Christianity, Judaism, Baha'ism, and so on."

"Interesting and confusing, but I'm getting the picture."

"What to do?" I say with an Indian accent, shaking my head, smiling.

He smiles back.

✹

The plane's front wheels have barely touched the runway when the bearded man wraps the rosary beads around his wrist and stands up. He loosens his belt, sticks his hand halfway down his pants to tuck in his shirt, grabs the waist back up, and tightens his belt. He then steps out in the aisle and opens the overhead compartment to take out a huge, overstuffed plastic bag, all the while trying to keep his balance, while the plane is still moving, taxing to the gate.

The flight attendant welcomes us to "the beautiful Kish Island" over the PA, and reminds us that the importation of alcoholic beverages is not permitted to Iran. And, the lady passengers are asked to kindly observe the mandatory Islamic attire.

As we leave the airplane and enter the main airport hall, the Filipino ladies help themselves to the robes and headscarves provided for them by the Kish authorities in a plastic bag.

I am relieved when Mark exits passport control without being hassled, and we make our way outside to the taxi station.

"That was easy. No questions asked," Marks says. "The visa officer even welcomed me to Kish and smiled at me."

"Of course. I told you. Foreigners are more than welcome, you will…" My phone rings. Maurice's name is flashing on the screen. "Sorry, one second, I have to get this."

"Go ahead," he says.

DESERT MOJITO

We get in the taxi.

As soon as I push the green button I hear Maurice's screech, "Where are you? I've been trying to contact you for the past two hours." I can barely hear him over an odd continuous sound in the background.

"I just landed in Kish. I'm in a cab. Where are you? What's that droning noise in the background?"

"KISH?!" he screams out.

Mark, who must have just heard that very audible shout, glances over at me and smiles before he goes back to looking out at the scenery. The road leading into town is tastefully decorated with miniature lights and colorful flower pots, distracting one's attention away from the dry, barren land all around.

"Why do you keep moving in the wrong direction?" Maurice says. I can hear the irritation in his voice. "You're not only supposed to move away from that region, you're supposed to stay away from Iran in particular."

Over the years Maurice has developed a love–hate relationship with Iran; he loves Iran, the country of his birth, but without the "Islamic Republic of" before its name. And, to add wood to his already flaming stance, the country's claim that it is solely composed of heterosexuals is absurd. He gets restless and worried every time one of his family members or friends visit Iran.

"Where are you?" I say. "And what is that awful sound in the background, for God's sake?"

"I'm on the inter-terminal airport train in Zurich. And that sound is..." he chuckles, "that is a cow mooing over the speakers on the train. It must be some kind of advertisement for Swiss tourism."

"Wow! Who knew the Swiss had a sense of humor?" I say, laughing. "I'll be in Kish only for a day. I'm playing tour guide to a friend."

"You and your crazy friends!" Maurice says, still sounding annoyed. "It's beyond me why anyone in their right mind would want to visit Kish."

I sneak a peek at Mark. He is staring out the window, engrossed in Kish's famous Jamshid Hotel, which has just come into view. Its imitation-Persepolis pillars, statues, and intricate carvings announce its out-of-place presence on this semi-pristine island.

"Oh, come on. We're here to dive. Believe it or not Kish has the best coral reef sites in the area."

"Whatever," Maurice says, irritated. "Maya listen. I may be able to come to Dubai for a quick visit in six weeks after all. You better not be in Kish or Tehran."

"Great. I promise I'll stay put. If…"

The line is cut off.

Mark looks over at me and says, "Your friend sounded very excited."

"Yeah, Maurice is usually excited. I've known him since elementary school. He called to say he's coming for a visit to Dubai.

"Does he live in Iran?"

"Oh, God no! He lives in New York. He's some hotshot executive. Can you believe he gets flown to meetings in a helicopter?" I'm hoping to impress Mark with the VIP circle I keep.

"Nice. Is he married?"

"He almost got married once but it didn't work out. I'm sure he'll be married one day soon. He's a good catch."

Mark looks over at me, grins and says, "He's not your type?"

"Not really, considering he's been gay ever since I've known him. Well…" I hesitate, uncertain about how much I need to share. "Now we know he was gay all along. But when we were kids, back in the elementary school…"

"Oh! I see. I guess that wouldn't be your type, then," he says as he runs his fingers through his hair.

Since he brought up the subject I think this is a good time as any, and say, "Why aren't *you* married?" I try to sound as carefree as he just did. His nervous laugh and the uneasy look in his eyes surprise me.

"Where did that come from? Well…" He clears his throat. "Maybe we can discuss that whole grey romantic area over drinks another day." He then raises his eyebrows and rolls down the window. "Great island breeze," he says.

I nod and say yes. I must have hit a sore spot.

I turn to our driver, who has been looking at us in the rearview mirror more often than he has looked at the road. He's a friendly-looking man in his early thirties. As soon as he sees me looking at him, he says in Farsi, "Did you just come from Dubai?"

"Yes," I say, and we start chatting. Ali is from Shiraz and has been living in Kish for the past six years. He asks me where Mark is from. At the sound of the word "America," Ali's eyes sparkle and a huge smile spreads across his face.

"Welcome to Iran," Ali says, looking at Mark through his rearview mirror.

"Thank you. Happy to be here."

"My name is Ali. You?"

"Mark."

"Mark. Very nice. Very nice. You like Obama?"

Mark is taken back and looks at me nervously, uncertain how to respond. I give him an okay signal.

"Yes. I like Obama. I voted for him," Mark replies, firmly.

"Excuse me?" Ali turns to me for clarification. I translate what Mark has just said. Ali smiles happily again and says, "Obama, good man. Iran people like America." He looks at Mark. "Like Obama. OOh BAA MAAst," Ali says, cheerfully. He laughs out loud and asks me to translate his play on word for Mark.

Mark looks over at me and waits for my explanation.

"He's a funny guy. He's doing a play on words," I say, "with Obama's name. Instead of 'O' he says 'OOh,' which is a pronoun in Farsi meaning he or she. So 'ooh baa maast' translates into 'he's with us.'"

Mark's wary and lost expression immediately softens, and is replaced by a pleasantly surprised one.

"Yes. Yes," he says, looking back at Ali in the mirror.

Men! Forget Obama. We have more important matters at hand. I need to find out what 'grey' romantic matter Mark is hiding from me. Before Ali has a chance to further expand on his love of Obama, I ask him whether he can help us get some alcohol. He says he will do his best, but not to keep our hopes up high since smuggling alcohol is very difficult to the island. Mark asks what we are discussing and I tell him we are still praising Obama. He grins. Ali gives me his mobile number, drops us off at the apartment, and sets out on his alcohol-scavenger-hunt.

✪

We decide not to waste time and head out to the dive-center right away to reserve spots for our early dive tomorrow morning. Heading down the main street, we walk past the part of the island that is crowded with shopping malls, sidewalk cafes, the Go-Cart racetrack, the bowling alley, and the billiard hall. Mark continues to express his amazement at what he sees. We

DESERT MOJITO

cut through a barren field and make our way to the beach, heading to the Persian Gulf Dive Center, all the while chatting about the way of things in Iran.

As we approach the dive center I see Hashem, my dive instructor, busy filling up the scuba air tanks. He spots me.

"Maya!" he says, excitedly, his bright white teeth flashing across his tanned face. "Long time. We thought you had moved back to America without saying bye." He shakes my hand and acknowledges Mark, nodding.

I introduce Mark. "Good to see you," I say. "I was here last year for three days. Stopped by to say hi. Amin said you were on vacation in Tehran."

"That's right." He pauses. "Things have changed a lot since you last came diving. I hope you're not here to dive."

"What do you mean?" I say, already guessing the bad news. "We wanted to reserve a dive for tomorrow morning."

"He can go," he nods at Mark, "but you can't. Male instructors aren't allowed to take women diving anymore, and our female diving instructor is on vacation." He sighs. "I'm sorry." He sounds frustrated and genuinely sad.

Mark sees the expression on my face.

"What's the matter?" he says. "Bad weather?" He winks at me, smirking.

I nod. "Very bad indeed. Women can't dive with male diving instructors."

"Are you serious? What can happen under the water?" he asks surprised.

"Don't you know? I can striptease for you and the fish under the water," I say.

"Hmm! I see. A bit difficult with the tank on, but still manageable if you really set your mind to it, I suppose." Mark says, teasing me back. "Oh well. We can do something else."

"No way. Why should you be penalized for my sake? You've come all the way to Kish to dive. You should go down and see the reefs. It's really pretty."

"Yes," Hashem says, smiling at Mark, "it is beautiful. You come tomorrow. Eight thirty. Maya see coral and fish before. You come and see. Many fish in Kish."

Mark looks at me uncertainly.

"You have to go. And that's that. *Khalas*," I say, and assure Hashem that Mark will be joining the morning dive.

"*Khalas!*" Hashem says, laughing at me. "You've become an Arab, Maya."

I shake my head and with an Indian accent say, "What to do?"

✸

We leave the dive-center for a tea shack next to the pier. The air feels softer and lighter than in Dubai. We get our teas and sit outside next to the bike track, which runs along the cliffs on the shoreline for thirty-five miles, all the way around the island. The scene is like any other typical day at a beach, in any other part of the world, except that the women are covered head to toe, and only men and children are in their bathing suits and shorts. The setting sun is painting its sky with hues of yellow, orange, red, and purple. The fishing boats, jet skies, and motorboats are making their runs, taking the passengers around the island.

Mark is quietly taking in his surroundings. I have no idea what he's thinking.

"So? What do you think of Kish? Pearl of the Persian Gulf," I say.

He sighs. "I'm amazed. It's beautiful. It's not at all what I had imagined or expected. People are enjoying life," he says, "except for how limited life is for women…" He nods in the direction of the woman waiting to get on the jet ski. The jet ski attendant has just handed her a long, oversized, blue-hooded raincoat to put over her clothes. "So… Women can't swim or sunbathe?" Mark continues to say, with a perplexed look on his face, frowning.

"Yes, we can. The ladies' beach is on the other side of the island. Tucked away in a secluded corner. Safe from the men," I add, playfully.

"Oh! So you get to enjoy the sun in your bathing suits, only not with men around?"

"Yes. Or, another way to put it is that men cannot enjoy us in our bathing suits." We both laugh and I continue, "From what I hear, long ago, Kish authorities dedicated this remote spot to women. Little did they know that special beach faced one of the richest underwater coral reef sights around the island. It is an amazing, pristine beach accessible to women only. A bit ironic, don't you think?"

"There's some universal justice after all, eh?"

"Maybe. They know about this well-kept underwater secret now, but have been too lazy to move it to another location. But I hear that's about to change."

"It all still seems very silly, not to mention unfair to women. I can't believe you can't dive with us tomorrow."

I look at him in silence, shrug my shoulders and say, "What to do?" I refrain from doing my favorite Indian accent. "No point getting worked up over it. It's just the way things are around here." I pause, and then utter the famous three words, the simplest justification for all that is baffling, unfair, illogical and paradoxical in this land: "This is Iran."

"Iran, indeed. I can't believe I'm here. And, you were right. Everyone's been so friendly and nice to me so far. But why do people stare at me so much?"

"Oh! That's right, the staring. Don't worry, it's not you." I chuckle. "You know, when I finally managed to get used to such an intrusive, odd social behavior, I missed it whenever I traveled outside Iran. I remember the first time I felt the stare-void was when I had been working in Tehran for a year straight. I finally went on a business trip to Paris and from the moment I landed at the airport, I felt something was missing. I finally figured it out after the second day. I realized that no one had as much as glanced at me. I felt invisible, like a ghost. I felt unattractive and asked myself, 'How could they just pass me by and not look at me?'" Mark starts smiling. I take a sip of my tea and continue, "Then I realized how this basic, albeit disturbing habit of staring had served its purpose on many levels, including the acknowledgement of my existence."

"Interesting. That makes sense," he says. "Is it okay if I stare back?"

"Of course. It's a social norm here. Everyone stares at everyone else. There's a lot of silent sizing up and communication going on. Iranians have truly mastered the art of speaking and hearing with their eyes if you ask me. But you're right. They love staring at foreigners in particular, not to mention shamelessly. They even point them out to each other. But I assure you, you're safe and there's nothing to worry about."

"I do feel safe, actually," he says. "I just need to get used to the stares. Now I know how Hollywood stars feel."

"Being a foreigner, you're already half as good as being one in Iran."

"Shame I'm not much into fame," he says.

"It wasn't really a choice for me," I say, jokingly. "I was born into it."

"You mean being born in the States or having an American mother?"

"It works both ways for me. You see. If I'm in Iran, I can use my American edge of fame, and when outside, my Iranian one. I'm covered either way." I raise my eyebrows and smirk.

"You're a troublemaker, Maya."

"I know. Let's get freshened up."

✾

We are back in the apartment. I'm in the bedroom changing when there is a knock on the front door. My heart drops. Who could it be? I come out to the living room to see Mark with his eyes wide open, standing frozen next to his rucksack. I tell him to stay quiet and point him away towards the bedroom as I nervously walk to the door. He tiptoes to the bedroom and shuts the door.

"Who is it?" I ask in Farsi.

"It's me. *Khaanoom*. It's Ali. Your taxi driver."

I let out a sigh of relief and open the door to find Ali standing there with a smile. "Here you go," he says, handing me a small black plastic bag.

"Good job, Ali. I can't believe it. What did you find?" I peak inside to see a bottle of tequila.

"There's a worm inside," Ali happily points to a brown thing floating on the bottom of the bottle. "I wouldn't have let you down. Your American fiancé should know about us Iranians and our hospitality. He is our guest."

"Yes. You're right," I smile at Ali, enjoying his diplomatic reference to Mark as my fiancé. "Thank you very much, Ali."

Mark is still hiding in the bedroom. I pay for the tequila, give Ali a good tip, and shut the door.

"You can come out now," I shout out to Mark.

"Was that Ali? What was he doing here?" He walks into the living room and sees me holding out the tequila bottle. "How on earth did you manage that?"

"Ask and you shall receive," I say. "Should we go get some lime and chips? We need to buy some bottled water, too. The tap water's not really drinkable."

"Sure, let's go." Mark cannot stop chuckling. "Maya. You're a troublemaker," he says again, putting on his shoes.

I laugh. "What do you mean? As Ali said, we need to take care of our guest and show you some Iranian hospitality."

"Thank you. I do appreciate it. And all the way from Mexico, too. This stuff must be hard to get here."

"To be honest with you, I was very surprised, too. Tequila's hard to find even on the black market in Tehran. No idea how he got this. Your luck, I suppose."

"Hey, is there a place where I can check my e-mails?"

"There sure is," I say, "which reminds me, I also need to photocopy my Iranian ID card to mail to my father while we're here."

"Let's go," he says. "Can I see your Iranian ID?"

Crap. Why did I have to tell him? "Yeah, I'll show it to you in the cab," I say calmly, disguising my concern. I can't show him my lovely one-line-long name, my date of birth, and my horrid picture in the tight *hijab* bandaged around my head. I need an escape plan. As we head out the door I am wondering if I should take him on a boat-ride, and hope to get kidnapped by some Somali pirates.

❂

On the cab ride over to the Internet–photocopy center, I tell Mark that in the Islamic Republic of Iran, parents have the liberty of choosing their children's names from a state-approved name list. Foreign names, names of corrupt figures related to country's pre-Islamic past, and names of Zoroastrian gods and goddesses are also banned. What shocks him the most is when I tell him that it is customary for a woman to keep her maiden name after marriage.

"Huh. A very liberal country indeed," he says.

"Yeah, right." I roll my eyes. "But get this—when a women marries a doctor or an engineer, she insists on using her husband's title and last name. She is referred to as Mrs. Doctor or Mrs. Engineer plus the last name."

"Interesting. How'd you be able to tell the difference between a woman who has adopted her husband's title and one who actually *is* a doctor, herself?"

"Great question, Mr. Clover. You can't. At least, not just by hearing the name, not until you see or meet in person. Usually, the title-adopter doesn't look like the kind of woman who would've bothered spending all her precious, youthful years going to medical school to earn a title. It's easier to just adopt your husband's title, instead," I say, chuckling.

"I see. Smart women," he says. When he sees me look at him in surprise he says, "Or not. All right, all that said, now, let me see your Iranian ID."

"Let me give you some background info on the ID before showing it to you."

Please someone help me get out of this one. The day I took the ID picture was a hot summer day, I had been stuck in Tehran traffic for two hours, shouting, swearing, swerving, all the while trying to keep my scarf from slipping off my head. By the time I made it to the photography studio I was sweating and ready to kill someone. "They won't issue the ID even if one thread of hair is showing," the studio photographer kept reminding me, after I ruined many shots by trying to cheat, pulling my head scarf back, just a little when he wasn't looking. I finally surrendered and wrapped the scarf tightly around my head and stared into the camera with a resigned look on my face.

I knew that the picture would cause me my demise when I least expected it. And now, I'm wishing for a divine or even an earthly intervention. My only choice is to continue blabbering to keep Mark distracted until help arrives.

"First of all, anyone who's Iranian, either by birth or through naturalization has to apply for one of these IDs, which is called *shenas-nameh*. It's the most comprehensive identification booklet-slash-birth certificate I've ever seen. In addition to the birth details, one's most important civil activities in a lifetime are marked from birth to death in this little red booklet. Can you believe that?"

He doesn't respond. I look at him and see that he's distracted by a group of kids waving to him from across the street, shouting out, "Hello, mister!"

He waves back at them happily, and says, "Hello."

They giggle and keep waving at him.

"Cute kids. Sorry," he says, turning to me. "You were saying. A comprehensive, birth-to-death booklet. How?"

"Here's how. To begin with, your fingerprint is on the inside of the cover page. The first page has your first and last name, date and place of birth, parents' first names and the identity certificate number. Quite typical of all ID cards, except that both parents' birth certificates need to be presented at the registrar's office to prove they're legally married when they apply for their newborn's ID. That's why children of immaculate conceptions will have difficulty documenting their existence."

"So, what do unmarried women do if they get pregnant? I'd think getting an abortion is out of the question for religious reasons. Isn't it?"

"Sure is. But it's also much easier to get an abortion than to be an outcast for life."

Mark nods, with a serious look on his face.

There's not an iota of celestial help in sight, so I have to continue rambling on. "Flipping to the second and the third pages of the *shenas-nameh,* we come across the happening sections, where marital actions, divorces, and children's names are registered. You'd think a polygamous system would dedicate more pages to this section. Right?"

Mark laughs out loud and says. "Right."

"Anyway, the inside of the back cover is dedicated to one's political activities, to be stamped when voting in elections," I say. "There you have it—your life summarized in a four-page booklet. And, all that information is handwritten in black ink pen. A person's life summary in calligraphy."

"Wow! Let's see yours."

I look him in the eye and say, "This would be a very sensitive document in the wrong hands. Especially if one is in the habit of lying about one's real name, age, marital status, and number of children. Most people like to keep this little red devil locked up in a very safe place."

"Maya! Are you hiding something from me?" he says, grinning, looking at me from the corner of his eyes. "Children? Age?"

I chuckle and say, "No kids or husbands, I reassure you. One last thing—and when you expire, upon taking your last breath, the booklet is taken to the morgue and a hole is punched through all those pages. *Khalas*! Much ado about nothing!"

Mark laughs and as we get out of the taxi he says, "I'll steal a peek at your *shenamese* tonight."

His mispronunciation is adorable. So is he.

I laugh and correct him, "It's *Shenas-nameh*. I'll hide it under my pillow," I say, naughtily.

✦

He heads out to the Internet center as I make my way to the photocopy office, silently giving the Divine a piece of my mind on the way for ignoring my cry for help.

The clerk behind the counter is a light-complexioned man with clear blue eyes—an unusual feature for this part of the country. I say hi and hand him my ID.

"Which pages you need photocopied?" From his accent it immediately becomes apparent that he is an Iranian Turk, or using the politically correct term, an *Azari*, from the Azerbaijan region in northwestern Iran. The *Azaris* play a crucial role in Iran's economy and are famous for their complex nature of opposing extremes—their unmatched intellectualism on the one hand, and illogical comments, deductions, and unexpected reactions on the other. They are an enigma to their Iranian compatriots.

"Just the first page," I say. "Because the other pages are empty," I add, meaning no husband or children.

He looks up at me in surprise and holds his stare. He may just be curious about my date of birth relative to my state of singlehood. Finally he snaps out of his stare, which was beginning to make me uncomfortable, and looks back down to open my booklet to the first page. I watch his fine *Azari* features progressively distort into a knot as he reads on, and at one point it appears as if he has stopped breathing (maybe he just saw that my place of birth is Oshkosh). He finally manages to pull himself together, takes a deep breath and looks back up at me. Again he stares deep into my eyes, perhaps making a face-to-age assessment this time around.

Another few seconds pass in total stare-and-pause mode. *Azaris* are famous for this mode, which is basically a blank stare ahead, void of any detectable vital signs. Then all of a sudden his eyes light up. A glimmer of hope is now shinning through his bright blue eyes.

I'm thinking, "Thank God."

He smiles and says, "*Inshallah*, soon the second page will be filled with a deserving man's name."

I smile back at him and say, "*Inshallah*."

✦

I see Mark seated at one of the Internet stations, deep in conversation with two twenty-something-year-old girls, who are hovering over him like vultures; pretty vultures in tiny, tight overcoats and designer jeans, and with custom-designed noses and flawless made-up faces. Tiny scarves barely covering their highlighted, long hair. They are your typical state-of-the-art, hip, hot and attractive girls from Tehran.

Mark is enjoying the attention. I'm not.

"There she is," I hear him say as I make my way to them.

"I see you've already made new friends." I acknowledge the girls silently, barely nodding to them, which in female lingo means, "Leave now, I'm here."

They both take a tiny step back, and start checking me out disapprovingly head to toe. Then they stare into my eyes blatantly, with a smirk. All this, translated from female lingo, is, "We are not leaving."

"Maya, this is Bahar and Nisha. Did I say that right?" Mark says, turning to the girls.

"Perfect, Mark," one of them says giggling. "No Nisha. Noushiiin, Noo Noo is easy." She smiles at Mark, batting her lashes.

Easy Noo Noo and her friend Bahar continue to ignore my eminent presence. I look at them with a blank stare, which means, My patience is running out. Your time's up. Make like a bird and fly. SHOO! SHOO! Noo Noo!

"My number and e-mail address," Bahar says, handing Mark a piece of paper.

I am in awe of these girls' ambitious, proactive approach to courtship. No wonder I'm still single.

With a heavy Persian accent, Easy Noo Noo asks, "You have Faceboooook?"

I must intervene before the situation gets out of hand. That is, out of *my* hands.

With my back to the girls, I put one arm on Mark's shoulder and whisper, "They're bad news, get rid of them," in his ear.

Mark seems confused, but obediently complies and politely tells the girls that he does not have a Facebook account, but that he will call them if he ever visits Tehran.

"I wait for you. E-mail me," Bahar says.

They throw me a you-bitch glance, wave to Mark, and wiggle away.

"Insistent little buggers," I say out loud as I watch them leave.

"Come on, Maya!" He is chuckling happily. "They were both very sweet and pretty. Beautiful eyes and hair."

"I leave you alone for a second and—did you notice how quick they were? Not only in approaching you, but slipping you their phone number in under, what was it? Five minutes?"

He keeps smiling and says, "Yeah, they were pretty fast. I guess you do need to be quick to avoid attracting the religious police's attention, eh?"

He sounds content and pleased. Is he charmed by the fact that he just got hit on by two young pretty girls? Or is he just glad to understand the dynamics behind the speedy pick-up techniques?

"Whatever. Whichever. That was a typical example of how good people have gotten at evolving with the system," I say, annoyed.

"I guess separating men and women only makes them more curious about each other."

"To say the least. You would've been making your wedding plans for next month if I'd gotten here five minutes later. You owe me one."

"Huh? Thanks, wow!" He shakes his head, rolls his shoulders back and says, "Hey, check this out." He points to a Yahoo advertisement on the corner of the computer screen. There is a picture of a buff rock-climber in her late twenties, hanging from a high cliff in a red t-shirt and khaki shorts, smiling into the camera, with the ocean and a vast green landscape and mountains in the background. "Israel, Where Else?" is written on the blue sky right behind her.

"I thought they didn't like Israel around here," he says with a perplexed look on his face.

"You thought, right, I know. I've seen this ad pop up on the screen in Dubai a couple of times, too. Pretty weird considering traveling to and from Israel is banned by most countries in the region."

"Just like it's odd to have you and me, two Americans, walking around enjoying life here," he says. "It's all about politics."

"I like to blame the media and their selective and biased news coverage, swaying the innocent people's opinion around the world, influencing the…"

"Climate," he finishes off my sentence. "Politicians control the media, too. Anyway, I'm so glad I came to Kish to see for myself. In just the past three hours my whole idea of Iran and Iranians has changed radically."

"In a good way, I hope."

"Yes. All good—friendly, English-speaking, American-loving people. And to top it off, pretty girls passing out their phone numbers willingly, effortlessly." He holds back a smile, throwing me a quick glance, waiting for my reaction.

"Ha!" I nudge him lightly. "That pretty much sums it up. You're going to like the food, too," I say. "Come on, let's go get our water and lime and relax a little before heading out to dinner."

"How do you say 'let's go' in Farsi?"

"*Berim.*"

"Maya, *berim*," he repeats after me.

My heart melts at the sound of him saying my name. Yes, *berim*.

✪

We stop by at the neighborhood convenience store, where Mark is warmly welcomed and interviewed by Mr. Behrouz, the owner, who speaks very good English. As we are leaving his store he comes running after us, holding a huge watermelon in his arms. He hands it to Mark and says, "For you, my friend. Come back to visit Kish. Come to my house for Persian food."

Mark looks surprised and uncertain as how to react. He takes the watermelon and gives Mr. Behrouz an American hug and pat on the back, thanking him.

Mr. Behrouz seems touched by Mark's gesture, and turns to me and says in Farsi, "He is a good man, take good care of him." I smile back and thank him for his kindness.

"Unbelievable. Amazing people!" Mark says in a daze as we walk away.

✪

DESERT MOJITO

I'm preparing our drinks in the kitchen. Mark turns on the television and starts switching through the channels.

"No way!" he shouts. "It's the NBA playoffs!"

"Are you a fan?"

"Not really. NBA's not that big a deal, but fun to watch if it happens to be on. That's not the point, though. I'm just super-surprised to see the Iranian national TV broadcasting the NBA." He leans back on the couch, brushing his fingers through his hair, looking baffled. "I wish I were a journalist and could report back on all that is kept from us back home in the States."

"Unfortunately, journalists cover all the sad and ugly stuff. Plus, they frown upon journalists here, and what happens in Iran stays in Iran," I say, handing him his drink.

He takes a sip, squints, shaking his head. "Whew! Strong tequila." He lifts his glass to mine, "Cheers," he says. He lowers his glass and says, "Can I ask you something?"

"Aha."

"Why did you say those girls were bad news, today?" He sounds genuinely curious.

"No reason," I say, shrugging my shoulders.

"I thought maybe they had a scam going, not apparent to me, but you knew what they were up to."

"Oh, they had a scam going all right." I smile. "Once they had your number and e-mail they'd find a way to get involved with you."

"And why is that bad? They were cute, innocent-looking girls." He grins, and looks me straight in the eye waiting for a reaction.

"I didn't know you were interested," I say as I look away, feeling uneasy. "Next time, I'll leave you to it." I not only fail to sound cool, but I come off sounding like a jealous fifteen-year-old girl. Before he gets a chance to further investigate the reason behind my possessiveness, I say, "So, now that you have your drink, do you care to share some of your romantic stories?"

"Hmm, change of topic?"

"Not really. It's still about women."

He takes a couple of big swigs of his drink and utters another, "Hmm," before he says, "All right, here it goes," he sighs, "I was engaged to be married before I moved to Dubai."

The sudden morose look on his face makes me immediately regret bringing up a subject he clearly would have liked to avoid. I feel horrible for manipulating him. I must change my name to Cobra, the wicked snake lady. I wonder if that is a state-approved name: Cobra.

"I'm sorry. Forget it. Let's talk about something else," I say.

"That's all right. I'm over it. No bruised ego there." His words and tone still do not correspond with the expression on his face.

"Sure?" I ask.

He nods. "Joanne and I were together for three years before we got engaged." He finishes his drink and gets up to refill his glass.

"What happened?"

"I'm not sure. She was older than me and didn't want to have children. But, I did. She finally agreed to adopting, but shortly after we got engaged she started coming up with excuses why we shouldn't go through with the adoption. We just started fighting a lot after that, and everything went downhill from there. We weren't getting along. So, we finally decided to break up." He lets out a loud sigh. His eyes are hazed over with a sad look. I feel like giving him a hug.

"I'm sorry. Did you really love her?"

"I thought I did, but…" He pauses. "But, I guess not enough to stay with her knowing she would never want to have kids."

"I think you did the right thing if you were really set on having or adopting a child. Why else should people get married? They can just live with each other instead, if they don't want to have a family," I say.

"Do you want to get married and have children?"

"Oh, Mark!" I say, batting my eyelashes. "I'm really touched, but we hardly know each other."

He chuckles, diverts his gaze and shyly looks down.

"Yes. I do," I say, seriously this time.

I do, I do, I do echoes in my head, heart, and soul.

"Why aren't you married, then?"

"Lucky strike, or bad luck. Still not sure how to look at it." He is waiting for a more solid, convincing response. "I think I wasted too much time with the wrong guy. And, living in the wrong country—Iran—didn't help, either. Wrong for my sort, that is."

"Did you want to marry that wrong guy?"

"At first, maybe. But ultimately, when it came down to it, I couldn't see myself with him. He was too much work for me. I lacked the complicated Iranian women's know-hows and skills of keeping a man in line."

"What kind of skills?"

"You know, calling him many times a day or night, policing him, mothering him, challenging him, admiring and loving him, and then ignoring him, all at the right times and places."

"Hmm. That does sound like a lot of work." He is silent for a moment. "You know what's ironic…Remember Sofia?"

A chill runs through my veins at the mention of her name. I wish I could put him on pause mode, forever, and not let him finish that sentence. I nod in silence, knowing that whatever he is about to say is not going to be good for my once-beating heart.

"We've been sort of seeing each other," he says.

There. It's official.

"Really!" I say, trying to sound happy. "Well, good for you. She seems nice." I feel dizzy and numb. It is not hard to appear apathetic after what feels like being shot dead.

"Seriously? I didn't think you liked her." He throws me a suspicious look.

"Why would you say that? Not so," I frown, shake my head in denial, and add, "I liked her a lot." I'm lying through my teeth, lips, and lipstick.

"Hadn't you told her about some beach party to which she wasn't invited, the night at Nobu?"

I look up and stare at the ceiling, pretending to think, trying to recollect the conversation he was referring to before I say, "I may have just mentioned how your Miami friends should check out the beach party at Breezy Beach."

"Hmm. Then she must have taken it the wrong way," he says, sounding convinced.

Phew. That was close.

I shrug my shoulders and say, "She must have. So, you were saying…What's ironic?"

The sad look in his eyes is now replaced with a serious one. "What's ironic is that she has a four-year-old daughter."

"NO!" I say, shocked. That was the last thing I expected to hear. "Who knew? She doesn't look like a mother. How old is she, anyway? Where's her daughter?"

"Her daughter is in Madrid with her ex-husband. She's thirty-two."

"You got a package deal, a kid and a woman."

"Right," he says. "That's the ironic part. I can't see myself with her."

Those last words are like music, nudging my heart back into life—bopbop. Bobup. Bobup, bibup, shoobie-doobie-pop, it starts pumping again, dancing with joy.

"How long have you two been dating?"

"Three, four months I guess. She wants to get serious. But I'm…I don't know, busy with work. I find myself using any excuse not to get too involved or committed to her."

My heart is now going crazy, banging, hip-hopping happily against my chest.

"You shouldn't push yourself in these things." Let *me* push you, I'm thinking.

"She's a nice girl. The full package," he says. "She's pretty and smart, but maybe I just need time."

"Maybe. But if you can't see yourself with her now I doubt you can, later." Oh, no, Cobra's back, and her sting is merciless.

"Maybe…"

"Maybe it's just not there." I say, raising my eyebrows. My venom surprises me. It is official; my tongue has declared an autonomous anarchist state, operating independently of my higher faculties. Before it overtakes my entire self, making me say more undiplomatically biased things, I excuse myself and take refuge in the bathroom.

I lock the door, take a few deep breaths, flush the toilet, wash my hands, take a few more deep breaths, and try to calm down.

Mark is busy cutting the watermelon when I finally leave the bathroom.

"This is the juiciest, sweetest watermelon…Here, try some," he says as he hands me a fork.

I take a bite of the red watermelon. "Wow! This is sweeter than sugar," I say. "Mr. Behrouz sure knows his watermelon."

"What a kind man. Maya. I'm buzzed. This tequila is strong."

"All tequilas are strong," I say, laughing. "A drunk American in Iran!"

"Sounds like a Hollywood movie," he says, cheerfully.

"I was thinking more like headline news," I say.

"You're bad. Stop trying to scare me." He takes another bite of his watermelon, dripping the juice all over the kitchen counter.

"I'm teasing you."

"Bad girl. How do you say cheers in Farsi?"

"*Beh salaamati*," I raise my glass to his.

"*Bes lam-ati*," he says.

"Close enough," I say, chuckling. "I need to change before we head out. You can enjoy watching your NBA. I'll be quick."

"Take your time." He picks up the remote, throws himself on the couch and shouts, "Go Celts!" He seems tipsy enough to enjoy the sports announcer's commentaries in Farsi.

❂

I go to the bedroom to get ready, thinking how having him near me is almost more painful than daydreaming of him from afar. His confession about Sofia does not make matters any simpler.

By the time I am ready to leave the room, I have semi-convinced myself that we are just friends, even though I believe a better way to define our dynamic would be one of iron to magnet. I'm the iron in this scenario.

"I'm ready," I say. "Who won?"

He springs up from the couch, almost falls back down, and says, "The first half just finished. Lakers are up by four."

"How are you feeling?"

"Not bad, nice, a little tipsy." He smiles. "Will I get in trouble?"

"The police are waiting outside the door to arrest you. This was all a setup. Sorry, Mark."

"Ha-ha. You're a troublemaker."

I'm putting my scarf on when he walks up to me and says, "Thank you, Maya."

"For what?"

His vicinity is making me nervous again.

"For doing all this. For being such a great friend and consultant."

"My pleasure," I say.

As I'm about to turn and look away, he bends down to kiss me on the cheek, or so I thought at first. Much to my delight, his lips brush past my cheeks and land on my lips. He starts kissing me lightly. I quiver from my head down to my liver. My eyes are still open and I look up to check his. They're closed. I close mine and kiss him back.

Finally! The divine intervention.

I am in heaven.

But where is he? I wonder.

○

He is not around when I wake up. It's eight thirty in the morning. I stumble to the kitchen to find a note next to the coffee maker: "See you after the dive. Mark."

I sit at the counter, disoriented, unsure of what to make of last evening's events.

Shortly after the long kiss of my death (poetically speaking) we left for dinner. Things got stranger as the night progressed. He was embarrassed, and I was confused. He kept apologizing, saying he must have had too much to drink and didn't mean to kiss me. I kept lying, reassuring him that everything was all right. We got back home sometime past midnight. He fell asleep on the couch. I tossed and turned for hours in the bedroom feeling restless, hopeless, and waging war on the divine force. I must have finally fallen asleep mid-battle at the break of dawn.

This morning I am still not sure how I feel, but I know it isn't good. If he considers kissing me a mistake, then where can we go from here? And to make matters even more dismal, my suspicions about Penelope were true all along.

A message beeps in interrupting the rattling train of my thoughts.

It's from Michelle.

HOW'S IT GOING WITH AHMED? SEDUCED HIM YET? ;-)

Good question. I knew that my intentions were murky all along when I had arranged for the alcohol. Now I regret not flashing some skin, cleavage, red bra-straps, and G-string. What am I to make of his post-kiss claims? I am wondering how to reply to Michelle's text when the landline rings.

"Hello?" I answer the phone.

"Hello," I hear my father's warm voice. "How are you?"

"I'm good. So glad you called. How are you?" I am relieved to be distracted from my useless thoughts.

"Very good," he says. "Is everything in order at the apartment? Mr. Nouri was supposed to clean it up before your arrival."

"Yes, thank you. Everything's perfect." I am trying hard to sound cheerful. I don't want him to hear the frustration in my voice.

"How's your friend? Is he enjoying himself?"

"He's out diving. I couldn't go. They're not allowing women to dive with male instructors."

"Ridiculous," he says.

"But Mark loves it here. He loves the people, the food, and…" I pause. "He is bummed he can't visit Tehran, and the rest of Iran."

"One day soon, *inshallah*," he says.

I'm wondering if he is insinuating that Mark and I will visit as a couple, or that Iran will soon be opening its doors to Americans.

"Maya, don't forget to mail me a copy of your *shenaas-nameh*."

"I already did. Yesterday. Baba, thank you again for everything."

"You're welcome. Tell your friend I said hi and that he's lucky to have you as his tour guide."

"He is lucky, isn't he? I'm sure he knows it. I'll call you from Dubai."

"Bye, darling."

I hang up the phone and aimlessly walk around the apartment. Mark's army-green canvas bag is in the corner, next to the couch. I notice a quarter-sized hole in the sole of one of his white socks on the floor. His sheets are bunched up at the bottom of the couch by the pillow and his t-shirt and jeans are hanging on the chair. He is even perfect in his imperfections.

As I am walking away from his corner, I notice a light flashing next to the couch on the floor. It's his mobile. I bend down to see Sofia's name flashing on and off across the screen. Why did he have his phone on silent? For an instant Cobra comes back to life, urging me to answer the call and tell Sofia that Mark cannot come to the phone, without giving her an explanation.

But what if all these theories and beliefs on karma, and energy recycling, and the universal consciousness are right? If any of these notions are remotely true, then I am sure to have my hands full for many years and lifetimes to come. Crap! There are so many things to watch out for when it comes to being bad. Isn't being bad part of living up to our human nature? Living out one of our many dimensions? What is so fascinating about behaving and being good at all times, anyway?

As much as I would like Sofia to disappear from the face of Dubai, I can't bring myself to meddle in Mark's personal life any more than I already have. I talk Cobra out of her malicious intent and walk away from Mark's phone.

✸

I get ready and head out to the dive-center. It's a clear sunny day and a cool breeze is blowing over from the Gulf. The water is calm and clear. It must have been a perfect day for diving. I cannot believe I am stuck out on the shore, when I should be underwater with Mark, swimming around the corals with colorful reef fish, turtles, and lobsters.

A message beeps in. It's from Janet: MORNING, HOW'S CLOVER? HOPE YOU'RE HAVING FUN. I'M AT THE AIRPORT. MAY NOT HAVE TIME TO TEXT YOU FROM RUSSIA. TA-TA.

It's past ten o'clock by the time I arrive at the dive-center. I see Amin in his bright orange shorts and white t-shirt hosing down wetsuits on the patio.

"Need some help with that?" I say, walking up the stairs to where he is standing.

"Maya! Have you lost your way?" He flashes his bright smile.

"Hello. Good to see you. I got in yesterday."

"Hashem told me. Your friend is out diving with two other guys." Amin's tanned, boyish face, curly hair, and toned body is typical of men in tune with Mother Nature, as opposed to unnaturally pumped-up men with gelled hair, Spandex shorts, and tight sleeveless shirt—all of which are only in tune with the gym equipment. "How's Kamran? He hardly comes diving anymore," Amin says.

"I saw him at a concert in Dubai. He seemed very much the same, except that he may be getting married soon."

Amin laughs out loud. "Kamran. Married?" he says. "There is a higher chance of world peace than him tying the knot. Stop spreading rumors, Maya."

I laugh along with him, maliciously.

Just then I see a diving motorboat appear from behind the cliffs, take the bend, and head towards shore. Mark, Hashem, and two Japanese guys wave to us from the boat. Amin and I start walking out to the beach to meet them. Mark is smiling giving me the thumbs up; I make a mental note to let him know that, in Iran, the thumb up gesture is equivalent to showing your middle finger in the West.

"You missed a beautiful diving day," Hashem says as he jumps down in the water, splashing us. "Mark is very lucky. He saw a blacktip shark."

Mark seems more serene and calm than usual. He is glowing and has the typical, content look of a diver after a great dive.

"The blacktip was just inches away from my reach!" he says, sounding like a little boy.

"That's great. Were you scared?" I ask him, smiling.

He sticks his chest out and clears his throat. "Of course not. I was surprised—couldn't believe it. It must've been at least five feet long. And it was just floating in mid-water, motionless, right in front of me." He pauses. "Oh. So sorry you missed it. Wish you were with us."

"Great. I knew you'd like it," I say.

"Gorgeous corals. Saw a huge barracuda, snappers, puffer fish, and a stingray," he says as he unzips his wetsuit. "No funny currents. Perfect visibility."

HE'S WITH US. I'M WITH HIM. WHO'S WITH ME?

I wish that were how I felt. My emotional report forecasts low visibility and turbulent currents ahead.

"Great. We should get going. Our flight is in three hours," I say, abruptly, feeling irritated and uncomfortable.

Mark puts his arms around me and whispers in my ear, "I understand how frustrated this no-diving-for-women is making you feel. I'm sorry. *Inshallah* next time the climate will be more suitable," he says.

"*Inshallah*," I say.

HAPPY GAY CELEBRATION AT PEACE TIME

I'm on my way to the airport to pick Maurice up. He could not have visited on a busier weekend—Asif's wedding party and Mark's restaurant opening are happening within twenty-four hours of each other. He is definitely not going to enjoy being dragged around. But, what to do?

My phone rings. It's Asif.

"Well hello groom, or is it bride-to-be? Ha-ha. Are you ready for tonight?" I say, cheerfully.

I don't hear any sound coming from my phone. I look at the screen, it is still displaying Asif's name. "Hello? Asif? Are you there?"

"Maya." I hear a whimper from the other side. "I want to kill myself."

"What're you talking about? Have you gone mad?"

"Flying Carpet FREAKING FLOODED LAST NIGHT," he screams out frantically. "The management just called to make us postpone our party to Monday night or have it tonight at the Falcon Beat—their ugly-ass sister restaurant, which is not even an option. I can't believe our luck. So much for planning three months ahead. What am I going to do, Maya? How are we to contact eighty guests on such short notice? Not to mention the ones who've flown in from overseas—our parents, friends, family...Can you believe this? We're a fucking mess. I knew—"

"Shh...Asif, shh," I say. I can still hear him rambling on into the phone. "Calm down, babe. I'm sure we can come up with a plan. Why not have it on Monday?"

"Monday is a freaking dry night. It's some religious holiday. What's the point of having a party if there's no drinking and dancing? And what about the out-of-town visitors? Half of them are flying back on Sunday. Monday is not an option."

I hear my call-waiting signal. I see Mark's name flashing on the other line. "How many guests did you say?" I ask Asif.

"Sixty-five confirmed. But we expect more, probably around eighty."

"Let me call you back," I say.

"Why? Maya, don't put me on hold. I need to talk to you."

"Then hold one second."

I put him on hold without waiting for his reply, and switch to the other line. "Good morning," I say, cheerfully.

"Hi, there. How're you doing?" I hear his manly man voice.

"I'm good. Congratulations. Last night was a great success wasn't it?" I say.

"I suppose so. Everybody seemed amused."

"Everything was finger-licking yummy. Exquisite, really. I think Peace Time will be a great hit in Dubai."

"*Inshallah*," he says, "but the private openings always go well. It's the public ones we worry about."

"I'm sure that'll be just as great."

"The staff's ready, but it would've been nice if they had another practice run."

"Oh my God. This sounds too good to be true," I say, thinking this is a miracle.

"What do you mean? Why is it too good to be true? The staff is more than ready. We have been training them for two weeks now."

"No. No. Not that. Tell me, what's Peace Time's capacity?"

"The restaurant capacity is around ninety, and sixty at the bar and the dance area. Why?"

"Do you think the staff can handle a small party of seventy this evening? Do you have enough food, staff, whatever?"

"Yes. Everyone is coming in and we were planning on doing another complete run-through tonight. Hell, we could've opened tonight, but we are technically closed till tomorrow's public-opening. Why? What's going on?"

"Do you remember the married gay guys? The ones in the picture with me at the film festival?"

"Yes?" he says, suspiciously.

"They were planning on having a small commitment celebration at the Flying Carpet tonight," I say, "but the venue flooded. They've been planning for this night for months now. They have people in town from all over and they need a low-key, cool venue. Mark...Please say yes." I pause. He is silent. "It'll be a win–win situation," I say. "Your staff can practice one more night and you'll make many people very happy."

"Hmm, well...Let me make a few calls and get back to you."

"This would mean a lot to many people, including me."

"All right. Let me see what I can do," he says. "So, you thought the food, service, and the music were all good last night? Any complaints?"

"No. Not really. Everything was perfect. We spent so much time figuring out all this stuff and it was just great to see it all come together." I chuckle and add, "I had the Paul Ré Chocolate Cheesecake. Nobody knew who he was at our table until they read the footnote on the menu."

He laughs and says, "Was he the American physicist, artist, peace activist?"

"Yup."

"Hey, we even had three orders of the Shalom Salad," he whispers. "Remember how worried we were about the name?"

I laugh and say, "Hallelujah. That means peace is just around the corner. Who ordered it? Did they look Jewish?"

"I'm not sure. They were Indian."

"Go figure, the peace-loving nation." I say. "But I'm pretty sure they'll make you change the name."

"If they do, we'll just call it the Salaam Salad. Doesn't that mean the same thing, peace?" he says.

"Sure does," I hesitate before I ask him what's been on my mind ever since last night. "Where was Sofia? I didn't see her around." When she didn't show up by the end of the night, I was pleasantly surprised, but curious.

"She…She said she couldn't make it because her daughter's in town," Mark says, sounding a bit nervous.

"Oh." I'm thinking, "What a boring, undramatic reason."

"And, she may also be mad at me," he adds, sounding annoyed.

Now that's more like it.

"Why?"

"Basically because I finally had a talk with her a while back about wanting to be just friends." He sighs. "That didn't go over too well. I'll tell you about it later."

YES! YES! YES!

I try to censor the jubilation out of my voice and say calmly, "Bummer. I'm sure you did the right thing. Anyway, please see if you can get things going for tonight."

"I'll let you know within the next hour."

"Great. Bye."

✹

Asif has given up being on hold. I decide to put off calling him until I hear back from Mark.

No Sofia. Yes. That is the best news, ever.

DESERT MOJITO

Now what?

I cannot get the grin off my face all the way to the airport arrival hall.

✺

It is no surprise that Maurice, always first in everything, is the first first-class passenger walking out. He wheels his Tumi carry-on behind him. He walks briskly, moving his head rapidly across the faces until he spots me among the Indian crowd. He smiles and shakes his head from side to side.

"I can't believe you've dragged me all the way to Dubai," he says. His adorable dimples are a reminder of my favorite feature in him, ever since we were nine. He kisses me and gives me a big warm hug and says, "If this isn't love, I don't know what is."

"This *is* love. How was your flight, my love?"

"Did you know there are lots of Jews in Dubai?" he says, titling his head, opening his eyes wide.

"This *is* the Middle East, darling. What did you expect?"

"They were serving kosher food in boxes to quite a few passengers on the plane."

"Well. You did fly in from New York. Plus, all religions are welcome but not all passports are. How long are you staying?"

"Just for the weekend. I have to be in London by Monday. I have our entire weekend planned—drinks by the beach, and I have a surprise for you."

"Me, too," I say, letting him enjoy the thought of his plans for us for a while longer.

"I'm taking you to a Googoosh concert tonight. It'll be my fortieth Googoosh concert, and I wanted to celebrate it with you," he says, waiting for an ecstatic reaction from me.

"Wow! I'm touched. You've seen her forty times? I can't believe I've never been to any of her concerts. I didn't know she was here this weekend." I am not prepared to break the news of being a no-show at the concert later. "Have you purchased the tickets yet?"

"No. But I have connections and he's arranging VIP front-row tickets for us," he says, cheerfully.

"Isn't that really why you are here? Googoosh is your first love, *pas moi*, *cheri*. You can't fool me." I raise one eyebrow, glaring at him.

"Don't be silly. Of course that's why," he says, and cracks up at his own joke. "Do I hear jealousy there?" he says, winking at me. "Maya. You know you are my first love, my funny Valentine. Now, tell me, what's your surprise?"

I take a deep breath and think this is a good time as any to tell him, when my phone rings. It's Mark. "Let me get this first," I say, relieved, as I push the answer button.

"I think we can accommodate your friends tonight," Mark says, happily.

"Thank you. Thank you. You're a life-saver, Mark."

Maurice looks over and mouths, "Who's Mark?" I smile and look away, ignoring him.

"Could you have your friend call me, please? I need to check a few details with him," Mark says.

"Sure, I'll do that right now. His name is Asif. He won't believe his luck. Thank you so very much."

"No problem. I'm glad to have a chance to do something for you for a change," he says. "I'll see you tonight, then?"

"That's really nice of you. Yup, see you tonight." I say and hang up.

"Well. Well." Maurice says, "Who's Asif? Who's Mark? Do you have a male harem service going on here?"

I raise an eyebrow, raise my chin up and say, "Maybe."

"Maya? Are you in love? That grin, and the glimmer in your eyes...I know you too well. Out with it. Who is he?"

"We're going to a wedding tonight." I say quickly, and watch Maurice's face freeze. Talk about calmly breaking the news to him. I need to work on that. He is staring at me in disbelief as I look away to call Asif.

Asif picks up and inaudibly whispers my name, "Maya."

"Hello, drama queen. Cheer up. I got you the best private venue in town booked for tonight."

"This isn't a good time to joke around," he whimpers.

"I'm serious, Asif. You will not believe when I tell you where."

"Are you for real?"

"Yes. I am."

"NO WAY! YOU GOT US BURJ AL ARAB?" Asif screams out.

"That would've been my second choice. No this is better, *habibi*. I'll text you Mark's number. He's the guy in charge of the opening of Peace Time Restaurant."

"Are you joking? Mark-Mark? The one you have a crush on?"

"Yes, Mark-Mark. And if you call my feelings a crush, I'll crush you when I see you."

"Oops. Sorry. No need for violence. Now don't tell me Peace Time is the confidential secret project you couldn't tell us about?"

"Yes. It is and now you know."

"OHH MY GOD. MAYA! You booked Peace Time? There's been so much buzz about this place around town the past couple of weeks. Is it true that their menu is all organic stuff?"

"Yes. Farmers' market produce and free range meat products. Honey, everything is fresh and in season. I was there last night for the private opening. You'll love it," I say as we get in the car. Maurice, who by now must suspect that Googoosh is not going to happen tonight, is ignoring me, pretending to be busy texting on his Blackberry. "Mark's waiting for your call. His number is 050-121309. Call him right now."

"I can't believe this. Maya. I will thank you forever if tonight does actually happen," Asif says.

"Let me know if you need any help calling up your guests or whatever else," I say.

"Could you just let Janet and Michelle know about the venue change?"

"Oh, that reminds me…Michelle had to go to Beirut. Her beau has chicken pox and wanted her by his side. She said to apologize for missing your party and that she wishes you the best. But, I'll let Janet know," I say. Next to me, Maurice lets out a loud sigh. "All right, I've got to go. Got a very impatient VIP guest in town sitting right next to me, huffing and puffing, giving me the eye. You'll meet him tonight. *Yallah,* call Mark. Good luck."

"Bye, doll," Asif says and hangs up.

✻

On the way home, I apologize to Maurice for not being able to make it to his fortieth Googoosh concert, and beg him to come to Asif's party with me. He is not at all happy about the situation, and complains about my plans being a waste of his precious vacation time, and how he had planned to spend quality alone time with me, albeit with Googoosh breathing down our necks…But by the time we have dropped his luggage off at home and made it to Moonlight Beach at the Sheraton, he has forgiven me. And, I finally get a chance to fill him in on Mark.

Maurice suggests stirring matters up at the party tonight by him posing as my boyfriend.

"If he's a real man, then he will react when he sees us snuggling," Maurice says. "It's in his DNA darling, trust me."

"Are you sure? What if I ruin my chances? What if he backs off, thinking I'm taken? By you, of all people," I say, smiling.

"I'm hurt," he says, as he sits back.

"You know what I mean."

He rolls his eyes.

"You really don't think he'll back off if he thinks I am with someone?"

"It all depends on his character," he says. "What do you have to lose?"

"True," I say, half-convinced.

"Finally I get to, well…more like, *finally I am being forced to* meet all your Dubai friends. What's Asif's wife's name?"

All of a sudden I realize that I have failed to mention the same-sex nature of the occasion tonight, and decide to keep it a surprise.

"Asif's wife's name is Mary. She's American," I say. "She's very sweet. They met here and fell in love. Got hitched in the States and now they're throwing a party to celebrate with their Dubai friends." A pink lie. It cannot hurt.

"Hmm. Sounds very boring," Maurice says as he takes a sip of his caipirinha and gazes up at the tall buildings around. "Dubai looks very different. Half of these buildings weren't here on my last visit two years ago. I'm impressed." He then lies back on his beach chair, shining like a neon sign in his fluorescent green bathing suit. "Don't get me wrong, though," he says, "I still can't stand this place." He opens his eyes just in time to check out three young guys walking on the beach.

"The United States is perfect for people like you. Everything's clear-cut, straightforward, and practical," I say. "You can plan your whole lives ahead. That is, until the market crashes unexpectedly."

"Crash aside. I love the States and feel at home. Yes, I do like to plan ahead and feel protected by the law. I cannot imagine living anywhere else in the world. I like to live in a place where my rights as a human being are clear."

"They're clear in Europe," I remind him.

"Europe's too congested and socialist for my taste. It's not the same. Plus, from my point of view, no other country embraces diversity like the US."

"You're right, but Dubai has put Middle East on the map, and in the news, for a reason other than war and terrorism," I say. "It's a breath of fresh air in the region."

"Whatever. Judging from the news, it seems like here they come up with laws as situations present themselves. Too unreliable and unstable for my taste. Not that I have any rights here as a gay man."

"It is a young country," I say.

"It's too tribal for me. And you better not get pregnant here." He glares at me, sipping his drink.

"Ha? Where did that come from?" I say, surprised.

He sits back and shuts his eyes, basking in the sun, looking like he is willing a rapid tanning process. We had to stop by the store to buy him two sunscreen lotions—an spf 40 for his face and an spf 10 for the rest of his body.

"I mean, *please*. By all means, *do* get pregnant here before it's too late. In fact, hurry up, but don't have your baby here. You know, in case he or she wants to run for the US presidency one day. He has to be born in the US."

I laugh out loud. "You're incredible. Thanks for reminding me. Speaking of which, whatever happened to your adoption plans?"

"It's on the agenda, within the next two years. Even if I don't have a partner by then I've decided to adopt. I'll move to

California and have my family's support in raising my child. I'd love to be a parent."

"You'll be a fantastic dad," I say. "Here's a question for you. Let's say they discover a way to test out homosexuality or heterosexuality of a child at birth and let's say you had a choice of adopting either one. Which one would you choose?"

"Either. It wouldn't make any difference." He sits up, his eyes now wide open, following a tanned, muscular guy in a leopard-print swimsuit. "Oh-la-la. I'd like to adopt him." He takes another sip of his drink and says, "I can't believe you're dragging me to this party tonight. Can we take him?" he says, nodding in Tarzan's direction. "Come on, let's get in the water."

"Trust me, you'll fit right in tonight." As I follow him into the water, I smile to myself, imagining the look on his face once he finds out he is at a gay commitment ceremony.

✲

We arrive at Peace Time at six-thirty. Spending the day at the beach reminiscing and laughing with Maurice has revived me. But as soon as I step out of the taxi, I begin to feel nervous. Is it because Mark may be innocently risking the restaurant's credibility for my sake by giving refuge to a gay reception? Or is it because he is now available, back on the market, without Sofia in the picture? Or, that my pretend-date, a clean cut, well-groomed man wearing a wrinkled white Ben Sherman shirt, Boss pants, and black Prada leather shoes may scare off Mark?

✲

Lately I have not been on good terms with the spiritual realm—the Universe, God, the Creator, Energy, and whatever other terms we have come up with. So, I make a deal with myself as we enter the restaurant: If all goes well tonight, I will volunteer to teach free English classes at the laborers' camp every weekend for three months.

For the nth time, my heart drops at the sight of Mark. He's wearing a tan suit, a white shirt, and a lavender tie. He looks irresistibly handsome. He is talking to Asif in the dance area, which is separated from the dining area by a floor-to-ceiling sliding glass divider. Peter is talking to a group of guests already seated at one of the tables. The waiters and waitresses are running around in their blue-green marble pattern aprons, a reminder of our planet Earth view from space. On the front of each apron is a shimmering golden peace sign, a reminder of what is missing from our little marble in space.

Asif sees me and waves me over with a huge smile on his face.

"Is that Mark waving you over?" Maurice asks.

"Yes, the olive-skin guy is Mark, and the tall blond guy standing next to him is Asif."

Maurice laughs at my cheeky sarcasm and says, "I'm sorry to break this to you, but your olive-skin Mark looks very gay to me." He winks at me, reaches over and holds my hand and says, "Come on, sweetie. Let's see what this Mark is made of." I muster a fake smile and walk along with Maurice, nervously. He leans over and whispers, "The purple tie has got to go."

❂

As we set off on our male-rivalry scheme, hand in hand, I reassure myself that Maurice could easily be mistaken for a straight man in a professional setting and a sober state. The question is how long he will last as my date tonight once he discovers that Mary is actually Peter, and that he is amongst other fellow gay men who are tipsy on champagne.

"Hi, Maya," Mark says.

He nods hello to Maurice.

"Hi." I let go of Maurice's hand to kiss Mark and Asif. "Mark, Asif... This is Maurice."

Of course, neither one knows that he is the same elementary school friend and hotshot executive they have heard so much about. Maurice greets them with a firm handshake and stands back with his arms crossed over his chest.

"Everything's working out. This is a miracle," Asif says, happily. "Mark is an angel here."

Mark pats Asif on the back and says, "It worked out for both of us. My staff gets a chance to practice one more night before the grand opening and you get to celebrate in peace."

"Peace at Peace Time." Asif says, glowing with joy. "Maya, the miracle-worker." He gives me a warm, heartfelt hug. "Now, where were we?" he says as he pulls himself away. "We were discussing the music with Mark."

I say, "I hear the band plays The Beatles, Bob Marley, and…"

"Oh! My dear. Please stop." Asif rolls his eyes at me. "Well, for your information, the band plays all kinds of music. Put on your dancing shoes, Maya. By the way, you look beautiful. A red halter neck dress... Nice. Very Marilyn Monroe."

"Thank you, darling," I say.

I'm hoping Mark will pay me a compliment, too, but instead, I see him checking Maurice out from the corner of his eye. Maurice must have noticed the same thing, because he hastily reaches over to hold my hand in his.

"Nice paintings," Maurice says, looking at the walls around. "Is this one an interpretation of John Lennon and Yoko Ono's

'Bed Peace?'" he says, pointing to the painting on the wall next to us.

"Yes," Mark says, curtly.

"Is the artwork for sale?" Maurice asks Mark in a stern, serious tone.

"No," he replies back in the same tone.

"Hmm. Too bad," Maurice says, haughtily. "This one would have gone really well with my latest David Hockney acquisition." He then turns to me and says, "Honey, why don't we go get some champagne and let them finish off discussing the music? Nice meeting you both."

"Sure," I say, playing along. "We'll see you at dinner."

We turn around and walk towards the restaurant. "Maurice," I say, "what was that? You're the worst straight man, ever. Now Mark thinks I'm dating a pushy, conceited guy."

"Isn't that how assertive straight men behave?"

"No!" I screech. "And since when do you collect art? What was all that about David Hockney?"

He chuckles, puts his arms around me, and says, "I met him at a gay charity event."

"Oh. Great. Way to give away your straight cover. If Mark has any idea who Hockney is…"

Maurice says, "I didn't give anything away. Straight collectors support gay artists all the time. But, all right. I'll tone it down. Maya. Our plan is working. I think Mark's very surprised and bothered to see me with you," he whispers in my ear.

"I know. I felt it, too. He had no idea I'd be showing up with a date."

"A good-looking, fit, sun-kissed, beautiful date."

"Oh no!" I say, hopelessly. "Maurice please, please try to stay in the straight mode a while longer."

"That was straight. The things you put me through…" He smiles, flashing his dimples. "So where's this Mary? The lucky bride." He looks around the restaurant. "I would've sworn Asif's gay."

"You think everyone's gay," I say, rolling my eyes.

He does. But, this time he's right.

We walk over to where Peter is standing.

"Hi, Peter," I say.

He gives me a big hug and says hi to Maurice.

I turn to Maurice and say, "Maurice, this is Peter, Asif's partner." I then stand back, waiting to see his reaction with a naughty grin on my face.

He shakes Peter's hand calmly, congratulating him, and then leans over to whisper in Farsi, "*Kheyli khari*," meaning, verbatim: Very donkey you are. The donkey accusation has been our favorite ever since fourth grade.

I laugh out loud and whisper, "I love you."

"Maya, you're our savior. I don't know what we would've done without you," Peter says, hugging me again.

"You're most welcome. It seems like all this was meant to be."

Maurice takes a seat while Peter introduces me to his family and friends visiting from the States.

As I'm making my way back to Maurice, I notice a six-foot apparition sparkling at the door. It is none other than the immaculate Janet in a curve-defining, asymmetric, gold dress.

I have missed her. "Wow, you look amazing! Truly sensational. And…very shimmery. Moscow has done you good." I fawn over the texture of her dress. "Fish scales?"

"Ha. Thank you. You look great, too. I've never seen you in a full-length dress. *And* in red. Very pretty, *habibti*."

"Thank you. I figured it's now or never," I say.

That is when I notice a tall blond guy with droopy eyebrows and baby blue eyes quietly standing next to Janet.

"Can I help you? Are you one of Asif and Peter's guests?" I say, wondering why Asif has been hiding his good-looking straight friends from me.

"Oh. So sorry," Janet says. "Maya, this is Jorgen."

"Hi. Nice to meet you," Jorgen says, extending his hand.

"Likewise," I say. "Welcome, follow me." I try to hide my surprise, and lead the way to our table.

Janet catches up with me. "Sorry, didn't have time to fill you in," she says. "We met on the plane-ride back from Moscow. He's shy but intelligent and a fantastic kisser. I really like him."

"Yay. He has interesting eyes. Where's he from?"

"Denmark."

"He does remind me of a duke. Nice." I wink at Janet. "Listen, here's a quick update. Mark and Penelope are off, Maurice and I are on, so just play along."

"I thought Maurice was gay," Janet says, puzzled.

"Not tonight. Play along. I'll explain later."

Janet looks around the restaurant. "Beautiful place. I must congratulate Mark. I love that chained-hands peace-sign picture."

"There are supposedly one hundred and ninety five hands representing all the countries in the world. I love the background more, the tiny pictures of other animals and living creatures on our planet."

"Very interesting," Janet says.

We take our seats. Maurice puts his arms around my shoulder, brings his lips close to my ear, and says, "I can't believe I'm in Dubai. Are you telling me this kind of gathering is allowed?"

"Please don't freak me out," I say.

"I'm sorry. I don't mean to worry you, but you do know that homosexuality is a crime and punishable by law here?" He gives me a light kiss on my cheek and says, "I'm sure everything will be fine. It looks like any other ordinary gathering. No one knows the real occasion behind the party. Plus I'm safe. I'm straight tonight." He sits back with a smug look on his face.

"That's right, you are. Hey, look. I think the lady in the emerald green dress is Asif's mother at that table."

"She's strikingly pretty. And young. Pakistani?"

"Yes. The quiet red-faced guy next to her must be her husband," I say.

Maurice is looking in the opposite direction of where I'm pointing. "I see some cute guys arriving," he says. He then turns to me and gives me a loving smile and lightly caresses my shoulders with his fingers, "Please let me know when I'm off my straight hook."

"I can't believe you. You're the one who put me up to this. You better not back off on me, now. Can you see Mark anywhere?"

He pulls my chair closer to his and says, "He's talking to one of the waiters and keeps looking over in our direction. Come here, hot thing. I want to eat you." He chuckles and pinches my arm lightly.

I cringe in disgust. "Eww. You sound like a dorky pervert. You're the worst straight person, ever."

We giggle like two little kids up to no good.

The glass sliding divider to the dance area is now open and the band starts playing a jazz medley. Mark is busy talking to the restaurant manager, John, whom I met for the first time last night. He is intently listening to Mark, nodding his head before rushing back into the kitchen, leaving Mark standing alone at the bar. He sees me looking at him, smiles and waves to me. I smile back and give him the thumbs up. He shows me two thumbs up, and looks away.

It's now eight o'clock. The restaurant is buzzing with people and most of the guests have arrived. Some are seated at the tables or walking around admiring the artwork. The ones at the bar seem to be having fun with the touch-sensitive screen on the counter, where famous peace quotes and messages light up underneath when triggered.

"Don't you think it's a funny coincidence that we are celebrating the union of two men in Dubai at a venue named Peace Time, serving ethically produced and sourced food?" I ask Maurice.

"I'm seriously shocked. But, I hope the ethical food doesn't interfere with my unethical motivations." Maurice grins as his eyes follow a handsome man who has just walked by. He raises his champagne glass. "Here is to ethics."

"Cheers," I say. "You're impossible."

"I love you, too. By the way, your figure looks great in this dress. Love the cleavage."

"What cleavage? I'm a B." I pause and say, "Was that your straight male comment?"

"No. That was a very gay me. You look very sexy tonight. Work it, my love." He looks over in Mark's direction and as soon as he turns our way, Maurice shoves a plump red strawberry in my mouth, which makes me nearly choke.

✪

Everyone is either tipsy or toasted by the time we are done with dinner. So far, so good—delicious food, plenty of wine and champagne, and lots of laughter. Everyone looks content.

Maurice is slowly but surely slipping out of his straight jacket, making his move on Peter's friend, Andy, who also happens to be visiting from New York. I can see Mark sitting far from us at a table with the Peace Time manager, John, and three other guys.

The band finishes playing "Mack the Knife" when Janet and I sneak out to the ladies' room.

"I'm having so much fun." Janet giggles as she takes her lipstick out of her purse. "The food was so yummy. I couldn't believe my waitress knew the exact ingredients of everything she was serving us by heart. Imagine…This kind of service and competence, in Dubai! Wow! I'm coming back here for sure. Good job, Maya and Mark."

"Thank you. I didn't have much to do with it," I say, redoing the strap behind my neck. "So, Jorgen seems really sweet."

Janet flashes her snow-white teeth and says, "I seem to have more in common with Europeans than Middle Easterners. I really enjoy my time with him. Everything flows."

"Good to see you happy again."

"I saw Mark looking over, checking up on you and Maurice a couple of times at dinner." Janet flicks her eyebrows.

"I know."

The bathroom door opens right then, and Asif sticks his head in. "I knew I'd find you two here. Come on girls. It's no time for gossip. Speech and toast time. Maya, do you have yours ready?"

"Yes. But it's a poem, not a speech."

Asif tilts his head to the side, walks in, gives me a kiss and says, "A poem. I'm so touched. You wrote us a poem. Ooh." He sees his reflection in the mirror, and immediately forgets all about me. "Oh, dear!" He pushes me aside and leans over the counter, checking himself in the mirror. "I look horrendous." He takes a napkin and starts dabbing his face.

Janet and I are staring at him in the mirror as he grooms himself, meticulously brushing his fingers over his eyebrows.

We are snapped out of our daze when a message beeps in from my purse.

"Who could it be? We're all here," Asif says, straightening his shirt and jacket.

I check the message. "It's Michelle."

"Why isn't she here?" Janet asks powdering her nose.

"She's in Beirut." I open her message and scream, "I KNEW IT! Listen to this. 'I'm engaged. Smiley face. Charbel proposed an hour ago and I said yes. Smiley face. Tell Asif I wish him well. Mwah.'" I look up and say, "She's engaged!"

"That's great news," Janet says.

"That's sweet. But tonight's my night. Let's go, girls." Undaunted, Asif holds the door open for us, making sure we leave with him.

✪

We find the dining area deserted. Everyone has migrated to the bar and dance lounge. Most of the guests are out on the dance floor, swaying, shouting, "I love you baby, and if it's quite all right…"

I spot Maurice and Andy dancing together. Andy is pointing to Maurice, singing, "You're just too good to be true, can't take my eyes off you."

I'm thinking so much for my pseudo-boyfriend plan, when I feel the touch of two hands on my shoulders. I turn around to find Mark standing behind me with that familiar tipsy smile on his face.

"There you are," he says and hands me a champagne glass. "Cheers to us."

"Cheers to you and an amazing night." I raise my glass to his.

"Look what I found in my pocket," he says, holding up a shiny golden object between his fingers. When he brings his hand closer, I feel a rush of blood to my face.

"My bumblebee! You still have it."

He smiles. "I haven't worn these pants since the night at the races."

"Oh. Okay," I say, disappointed that he didn't say he'd been carrying it around as a reminder of our love.

"So that guy isn't your boyfriend, is he?" He nods in Maurice's direction on the dance floor, putting my bumblebee back in his shirt pocket.

"Not really sure what to call him. He is…"

He doesn't wait for me to finish my lame explanation. "*Bes alamti*," he says and raises his glass to mine. The champagne bubbles are fizzing around and out as he leans in close and says, "Here's to you, Maya. I'm really happy I've met you. I really like you."

I raise my glass to his and take a sip. "Thank you. I like you, too."

He moves back, looks me in the eye, then brings his face close to mine and whispers in my ear, "Can I kiss you?"

"Are you drunk again, Mark?"

"Yes. What do you mean again?" He smirks.

"Kish," I say, raising my eyebrows.

He chuckles and says, "I'm tipsy enough to…"

"Then no," I say, not letting him finish his sentence, "you can't kiss me. Plus I'm with Maurice."

He puts his hands around my waist, draws me close and says, "Why not? You just said that you liked me, too."

"Maurice may not like us kissing," I say.

I look into his smiling eyes. He is holding me close, and not letting go. I can feel the warmth of his breath on my cheek. Not sure what to do or say next. He presses me closer to his body. I want him to kiss me from now until eternity, but I cannot handle another drunken excuse—*I didn't mean to kiss you, blah, blah, blah.*

He is looking deep in my eyes. "Well? Can I kiss you or not?"

"Are you just going to apologize and say that the kiss was a mistake, and you were drunk and—"

I am shut up and shot down as his lips touch mine and he gives me the kiss of my life. Shooting stars, fireworks, jumping dolphins clapping, comets crossing a smiling moon, dizziness…He finally pulls his lips away from mine, and I land back down on Earth, and open my eyes to see his smiling eyes.

"I wasn't that drunk in Kish, either," he says, smirking mischievously.

I KNEW IT.

"You're bad," I say, smiling.

He kisses me again. I feel the warmth of his hand on my bare back. He brushes my hair away from my face and smiles. I smile back.

I feel at home in his arms. *This* is home.

I raise my head once again to meet his lips when I hear my name called out on the microphone.

"I have to read a poem I wrote for the occasion," I say, quietly.

"An ode to gay marriage?"

We laugh.

"No. I'm saving that one for Maurice's wedding," I say, winking. "Come on. *Berim.*"

Asif and Peter are standing next to each other, glowing in the middle of the dance floor next to their two-tiered wedding cake.

"We would like to thank everyone who has made this night even more special than we ever dreamt possible." Peter says as he reaches over to hold Asif's hand. "Thank you to our families and friends who have traveled far to celebrate this night with us. And, please raise your glasses to thank the man and the woman without whom tonight would've never happened. Ladies and gentleman, here is to Mark and Maya. Cheers."

Everyone looks in our direction, raising their glasses. I can tell Mark could have also done without the attention—he tightens his grip on my hand and nods his head in acknowledgement. We both raise our glasses, smiling, as everyone drinks to us.

"Before we cut the cake," Asif says, "we have asked some friends and family members to share with us what in their view is an important key to a happy relationship. And first on the list is my dear mother, my love, my joy, my everything."

Asif's mother walks up to the stage and takes the microphone. Every single word she says about the importance of love and passion seems to be the very voice of each indescribable fiber of emotion I am feeling. Mark has put his arms around me and his fingers are wrapped tight around my arms. I have dreamt of the past fifteen minutes for the past fifteen months. And now that the moment has finally materialized, I'm in disbelief. It feels as though I am having an out-of-body experience, as though I am the spectator of my own dreams.

Why tonight? What changed? Was it Maurice's presence sparking Mark's male-rivalry instinct? Was it the red halter dress stimulating his hormones? Was it the auspicious alignment of the moon and the stars? Was he attracted to me on some level all along? Did he first have to realize that the picture-perfect

Penelope was not so perfect in the picture of his life? Was it the magical bumblebee stinging his heart the night at the races? Was it fate? Or was it just a series of unrelated, random events leading to this random kiss? If so, I can only hope this is love and not some random, short-lived lust.

Regardless of the whys, which will remain a mystery, I make a mental note to contact the labor camp next week to arrange for the free English lessons.

❂

Miscellaneous family members and friends read out their tributes to trust, communication, compromise, selflessness, and kindness, and it is finally my turn to read my poem.

Earlier last week, Asif had begged me to do the knife-dance for his ceremony. This dance is one of main attractions preformed at the cake-cutting stage of every Persian wedding; the single friends of the bride—or in this case, Asif—take center stage, one by one, doing a seductive dance with the bow-wrapped cake knife in hand. The dance is a chance for the single ladies and the semi-horny, I-wish-I-were-still-single ladies to show off for the men. The movements are slow and sensual, and involve a lot of twirling hips, flipping of their hair from side to side, and holding sexy eye contact with the groom at all times. The groom—in this case, Peter—is supposed to bribe the luscious dancer into giving him the knife by showering her with crisp cash notes. The dancer playfully tantalizes and teases the groom by extending the knife towards him only to pull it away at the last minute, before passing the knife on to the next dancer. The knife is finally handed to him, usually by the bride's best friend or the best dancer in the group, which in Asif's case would have probably been me.

DESERT MOJITO

    This is all in line with the concept of the groom pursuing the hard-to-get bride, spending generously to win her over. Needless to say, this is also his last "permissible" chance to freely enjoy watching and paying for seductive dancers.

    I told Asif the chance of me doing a knife-dance is about as big as the chance of him becoming straight in this lifetime.

    I make my way to the dance floor and take center stage, standing next to Asif and Peter. Poem in one hand, microphone in another, I say: "This is called the Dance of Love," and start reading off my pink sheet of paper.

> *Dance of Love,*
> *Takes you above the peak of Everest,*
> *And ballets you to the Amazon forest,*
>
> *Dance of love,*
> *Flies you like a dove,*
> *Over the shores of the Red Sea,*
> *And jazzes you on the waves of destiny,*
>
> *This dance,*
> *You must do,*
> *And vow to be true,*
> *In every step,*
> *Be it waltz, salsa, cha-cha, samba, flamenco, or tango,*
> *Close your eyes,*
> *And just let go.*

For an instant I look up to see Mark's face in the crowd, gazing at me with an adoring smile. This all still feels like a dream. I feel lightheaded. I look back down to continue reading.

> *Rhythm will take you along,*
> *Through the highs and the lows and all the blows,*
> *Spin, dive, slip, step, and swirl,*

HAPPY GAY CELEBRATION AT PEACE TIME

> *Get dizzy in a whirl,*
> *Just let go and smile at the thrill,*
> *Enjoy the chill,*
> *At will,*
> *Until, You lose control,*
> *And let love do its stroll,*
> *Lift you up and put you back down*
> *In a haze,*
> *A daze of impossible ways,*
> *In its lightness, timeless, rightless ways…*

All of a sudden, I feel a chill electrifying my body from head to toe, and my hand holding the paper starts shaking. I hear Asif asking someone to turn off the fan that seems to be blowing in my direction. Someone tells him there are no fans around.

I avoid looking up at the quiet crowd, and turn around to meet Maurice's eyes.

"Are you okay?" he whispers, as he hands me a glass of water.

I nod, and take a sip. I hope to get through the poem before getting hit by another jitter-attack, sending the microphone flying off into the crowd. I take a deep breath as I continue reading:

> *Slow…it will get…so you can forget,*
> *Till you look it in the eye and say,*
> *"Yallah! It ain't worth a thing…"*

I hear many in audience laugh out loud and some sing out the second verse: "*If it ain't got the swing.*" I look up, smile, and continue:

> *Yeah baby!*
> *Dance! Fly! Leap! Jump! Wave!*
> *And flow like a feather in the stormy weather.*

DESERT MOJITO

I hear someone shout out, "Bravo!" as I read uninterrupted to the end:

> *The curtain call is up,*
> *And they're playing your special pop,*
> *You're on top,*
> *Never, ever, ever give up,*
> *Leap up,*
> *And take your stance,*
> *For it's your turn to dance,*
> *Without a glance*
> *This is your chance,*
> *This is your dance,*
> *Dance, dance,*
> *This is your dance of love.*

EPILOGUE: LOVE POTION

It is a popular belief that the "second" key to a man's heart is through his stomach. (The first key is also in the vicinity.) The idea is that if a woman knows how to cook her man's favorite meal to his liking—though to save time, she should just go straight to his mother for his favorite recipe—chances are they will live happily ever after.

Right here at your fingertips is the recipe to steal any man's heart. Yes. Any man's, anywhere, any size, any creed, and any breed. This omnipotent potion has the power to allure, bewitch, and win over men, the world over. It should have been banned eons ago due to its trance-inducing effects. But, its magical powers have also protected it from annihilation, so much so that it has made its way to being the second-most-popular national dish in Iran, after *chelo-kebab* (rice and fillet of lamb). So, take heed:

> Women of the world,
> Throw away your tarot cards,
> Ouija boards,
> And astrology charts.
> Forget your fortunetellers,
> Palm and dream interpreters,
> Tealeaf and coffee readers.
>
> No need for black magic and Devil's reassurance,
> Or to Istikhara for guidance.[*]
> No more long journeys to the holy wishing well,
> Or deals with God and his buddy in hell.

---

[*] A practice by Muslims of seeking God's guidance before undertaking an important task, asking for guidance.

DESERT MOJITO

Say goodbye to your voodoo dolls,
Crystal balls,
And psychic enthralls,
Witchcraft and all.

No more drama,
Or a murky karma.
The answer to your prayer,
Is right here,
A gift from me to you for free.
And it is called GHORMEH SABZI.

To remember the name, just think of the French word *gourmet*, and then just remember the Persian word, *sabzi*, meaning herb.

Men who have had the good fortune of tasting *ghormeh sabzi* will admit to its being their favorite Iranian dish. When asked exactly what it is they find so enchanting about it, they get this dreamy look in their eyes and say, "It's just good stuff." They compare its effects to one of a hallucinogenic drug, changing their state of consciousness, body, and soul, and transporting them to another level of existence.

For optimum results, ladies (or gentlemen), be prepared to spend at least three hours preparing, chopping, slicing, dicing, cooking, and frying in the kitchen—in addition to another three to four hours hanging around the stove to occasionally stir the potion. You can purchase a canned version, which, needless to say, lacks the desired magical power.

Furthermore, popular belief has it that in order to bring out the finest taste, and enhance this potion's potency, it should be prepared and left overnight, only to be reheated prior to serving the next day for lunch. Another advantage to preparing this dish a night in advance is that you will not only be able to sleep in and spend your time beautifying yourself for the bewitchment feast, but you will also have a chance to rid yourself of the strange, awful smell of the herbs: fenugreek being the main culprit. A stinky woman will defeat all magical effects and purposes.

So, ladies, cook away and watch your man as he transforms right before your eyes. The potion will kick in usually when he is halfway through his first serving. There are obvious signals to let you know the potion is working its magic: His eyes glaze over and lose focus, he finds it hard to sit up straight on the chair, and then he starts sliding down, sinking lower in his seat. Upon finishing his first serving, his body goes completely limp and his speech becomes audibly slurred. After the second serving, he can barely keep his eyes open and he feels completely paralyzed. He has slid all the way down the chair, with his head tilted back. His eyes are closed and a huge smile of utter satisfaction spreads wide across his face. The only thought he can afford to keep is of how to hold on to this state of ultimate bliss and, more importantly, to the person who has caused it—YOU—for an eternity!

❂

I have invited Mark over for dinner tonight. Although we have been together every night since Asif's wedding two months ago, I figured it would not hurt to have him try my homemade *ghormeh sabzi* to seal the deal.

GHORMEH SABZI (serves 5–6 people)

Lamb stew, ½ kilo
Onion (finely chopped), 1
Herbs: garlic, chives, and parsley in equal amounts, and a little fenugreek. All finely chopped, ½ kilo total.
Black-eye or kidney beans (soak in water 1–2 hours), ½ cup

Dried (Persian) limes, 5–6
Oil
Salt, pepper, turmeric

Sauté the chopped onion over medium heat in oil (2–3 tsp.) in a pot until golden. Add turmeric (½ tsp.) and fry for another minute before adding the chopped meat.

Toss the meat for 10–12 minutes until well coated and browned on both sides. Drain and add the kidney beans and water (6 cups) to the meat pot. (If you are using black-eye beans, add them after the first hour or cook separately and add later.) Bring to a boil, turn the heat down to low, and cover the pot to cook for three hours.

Add the dried Persian limes with some salt at the end of second hour. If you add them earlier, your stew will be bitter.

Meanwhile, fry the herbs in oil (6 tsp.) and stir with a wooden spatula for 20–25 minutes until the water is evaporated and the color is deep, dark green (not black). Add this herb to the meat pot at the end of the first hour and stir well with sufficient salt and pepper to your liking. Let the concoction simmer over low heat, with the lid partly covering the pot.

Serve with white Basmati rice.
Good luck!

ABOUT THE AUTHOR

Nazli Ghassemi was born in Iran and has traveled extensively in Europe, America, and the Middle East, living among people of many cultures and creeds. She has worked variously as a dance instructor, hotel receptionist, businesswoman, translator, simultaneous interpreter, ghostwriter, and ESL teacher. She also has a degree in Biomedical Engineering from University of California, San Diego. She wrote her first novel, *Desert Mojito*, while working and living in Dubai. She now lives in Southern California and continues to teach ESL and is working on her next novel.

CPSIA information can be obtained at www.ICGtesting.com
Printed in the USA
BVOW081307310313

316874BV00001B/2/P